The Low Road

A Novel

Chris Womersley

SILVEROAK
New York / London

SILVEROAK
New York / London

An Imprint of Sterling Publishing Co., Inc. (New York)
and Quercus Publishing Plc (London)
387 Park Avenue South
New York, NY 10016

ISBN 978-1-4027-9863-4

Distributed in Canada by Sterling Publishing
ᶜ/o Canadian Manda Group, 165 Dufferin Street
Toronto, Ontario, Canada M6K 3H6

Originally published in Australia in 2007.

First published by Sterling Publishing Co., Inc., 2012.

For information about custom editions, special sales, and premium and corporate purchases, please contact Sterling Special Sales at 800-805-5489 or specialsales@sterlingpublishing.com.

Manufactured in the United States of America

2 4 6 8 10 9 7 5 3 1

www.sterlingpublishing.com

For my mother, my brother and my sister
who know something of the roads I have travelled.

A man's character is his fate.

—Heraclitus, *On the Universe*

Part One

Sometimes they lay on their beds, stared
at the marks on the ceiling and wondered
about their lives and how they had ended
up here.

1

L ee woke slowly, coming to consciousness from seemingly oceanic depths. Almost just a dream of waking, fluttering and knock-kneed. The room was quiet, as if waiting to accommodate him. He lay on the bed with his eyes closed behind quivering eyelids like a backyard golem, stiff and ancient.

When he was a child he would lie in bed at night afraid of something, afraid of everything, and try to breathe in such a way that whatever was out there wouldn't notice him in the dark. Just shallow inhalations and exhalations. As if he could remain invisible to the phantoms that roamed the highways and byways of the night searching for children to devour. There was even a stage, when he was about fourteen, when he would awaken with the sensation that the entire night, having been torn from its hinge, was barrelling through space. When this happened his sister, Claire, would appear at his bedside, place a hand firmly on each of his shoulders and wait until he ceased his whimpering. She wouldn't say a word. There was nothing, they both knew, to be said. Not after all that had happened.

And Lee tried now to remain as still as possible, to make himself small in the universe, convinced that the potential disturbance of his waking could ripple outwards and determine the manner in which this day would be lived. He would need to get it right. He remained still a little longer. Warm air murmured in his lungs. He licked his dry and flaking lips.

After some time he allowed himself to breathe more evenly and opened his eyes. The unfamiliar room had a bloodshot cast to it, of morning light filtered through a thin gauze curtain. Grimy yellow paint on the wall, aluminium window frames. A motel room, by the look of it.

His body felt constructed of material other than skin and bone, something altogether more industrial, like canvas and wire. Pieces of ill-fitting wood, things scrounged from beside the road and ragged ends of sticky tape. A low, grieving pain had taken up residence in his joints and he became aware of a space in his body where memory would normally reside, a solid persistence of sorts, but of what exactly he couldn't tell.

He felt he had been here for a long time, lying on the bed wearing bloodstained clothes, waiting for his life to come back to him, waiting for his situation to make sense. Was it days or merely hours? Occasionally an elderly woman muttered about the room. She leaned over him and appeared to listen for his breath. Checking if he was still alive. She smelled of cigarettes and talcum powder.

Now alone, he stared at the ceiling. Waiting is laden with possibility but he was unsure if this was even waiting. He heard the hum of distant traffic, occasional voices talking nearby. A woman called out, as if to a dog. The curtain billowed out from the window, looming with the promise of life. Is this what it's like to be as yet unborn? Everything was ruined. If it wasn't before, it surely was now. He closed his burning eyes and stared into the darkness. Fuck.

2

Although it was sudden, Wild wasn't entirely surprised to find himself leaving the house he had shared for so long with his wife and daughter. He'd long ago lost track of the man he was supposed to be, anyway. Even leaving in the middle of the night was now in character and he consoled himself with the thought that everyone else had fled, so why shouldn't he? But really, he knew some departures couldn't be undone, and this was one of them.

He moved through the grey, unlit house, negotiating past furniture and around corners by memory and touch alone. Through the warm bedroom doorway and along the narrow hall with its framed black-and-white photographs of family life: Alice as a stern toddler, the prototype for the teenager she had eventually become; Jane on a wind-blasted cliff in Greece. To the right his study emanating its comforting smell of ink and paper, with its hundreds of books brawling for shelf space: medical books, art monographs, biographies, poetry. So many books that there were tottering stacks of them on the floor, waiting to be sorted. All that learning, of so little use to him now.

He packed a bag of clothes, hoarded as many medical supplies as he was able, turned out the lights and locked the door. When he squinted into his rear-view mirror as he drove away, there was just a bruise of grey exhaust, lingering on the night air.

Wild slept in the back of his car for two nights before checking into a motel at the frayed hem of the city, where buildings are practical and low to the ground. He knew he should try to get further away but was unsure of where to go. He had never been on the run before. Besides, it would just be one night. Just enough space to allow him to think.

The crone on reception peered at him for a long time through her cloud of cigarette smoke before leading him to a room on the first and uppermost floor. There were no forms to fill out.

I'm Sylvia, she offered over her shoulder. I run this place.

Wild nodded. Where's the park?

What?

The park? Isn't this place called Parkview Motel?

Sylvia ignored him. She coughed into her fist and listed the attractions in a flat drawl. You've got most stations on the TV, even though it's black-and-white. Fiddle with the antenna if it plays up. Hot water, 10.00 a.m. checkout and all the peace and quiet you can stomach. Forty bucks a night, she said as Wild put his bag on the sagging bed. Cash only. Payable in advance.

He handed over two nights' rent. Sylvia counted the money, grunted and left without closing the door. The sound and rhythm of her slippers as she shuffled away along the concrete walkway was like sandpaper.

He scratched at his thin beard and looked around the tiny motel room. It smelled of old people. A few desiccated moths and flies lay curled on the aluminium windowsill. He opened the wardrobe and considered the jangling wire coathangers. The shower dripped onto the tiled shower recess in the bathroom, making some sort of mysterious, monotonous point.

Wild had stayed in plenty of motels in his life. Usually, the first few moments offered an erotic charge of being somewhere new and private, where you could bounce on the bed and burp without reproach, jerk off over the big-haired, daytime soap actresses and take half-hour showers. Not this place. Normally, he would switch on the television for the reassurance of some ambient technological murmur, but he was sure it wouldn't even work here. It was better, he reasoned, to save some disappointments for later.

In the bathroom, he splashed cold water over his face and flushed the toilet just for something to do. The pipes groaned as the cistern refilled, as if some massive, distressed creature were embedded in the foundations. His black medical bag sat on the bed. He didn't really remember packing and wondered if he'd brought enough clothes or toiletries. Enough for what? It was cold.

He stepped out onto the walkway overlooking the car park and rested with his hands on the wet railing. Stretching into the distance was a relentless urban grammar of rooftops, antennae, wires and flickering lights. A flock of birds rose and arced against the clouds like a slow throw of pepper. A horseracing call whined from a nearby room.

The world is full of these kinds of places, he thought. The suburbs that fringe every city of a certain size look pretty much the same. Sites of halfway use. Places of failure and suspicion and neglect. Car parks humming in their fluorescent silences, all angles and dark solids. Ribbons of highway unravelling through neighbourhoods. The bus shelter with a scuffle of soft-drink cans beneath wire seats and the stink of domestic misfortune. There's always an abandoned rail yard with rusted segments of track lying in the long, damp grass. The rotunda of a local park where, once upon a time, a kid was raped by a bunch of other kids. Airports with their undersound of TVs and language that one becomes aware of through senses other than hearing, a process of bodily absorption, like a photograph developing in a tray. Shopping centres, churches. Hostels with their congregations of wandering men. It isn't that things don't happen here, it's just that different sorts of things happen, and to different sorts of people. And now perhaps I'm one of those people, he thought as he gnawed at a thumbnail.

Wild was able to afford a more salubrious place, but the Parkview suited him in ways he was only dimly able to articulate. He went back inside and shut the door. Nobody would think to look for him here. He could stay out of sight. Besides, if he was going to escape one punishment, then perhaps he deserved another?

He sat in his underwear on the only chair in the room and devoured a chocolate bar. So many types of hunger, he thought. It was a many-headed thing.

He sensed the organic precision of thousands of hairs rising in unison all over his body. Horripilation, or *cutis anserina*. From the Latin for skin and goose. The *arrector pili* muscles beneath his skin kicking into action due to intense fear or cold, his body carrying on without his direction, doing what it thought best. He scratched at his generous belly and wondered which it was. Cold or fear. Both, most likely. He idly tried to think how long it had been since he'd had sex. Could he even remember? God, it must be more than a year. He sniffed at his underarm. I need a shower.

Like all people in free fall, Wild had been the last person to realise. Those around him nodded sympathetically, hid their wallets and lost his phone number. He had relinquished initiative, become someone to whom things just happened. He tallied all he'd lost. It seemed a mountain. He wondered about his wife and daughter, how they would roll their eyes at each other when they heard of this, his latest stunt. I've done it now, he thought with morbid satisfaction. If I wasn't in trouble before, I really am now.

A day or two later, Wild was sitting on the bed when there was a rapping at his door. Beside him on the side table were food wrappers, a toothbrush, empty glass ampoules and a handful of spare change. He'd been sitting like that for some time, sort of ruminating. Some writer he'd read in his undergraduate days had mentioned the stoned pleasure of staring at one's toe for hours on end. Back then it seemed funny and bohemian. It didn't seem anything in particular anymore.

He sat upright and stared at the closed door. He slid his tongue across his front teeth, which jostled in his mouth like a row of beggars. He hardly dared breathe. He clutched his bag to his chest and stood behind the door, in preparation for what exactly he was unsure. Did he think he was going to make a run for it, for God's sake?

He put his ear against the chipped door. The smell of cigarette smoke. Surely if it was the police, they'd have to announce themselves? Would they be allowed to smoke? He tried to recall how it had happened last time—the only other time—when the police had come to his door. Did they do the whole *Open up, this is the police* routine, or was it actually more discreet? So much for his great escape. Brought to a dramatic conclusion after just two days.

Again the knock, this time followed by a woman's voice.

Mr. Wild? Are you in there?

It was Sylvia. Didn't she have a motel to run?

He sighed, relieved. Yes.

Slippers shuffled on the concrete outside. Wild put his eye to the gap between the door and the jamb but could only make out the lean wobble of the day outside. At least she seemed to be alone. Finally he opened the door partway and peered out, blinking in the morning light.

Sylvia propped against the metal railing with a cigarette jammed between her fingers beside her mouth. In daylight, he saw that her eye shadow was aquamarine.

She looked Wild up and down and smiled, revealing a haphazard collection of teeth. How you settling in?

There was nobody else in sight. Fine. Thanks. He waited. Is there a problem?

Sylvia scratched her neck with long fingernails and coughed. Not exactly. Although you do owe me some rent. It's in advance, remember? But listen, I need to ask you a sort of favour?

Wild ran a hand through his straggling hair and down across his face, attempting to smooth his collected wrinkles. Unwilling to offer too much, he shrugged, but said nothing. How many days had he been here? Could it really be a few days since he'd first arrived?

Sylvia considered him. Got a bloke, she said, tossing her head to indicate a nearby room. Needs a bit of help.

What kind of help?

Sort of . . . medical help. And she dropped her butt and ground it out before flicking it over the edge of the walkway with the toe of her slipper.

Wild looked around. The door was still only open wide enough to allow for his head to protrude, tortoise-like, into the cold morning air. A vague panic buzzed within him, the intimation of some sort of chaos. He didn't like the sound of this at all. Medical help?

Yeah. Got a small—

Sorry, but what makes you think I can help you? Help him?

Well. You're a doctor, aren't you?

He wondered what he might have said to give this woman that impression. His memory of checking in was rather hazy. Perhaps he'd announced something or other about his qualifications? Signed in as Dr. Wild? Anything was possible. He rubbed the end of his nose and began to close the door, inch by tiny inch, in the vain hope that this woman wouldn't even realise. I really don't think I'm the right person to be asking about this. You might be better off asking someone else. Someone better.

But you *are* a doctor.

Wild held up a palm. Well . . . yes. No. Not really. I'm sort of . . . finished with that part of my life. Sorry but I think I have to keep out of this.

Sylvia put out a bony hand to stop the door from closing. Wild felt curiously helpless, could almost see the way things would turn out even as they were just beginning to unravel.

Thing is, she said in a low voice, I don't want to call the police or anything. This guy's hurt bad and I'm not sure how he got here and it looks kind of . . . Well, it would just be kind of unfortunate if that happened and, no skin off my nose if the cops snoop around here, I run a pretty decent place, but you know—and here she fixed both stony eyes on Wild—some people might not be so keen on the idea, know what I mean?

A cold breeze trembled across his face. He wondered for a second, just a second, about this woman in front of him. Finally, he nodded slowly and followed Sylvia to a room several along from his own.

The room was murky. On the bed was a shape like luggage. Sylvia waited by the door, cutting off any escape. Wild edged inside and, as his eyes adjusted to the gloom, realised that the form on the bed was that of a young man, perhaps twenty-three or twenty-four years old. The man wore a leather coat over a blue t-shirt, the lower part of which was dark and glistening with blood. He panted for breath.

Sylvia brushed past Wild and hovered over the man on the bed. She listened to his breathing and turned to face Wild, who remained near the door. Well? What are you waiting for? Here he is. You waiting for a written invitation or something?

Wild approached the bed as Sylvia closed the door and turned on the overhead light. The entire scene frightened him: this supine man with his feet together like a saint; the thick and brackish air. Sylvia bristled behind him, waiting and watching. He feared she knew more than he was comfortable with. Again she told him to hurry and eventually Wild shambled across the room to the bedside.

The patient with fluttering eyelids. Just a boy, really. With thumb and forefinger, Wild lifted the blood-heavy t-shirt and inspected the area where it seemed he was hurt. Wild grimaced. There was a lot of blood, smeared greasily across the boy's stomach, but mainly over his left side. In the midst of it, beneath his ribs, a black puncture slightly larger than a thumbtack.

Jesus. Has he . . . ?

Sylvia nodded.

With what exactly?

Gun's a gun to me, mate.

Wild pursed his lips with distaste and peered at the boy's stomach before allowing the t-shirt to drop with a muddy sound. He wiped his hands on his trousers. Well, there's nothing I can do if he's been shot.

Sylvia picked something from her tongue and folded her arms across her chest. Come on, mate. You can do more than bloody look at him. I don't think he's going to hurt you in his condition. Her voice had the mild lisp of a mistuned radio.

Wild sighed. Insects made dainty sounds as they collided with the bare globe above his head. Ignoring the boy's moans of pain, he did as he was told. Again he lifted the t-shirt, then turned the boy as gently as possible onto his side to inspect his lower back before returning him to his original position. He was strangely relieved that his inability to be of any use was not a matter of reluctance or incompetence, but was of a rather more practical nature.

I can't do anything about it. There's no exit wound, as far as I can tell, which means the bullet is still inside him. It needs to be taken out. This is not really my thing. You need to get him somewhere where they can operate. Was he shot here? In the . . . luxury suite?

She shrugged. No. Don't know where. Someone dumped him here last night.

Dumped him?

Yeah. It happens.

You know him?

Not really. Just from around the traps. Lee's his name. She produced a packet of cigarettes from a fold in her clothing and lit up. Can't you do *something*?

Wild regarded Sylvia's chicken neck and parchment cheeks. She could be aged anywhere between fifty and one hundred. One of those people who, having no use for youth, emerge straight into midlife. Born on the kitchen sink, smoked from age five, run this motel forever. He recalled the Greek myth of the oracle granted eternal life, but who was subject to mortal ageing and shrivelled over time until small enough to fit into a jar suspended from a tree.

Where's your bag? she asked.

What?

Your. Bag.

He held up his hands in a final attempt to dissuade this hag from involving him. Look. I'm not a doctor. I mean, I am, but . . . There is nothing I can do here for this kid. You're going to have to call someone. Call an ambulance or something.

No. *You* got to do something.

In an effort to keep the panic from it, Wild lowered his voice. Look, lady. I don't know where you got your information from, but while it might be true that I have some medical training, I'm not really equipped in any way, shape or form to deal with something like this. I was a GP, for God's sake. If the kid had a broken arm or needed a tetanus shot or even if he had an ingrown toenail, I might be able to do something, but this? No. Even if it wasn't out of my league, it would *still* be out of my league.

What about that oath you all got to take?

Wild sighed. She was obviously not to be underestimated, even if she was a thousand years old. And how on earth was it that every man and his dog had heard of the Hippocratic Oath? This woman was really irritating him. He should never have opened the door. He should never have come to this crappy motel. He should only have stayed one night. There were a lot of things he shouldn't have done. He could go some way into the past with this line of thought, but it wouldn't help him return to the place where it all went wrong, if there were such a place.

It's a long story.

Yeah. It always is, sweetheart. Isn't there somewhere you could take him? Someone you know?

Gee. How about a hospital? Wild wiped his hands on his trousers and moved towards the door, shaking his head, hoping to convey the impression that he'd love to stay and help but would have to leave her to it. He brushed past her.

Sylvia crossed her arms. Come on, mate. No use being all high and mighty anymore. Look around you. You two got more in common than you might like to think. I been around a while. I reckon you can smell crime on a man and you boys *both* need a good scrubbing.

Wild hesitated with his hand on the door handle. What are you getting at exactly?

I've heard of you. The Junkie Doctor, they're calling you.

He turned to face her. You've heard of me? The *what*?

I read the papers. Yeah. You're in a spot of trouble, I reckon. Man like you must know somewhere a man like Lee can get some help. Look, just get him the hell out of here and stop fucking me around. I tried to be nice about this, but let's be clear: you owe me money, I need a favour. You're on the run, big fella. You don't have any cards to play. This kid isn't going to die in one of my rooms. He's just not. And I'm not someone to mess with.

So I see.

Don't get smart.

He scratched at his throat with bitten fingernails. The kid on the bed arched his back and muttered. There is somewhere I could take him. Out on the plains. An old doctor friend of mine. Fellow called Sherman. I used to go there a lot to . . . I used to go out there but I haven't been in a few years. Not sure if it's still safe out that way.

Nowhere is safe these days.

No. I suppose not.

Where's your bag?

What?

Your bag. You want to maybe put some dressing on him or something before you go.

Wild sighed. It's back in my room. I'll go get it.

I'll get it.

No, it's OK, I'll—

I'm not being polite, mister. I'll get it. Don't move.

Wild remained where he was. He averted his gaze from the kid on the bed and instead watched the progress of a cockroach as it clambered along the skirting board, stopping here and there to measure the air or whatever with its antennae. *Survive the Bomb*, they say of cockroaches. The poor bastards.

Sylvia returned a minute later with his bag and handed it to him before closing the door. Wild squatted by the bed and prepared an injection of morphine. He drew the liquid from an ampoule into the syringe and tapped the chamber to clear it of air bubbles. Saliva flooded his mouth, the expectant prick of bile.

You giving him all that? Seems a lot.

Wild laughed as he looped a tie tightly above his elbow and set about hunting down a vein. Nope. This is for me. Doctor's orders.

He had his hit, absorbed its pillowy impact and began cleaning Lee's wound with shaking hands. It always amazed him how much blood a person carried inside them. Gallons of the stuff. The bullet appeared to be lodged under the skin just below the kid's left ribcage. The area was swollen and badly bruised. Most likely there were a couple of broken ribs but he might have avoided any serious tissue damage. There was almost certainly some sort of internal bleeding. He daubed the area with disinfectant but decided to apply a dressing after the wound had dried out slightly.

Will he be alright?

He shrugged. Depends what you mean by alright. Infection is maybe the danger at this stage. Hard to tell if any organs were damaged, but I guess we'll find that out. What do you care, anyway?

Sylvia smoothed the front of her dress and made a sound in her throat. I don't like to see anyone die. Specially not a kid like this. How far is this place you're heading?

A day's drive, more or less.

When you leaving?

He hadn't thought about it. I might wait an hour or two. When it's starting to get dark. That OK?

Sylvia nodded, her eyes fixed on the kid on the bed. She looked depleted. Yeah. But no longer. I got to get rid of these sheets and scrub the place.

Wild indicated a suitcase on the floor beside the door. Is that his?

Yeah.

What's in it?

Sylvia shrugged. Don't know.

His nose and face itched. Trouble breeds trouble, he thought. Like those bloody organisms that divide and divide again until there's a billion of them before you know it. Still. He wondered why he hadn't thought of Sherman before. It would be the perfect place to stay for a while until things blew over, if they ever did. He was almost cheered at the thought of Sherman's crinkling half-smile, the way he rubbed his eyes without even removing his round glasses.

He wondered about Lee. It seemed unlikely he would be able to get him to Sherman's before he died. Inside the tiny bathroom he washed blood from his hands and considered himself in the mirror. Am I the kind of person, he thought, who could dump a man beside the road and keep on driving, or is that yet to come?

When Wild returned to the room, Lee murmured, stiffened slightly and sagged once again onto the bed. In the ghastly afternoon light, the kid appeared insubstantial, as if about to dissolve into the bloodied bedclothes. Wild detected a strange sensation within his chest, like a small animal turning in its sleep. It was, he was surprised to realise, pity.

He drew a chair up to the bed and lowered himself into it with a great sigh. Lee, now apparently conscious, raised a hand to his face as if checking on his existence. Dried moons of blood had hardened under his fingernails.

The kid's eyelids flicked open and he looked first at Wild and then Sylvia, his gaze sliding from one to the other. His brow furrowed and he gasped for air. I don't think I'm meant to be here, he said at last, in a slender voice.

Wild wiped his forehead with the back of his hand. Despite the cold, his skin was damp with perspiration. Believe me. I know exactly how you feel.

3

With one hand, Lee gingerly touched the left side of his torso, where the escarpment of ribs slid away to the softer flesh of his stomach. He felt the dark heat of a bullet wound and levered himself into a sitting position to see better. With a grimace he lifted his blood-soaked t-shirt to expose a black, pea-sized hole, fringed by a mineral crust of dried blood. The surrounding skin was swollen, tender. There was blood all over his hands and smears of it on his jeans. His own blood, presumably, although he couldn't be entirely sure. He flinched at the memory of that woman and the jump of her gun. That blunt truck of surprise. Her slow blink. Bang.

He sat on the edge of the low bed, to see what it felt like, preparing for a more committed movement. The linoleum floor was cool beneath his toes, almost like water, and he licked his lips. He would love nothing better right now than to dangle his feet in lake water, but that seemed a long way away now, more remote than ever. With one hand behind him on the bed for balance he eased back to relieve the pressure on his wound. He breathed heavily and gritted his teeth, now fully alert to the regiments of pain marching through him. He held his breath until the pain subsided. Perhaps he would die here, right where he was.

He inspected the backs of his hands, as if surprised to find them there. Small and bloodstained. He turned them over, unintentionally assuming an attitude of half-hearted supplication. The lines crisscrossing his palms. Once with his sister he visited a fortune teller at a country fair, a woman who wore a suit and smoked a pipe, a woman who, when Lee had inquired after his future, said—without the merest change in expression—*What makes you so sure you got one?* And it was her voice more than anything he could always recall, a sound like a knife shredding cabbage. That, and the look of horror on Claire's face as she dragged him by the wrist from the dusty tent.

His gaze travelled along his forearm, tracing the creamy plank of flesh with its submerged design of blue veins, the indecipherable map of his inner architecture. The workings of his own body were a mystery to him. He turned his hands back over and balled them into fists before splaying them as much as he could. The tendons and muscles slid and arched beneath the skin, creating tiny ramparts across his knuckles, an entire language of movement as unknown to him as Sanskrit or Ancient Greek, deep in conversation inside his body.

Awkwardly, Lee removed his leather coat and t-shirt, slung them on a chair and staggered into the bathroom to inspect his torso. Under the fizzing fluorescent light, he could see the skin around his bullet wound was swollen but also discoloured with what appeared to be disinfectant. Someone had attended to him while he slept. He caressed the yellowed smear and raised the finger to his face. A hospital sprang up within his senses, a kingdom of wards and machinery, of hallways and steel. He inhaled slowly, seeking damp mops and dry bandages, the odour of laundry and steamed broccoli and inside that again he expected to hear the squelch of nurses' shoes on linoleum as they made their rounds during the night. He rubbed his hands on his jeans and bent to the sink to slurp water from his cupped hand. The water tasted of mildew.

With thin and innocent fingertips he traced his surfaces, from the bony meat of his chest down across his stomach, searching for further signs of violence or distress. Nothing. Just skin and hair, the distinct fabric of human flesh with its topography of ridges and bumps. Some minor scratches and the strangely glossy scar from a childhood car accident that ran down his right side. Otherwise his skin appeared almost without texture. He angled his head and looked into the mirror with dark eyes, relieved to observe his hair had at last grown free of its prison severity. A squadron of mosquitoes hummed in the shower recess.

At the bedroom window, in the bruised afternoon light, he could see a car park below, around which the motel was constructed. Goosebumps rose on his naked skin. Lights were coming on in the distance. The world turned on its hinge.

Holding the curtain to one side, he could make out dislocated segments of walkway outside his room and the other rooms of the first floor. The windows of the rooms opposite his own, a slice of rusted roof. There were few signs of life, apart from the occasional flock of birds that spattered across the darkening clouds. The roofs that stretched into the distance were unfamiliar but not entirely foreign and he scanned the horizon for a landmark by which he could orient himself: a building, a hill, a neon sign, anything. But there was nothing. He wondered how long he'd been here.

A couple appeared below him in the motel car park, arguing in low tones. It was clear they had done this before, this arguing, perhaps many times. Their gestures were tired. Although the man had his back to Lee, he looked familiar. Perhaps this was the person who had daubed his stomach with disinfectant? He allowed the curtain to drop and stood as far as possible to one side of the window while still able to observe them. He waited for the man to turn around, but he never did. A trio of thick-chested dogs lay patiently at the woman's feet like luggage to be loaded into the car. The woman raised a hand to her mouth and looked away across the highway, perhaps hoping to see something on which to focus. It seemed a decision had been made, one she was only reluctantly agreeing to. She was small and wiry. Middle-aged. She wore a loose, white shirt, a man's shirt by the look of it, several sizes too large. It billowed about her waist in the wind. A tendril of dark hair bisected her features from one temple to the opposite side of her jaw. After a minute she shrugged, clicked her fingers at the dogs and walked to the car with them trotting around her, their tongues lolling like lengths of salmon.

Lee stepped away from the window and it was only then that he noticed the suitcase on the floor beside the door. He stared at it, disbelieving. Surely not. He looked around and swallowed. It was unmistakably the same one, the one he'd taken from Stella. His breath quickened. Brown and battered, with a rounded metal edge on each corner. A faded sticker on one side showed a woman frolicking in the shallows of a beach with a red ball. A grinning fish. *Je me baigne à Agadir,* whatever the hell that meant. He rested a hand on the aluminium windowsill. Again he remembered the woman with the gun, the way she shook her head and blinked slowly before pulling the trigger, before he could say even the tiniest word. *No* or *Don't*. No time for any sort of plea.

Ignoring the pain across his side, he lurched over to the suitcase. He crouched down, lay the suitcase flat and opened it. Inside, arranged head-to-toe like bodies in a grave, were coloured bundles of money. His gun, the one Josef gave him, rested on top of the cash. He skimmed a palm over the money, as if across water, and chuckled. I don't believe it. I don't believe it.

And then the scraping of the door against the linoleum, a blast of cold air on his naked back. He turned to see a large man in a tattered overcoat step into the room.

Ah, the man said in a deep voice. You're awake at last.

4

L ee lost his balance and fell to his side, but was able to grab the gun. It seemed heavier than it should be. He fumbled with it and pointed it up at the man standing over him. Should he just shoot him? It was then that he realised that the safety catch was probably on, but it was too late to investigate. He wasn't even sure where the safety catch was. His heart beat about in his chest like an injured bird.

The man had a large black bag in one hand and held up his other hand, palm outwards. Whoa, fella. No need for that.

Who the hell are you? Lee asked. Fresh blood sumped from his bullet wound into the folds of his stomach. He withheld a grimace but was sure he'd betrayed the amount of pain he was in by the airless quality of his voice. He feared he might throw up.

The man shrugged but made no other movement. He seemed both grave and uninterested. He wasn't wearing shoes. The hems of his trousers were torn. Lee motioned with the gun for the man to close the door, which he did with his bare heel, still holding one hand at shoulder height.

That's quite a hole you got there.

Overcome by pain, Lee didn't answer but unwillingly inspected himself. His right hand, the one clasping the gun, was sticky with blood.

The man joggled his bag. You must be in quite a lot of pain? A bullet inside you, right beside your ribs? Got something here might be of help. Some bandages and disinfectant. I took a look before—

You what? Who the hell *are* you? Where are we, anyway?

The man dropped his bag to the floor with a thud and held up both hands. It's OK. I'm not armed or anything.

The man swayed, as if on a boat. It made Lee wonder if, in fact, the world itself were pitching slightly. It wouldn't surprise him. Nothing would surprise him.

Lee remained where he was on his haunches, shirtless, the gun in one nervous hand while his other rested on the floor. Microbes of grit pressed into his palm. It was an almost pleasurable sensation in the presence of such other enormous discomforts. The suitcase was open beside him. Some of the money inside was spattered with blood. He looked at this large stranger with his thin, greying hair, pale beard and doughy face.

Finally, Lee struggled to his feet, patted the stranger down and shoved him into the chair. The man smelled of alcohol and chalk. Lee grabbed the man's bag and emptied it onto the bed.

Hey. Don't do that—

Shut up.

Bandages, underwear, syringes, a toothbrush, ampoules, wads of cotton wool and a dozen bottles of pills clattered onto the bed like cheap jewellery. Lee stood and wondered what to do.

As you can see, the man said, I'm a . . . doctor.

Because you got a doctor's bag? You're not even wearing shoes, for fuck's sake.

Look. We've got to get out of here. The manager wants us out tonight or she'll call the police or something. She's crazy.

The man was much older than Lee, maybe fifty and sort of heavy with disappointment. Handsomeness clung like rags to his face. Lee waited for something to make sense, for that moment when the world slotted into a familiar view. The stranger sat there with one bare foot slung over his opposite knee, chewing at a fingernail.

Lee straightened. How did I get here?

Someone dumped you here, apparently.

Dumped me here?

Last night. I don't know. That's what the manager told me.

Who's that?

Some crone called Sylvia.

And Lee recalled things: the view of streetlights passing overhead from a speeding car, a man and woman arguing in the front seat; the cold, hard touch of concrete and dew against his cheek. Why?

The stranger sort of laughed. It happens, apparently.

Where are we?

On the outskirts. A motel. Parkview, not that I would hold your breath about the park or the view.

Lee began to feel faint. The room began to lose colour and shape, as if dissolving into more liquid form. He blinked and shook his head. And who are you, again?

Wild.

A doctor?

The man called Wild made an indeterminate motion with his head and scratched his nose.

Lee gritted his teeth. He stepped forward and placed the muzzle of the gun against the man's cheek. The man's teeth clacked together. Who do you work for? You with Marcel? You come after me?

The man shook his head a fraction. His eyes were wide.

What about Stella? You know him? He send you?

The man tilted his face away from the muzzle. I wish that I worked for someone, but I don't. I don't have a clue as to what you're on about. I don't like it as much as you don't like it. Fact is, I wish I never set eyes on you but there's not a lot we can do about that now.

Lee leaned in until his face was barely an inch from that of this man called Wild. He could smell the damp wool of his tatty overcoat, something a bum would wear.

Why are you trembling? Wild asked.

Lee paused with the gun still jammed into Wild's cheek. You can't have that money. That's mine. That's my trip out of here. You understand me? Shaking, he took the gun away and stepped back.

Wild rubbed at the thumb-sized imprint of the gun muzzle on his cheek. I really don't care about your money.

Then what do you want?

I just want to get out of here. If I wanted your damn money I would have taken it while you were passed out on that bed all day. If I wanted your money I wouldn't have bothered cleaning that wound of yours. How much you got there anyway?

Should be eight grand.

Wild scratched his jaw and raised his eyebrows. That's hardly money. Might last me two weeks if I'm lucky. Or unlucky.

Well, you look like you could use it.

Oh, I could always use it. I take it it's not yours?

It's mine now.

With effort Lee went to the window. His breath fogged the glass and he rubbed at it with his sleeve, like a man cutting a hole in ice. Nothing had changed. There were just the same rooftops and electrical wires. The sky thickened as darkness took hold. Through the rattling window he could feel the intimation of the evening and wondered what on earth was happening. Lights flickered in the distance and cars cruised past with headlights on. He wondered briefly about Josef, with his scent of cheap hair oil and violence, the suit that always needed cleaning. The way he sucked at that gold-capped tooth of his. Lee imagined his rangy figure striding across rooftops and edging through doorways, batting obstacles aside with the back of one hand as he searched. It wasn't a comforting thought.

One of the cars parked below reversed from its parking bay and nosed out into the traffic. It was the arguing couple, with their dogs scrabbling on the back-seat vinyl. Lee ran a hand through his hair and slumped on the bed among the medical wreckage. His stomach was smeared with his own warm blood. He licked his lips. A metallic taste had leached into his mouth. His body felt like wet sand. Again he looked around, trying to anchor himself in the room.

And someone wants their money back? Wild asked.

Lee ignored the question. You said you already looked at this . . . at this hole?

Yes.

What can you do? It's fucking killing me.

Like a cat on a sofa, Wild sat back. Here? Nothing much. I'm not qualified for this kind of thing.

So what use are you?

Wild offered a slight shrug, accompanied by a twitch of his hands. That's a good question. He looked embarrassed. They sat in silence. Someone called out in the car park below. A car door slammed.

So why should I trust you?

No reason at all, but it seems like you're a man without too many options. Anyway, you're the one with the gun.

Lee's thoughts were logjammed. Guess I'm damned if I do and damned if I don't.

There you go. Your options. Besides, Wild continued with a sweep of one large hand, believe it or not, but I'm a desperado as well.

And you don't want my money?

My concerns are of a different sort.

Like what?

I just want to get the hell out of here in one piece. Keep a low profile. Escape.

You sure? Lee swallowed. Because I'll kill you, he added in what he hoped was a menacing tone.

Quite sure.

So is there a plan?

A plan?

To get away from here.

There's a man I know who will be able to help you.

Where?

Out on the plains. A day away.

A man? Who is he?

An old friend. A great doctor called Sherman. He's sort of helped me out lots of times. It's a safe place.

Safe?

Well. As safe as you get these days.

And he can help me?

Absolutely. Fine doctor.

Isn't there somewhere closer?

I would have thought distance was an advantage?

Lee pondered. You got a cigarette?

No. Bad for you. It's Lee, right?

Yeah. You got a car?

Yes. Outside.

What's your name?

Wild. I told you.

Lee was exhausted and the pain across his body was immense. Within the ribbing of the thin blue carpet, an insect made its way from fibre to crosshatched fibre, some pale, carpet-eating bug going about its tiny business.

He licked his lips and steadied himself. Am I going to be OK?

Wild got to his feet. Automatically, Lee raised his gun. Wild stopped but said nothing. Lee watched him. What are you doing?

We need to clean you up. Don't want you bleeding all over my car.

Lee stared into Wild's pale blue eyes. He still wasn't sure he trusted him. The guy's hair was like the end of a coarsely cut rope.

Look. I'm more than happy to leave you here with your fortune and a bullet in your belly but, you know, old Sylvia has got the exits covered so whether you like it or not, you're coming with me. The sooner we can get you somewhere, the sooner we can fix you up. Besides, I think you've still got the safety catch on.

Lee felt himself being dismantled from within, piece by tiny piece, and recognised the childish urge to weep. He lowered the gun and lay back on the bed.

You know who shot you? Wild asked as he scrabbled through the items on the bed.

And again Lee remembered the woman with the gun and her slow blink. He wondered if Josef had set him up for some reason. Not exactly. A blonde woman is all I remember.

Wild began daubing Lee's stomach with a circular motion. Goodness, how romantic. Don't *move*, for God's sake, it's hard enough without you wriggling around. But I take it this has something to do with that money over there?

Lee held his breath and clenched his fists against the pain that splintered through him. You could say that.

You don't know her?

No. Never seen her before.

What's this other scar here, on the other side? Your right side?

Nothing.

That's a big nothing.

Lee shook his head and tried to ignore the smell of alcohol and bandages as Wild dressed his wound, which he seemed to do with much anxiety. He doubted this guy was a doctor at all. Probably swiped the bag from someone. It was, however, an act that seemed to require an exchange of minor intimacies.

I'm meant to be at my sister's.

I see. And where is that?

Lee hesitated, unsure of how much he should reveal to this stranger. Out near the ranges. Small town.

Ah. The country.

Yeah. There's a lake. She's expecting me.

Wild stopped what he was doing, as if reminded suddenly of something unpleasant. Well. That's nice. Perhaps you could go there when you're better.

Yes. I think I will.

With your ill-gotten gains.

Lee allowed himself a smile. Yeah. Wild's grizzled profile hovered above him and he could feel the old guy's anxious breath on his chest and the tight warmth of bandages being strapped across him. The burn of antiseptic. The bandages felt secure. Perhaps it would work out after all.

And where are you meant to be?

Wild straightened. What?

Can't imagine anyone ends up here because they want to.

He shook his head. We don't have the time for that particular conversation.

When Wild had finished, Lee fumbled his way into his bloody t-shirt and grabbed his leather coat and the suitcase. He picked up the phone.

What are you doing?

Calling my sister. I should tell her everything is OK, that I'll be there soon, in a few days.

Wild shook his shaggy head. I don't think we have time for that either. Do it later.

Lee wondered about Wild. Was it foolish to go with this stranger, or no more foolish than anything he'd done in the past day or so? He knew there were moments in life when everything changed but invariably they emerged from nowhere with their own logic, from angles never considered. Accidents and disasters and acts of God. Then there were other occasions when you felt the breeze and all it required was a step. A particular and terrifying sort of abandonment. This was one of those times. He grabbed the suitcase. OK. Let's get out of here.

Wild was already standing by the door with his bag. Yes. Let's sally forth.

What?

Let's go.

Lee nodded and they stepped into the cold night air.

5

J osef made tomato soup from a tin. It plopped into the saucepan with a fleshy sound. He heated it and ate with concentration, blowing on each mouthful before sliding the spoon into his dry mouth.

It fell dark and he drew the curtains. Some neighbours talked loudly on the stairwell outside his door. There was laughter, followed by frantic shushing. It would be that idiot from flat seven. He had the sense of a tiny bomb detonating within his chest. What was it about the laughter of others that could be so devastating? He ran a finger around his collar and sucked at his gold-capped eye tooth, fondling the surface expertly with his tongue. The noise died down, but irritation swirled in his chest, like mud stirred from the bottom of a lake.

After eating, Josef sat smoking hand-rolled cigarettes at his kitchen table. White Ox tobacco, a prison habit. He wore only trousers and a white singlet. His skin was pale. Beneath a prominent collarbone was a clumsy scar, a splash of differently coloured skin, where he had been shot a long time ago. A woolly cross was tattooed on the inside of his left wrist. The tattoo's longer line was about two inches in length, easily hidden beneath a shirt cuff. He traced the faint threads with the fingertips of his right hand, sensitive to the ink beneath the surface. Occasionally, the tattoo hummed, a sound to which he alone was sensitive, in the same way that only the musician is aware of the vibration of a cello's string long after the audible note has died away.

One of his clearest memories of prison was of the monotone whine of tattoo guns assembled from a thick guitar string, elastic and a small motor. It was constant, a sound that accompanied men calling out to each other and the clatter of tin plates and cups. He had watched men being tattooed, their mouths tight with discomfort, and he could recall many recurring designs: dragons, naked women, flowers, barbed wire, teardrops, tigers. Hundreds of women's names, thousands of *LOVE* and *HATE*. Stars and pit bulls. Men bearing Christ upon their backs.

Of acquiring his own tattoo he had no memory, not even of the scabbing that occurs afterwards. It was as if—like the skin itself—it had always been there and sometimes as he rubbed at it, he believed it had just floated to the surface, some thin wreckage washed up on the shores of his body. Periodically he would be compelled to rid himself of the damn thing and spend hours rubbing at it with rags soaked in various solutions: bleach, milk, vinegar, mineral turpentine. Once, even sandpaper, gently back and forth, with no result aside from a predictable and embarrassing graze on his inner arm. All of this was, of course, to no avail; the fucking thing would be there forever.

He drummed his fingers on the laminated tabletop. The kitchen possessed the sepia odour of last week's dinners, of cuts of meat nobody cooked anymore and beneath that, faintly, of fly spray. A transistor radio in leather casing burbled, its volume too low to discern actual words. He listened only to current affairs or Test cricket; anything else seemed too frivolous. He'd never possessed an ear for music and failed to understand the point of it. A week-old newspaper was on the table, along with the makings for a cup of tea and his packet of tobacco. Steam unfurled from the teapot. He poured himself a cup and added his customary dash of milk, his movements almost ceremonial through long years of repetition.

A tea-leaf circled on the surface of his drink. It sank and reappeared in the milky currents. He knew a tea-leaf floating on the surface of tea foretold a visitor. He also knew it was unlucky to kill a white swan or a white moth; that it was lucky to touch a hunchback; he knew not to place a hat on a bed and that a shoe on a table would only tempt death by hanging. He made sure to smash the discarded shells of hard-boiled eggs, lest witches use them to sail out to sea and drown unwary sailors.

His family were given to poring over the moist bodies of newborns, looking and feeling for signs of future career or personalities: a birthmark; a wayward blink; a caul to guard against drowning. When he was born, a grandmother shouldered into the room and held him up to her face as if preparing to devour him, before announcing he would remain a lifelong bachelor, alone and uncharmed. How she arrived at this diagnosis was unclear, but it was accepted nonetheless and woven without argument into the family fabric.

When he was a boy, the women sang songs of demons and love, of forests and oceans and blood. They were warned away from Jews, particularly at Passover when, as everyone knew, they held Christian children over vats and sliced their throats with butcher's knives to drink their blood. He believed in some vague and shifting version of hell. Thanks to his dry-fingered aunts, he also knew all about the saints. About Saint Dreux, the patron saint of those with broken bones, the owners of coffee shops and the deranged. About Saint Nicholas, who raised back to life three children who had been murdered and crammed into a vat of brine. Saint Francis, patron of those fated to die alone.

These offerings, this knowledge, was a love of sorts. Josef was never sure he trusted the signs his relatives insisted were scattered throughout the world, but he found them impossible to ignore. If nothing else, they gave shape to otherwise shapeless anxieties and were a personal bulwark against imminent disaster. After all, only those fears that remained unnamed retained their potency. Although he had not seen them in a long time, he imagined those aunts as they were twenty years ago, shuffling on slippered feet through darkened houses, forever haunted by ailments of obscure provenance.

The tea-leaf vanished beneath the surface. He wondered who the visitor could possibly be. Only on experiencing it did he realise how rare expectation had become for him.

The phone rang in the lounge room. He rose slowly and answered it, already disappointed by the growing comprehension that it would undoubtedly be Marcel.

Josef?

Yes, Marcel.

We got a problem.

Josef lowered himself into an overstuffed armchair that was here when he moved in. It was an enormous thing, almost capable of swallowing him whole. He stifled a sigh. What is it?

You heard from Lee? You seen him?

Josef sucked at his gold tooth. No.

Nothing?

No. Why?

Because. Because neither have I.

Josef adjusted the phone receiver to hear better. He cast an eye about for his cup of tea, pointlessly because he knew it was still on the kitchen table, going cold. He opened his mouth to speak, but Marcel interrupted.

He was supposed to be here this afternoon by the latest. You saw him, did you? You gave him the right instructions?

Of course.

Of course. Don't give me *of course*, Josef.

Josef blushed. Motes of dust eddied like plankton in the lamplight. Well, he said. I'm not sure what could have happened out there. It was pretty straightforward, you know.

Yeah. I know. You know. But does that fucking *kid* know?

Well. It was . . . uh, I explained it all.

Great. You explained it all.

Gave him the piece, wrote the address. Josef sucked at his tooth. If language was how the world was defined, their use of it was the inverse: a means not to describe things or pin them down, but to break them into something more haphazard. Information was not conveyed but rather whispered or scattered in unlikely places, thickly coded, freighted with ambiguity. The world was almost always approached from the side.

Marcel went on. Well, Sammy's been around today and seen Stella with some woman—

A woman?

Yes, a woman. Blonde thing. A fucking blonde woman.

Josef nodded. He needed to say something and listened to Marcel listening to his silence, imagined him screwing the phone into his ear in an effort to detect its meanings. You think . . . You think he, uh . . . What you think happened?

If I know I don't have to ring you. Tell me what you think. You're the man who brought this guy in. Said you had high hopes. Reliable, trustworthy. Write the guy a fucking—what is it?—a *reference*. This is your thing here, Josef. He's *your* guy.

And Josef felt the chill of implied threat. It was true: Josef had courted Lee upon his release from prison with the promise of easy money. Marcel gave him simple tasks for a few months to try him out before the Stella thing, the thing that the kid had obviously fucked up in a big way. Josef had assured Marcel the kid would be fine; after all, look what he did to that mate of his in prison. And besides, the kid had nowhere else to go. His family were all killed in a car accident years ago. This was the clincher. He was theirs.

Marcel was breathing furiously on the other end of the line and Josef imagined him rocking forward and back on that office chair of his, adding to the furrows already worn into the carpet.

You think he'd run off with that sort of dough? Josef said at last, trying to sound incredulous.

Why not? You tell me. You think he was OK?

Well, yes. Of course or I wouldn't have brought him in. It's only, what, eight G? Hardly worth the risk. Small change. Must be some other reason. Must be. Might be asleep or something?

Marcel harrumphed. Maybe not such small change for someone like that. Maybe for me. Maybe for you. When you spoke with him yesterday, was there anything that made you think he's not up to something like this? Anything? This job wasn't just stealing, after all.

I know it's not, Marcel.

So, was there anything made you suspicious?

No. Kid seemed fine. He's got nowhere to go. Probably at his flat. Maybe he misunderstood or something.

Maybe.

I'll go there tonight. Go there now.

Damn right you will. Go there now.

There was silence. Josef jammed the phone between his chin and shoulder and scratched his tattoo. He recalled the encounter at Lee's dingy flat with its furniture obviously found in the street and the flickering television on a milk crate. The clumsy way Lee handled the gun, like it was a dead animal. No real surprises for a kid his age.

Marcel cleared his throat and when he spoke at last, his voice was softer. I want you to sort this out. This is—how should I say? This is not the first thing that's sort of gotten away from you, you know what I mean?

Josef looked at his watch. It was getting late. Ten p.m. He badly needed a cigarette. He knew only too well what Marcel meant, could almost hear the sad shake of his old head. Foolishly, he nodded, managed a quiet *yes*.

You got to find this kid, Josef. You're losing your touch.

Yes.

You got to find him, or else.

I know.

I'll give you two days. Don't let me down on this. And take good care of him. Good care.

Marcel, it's only eight grand. Even if the kid has run off, it's hardly worth—Hey. Eight grand is eight grand. It's the whatsit—the principle. You can't escape this. You fucked up, Josef. Better make this right again. We can't have people doing this kind of thing. We just can't. You know nobody's—what's the word?—indispensable.

Normally they would talk of other, domestic things. Marcel liked to hear tips for the Saturday races or the best price for fruit at the moment. They gossiped about people they knew. Occasionally Marcel indulged Josef with a few questions about the cricket, a topic in which Marcel had only scant interest. But not tonight. They said their goodbyes and hung up.

Josef returned to the kitchen. His tea was cold. He assembled a cigarette with deft movements and lit it before returning to the chair in the lounge room. He thought about Lee. His angular face and dark eyes. His habit of insinuating himself into a room before anyone realised. He couldn't believe the little prick had let him down so soon, and after such an opportunity. And for such a petty amount of money. No. There must be a better explanation for this. The kid will show up. The kid will show up and everything will make sense and they'll laugh and even Marcel will chuckle and be embarrassed about threatening Josef on the phone like that.

But where would someone like Lee go? With no family? It amazed him that people seemed to move about all the time these days. Change jobs and houses and wives. Whole countries, just like that. Incredible behaviour. Where did these people go? Where could Lee go, assuming he had gone at all, and wasn't hiding out in his flat? Could be anywhere. The possibilities frightened him.

Smoke hung in a grey mass around Josef's head and shoulders. He felt heavy and tired. Heavy and tired and—for the first time in a very long time—in danger. An old man late at night, listening to the world going about its business outside his window. He'd known for some time he was getting too old for this whole thing, but now, unfortunately, Marcel suspected it too. He sucked at his tooth and smoked until the butt was soggy.

6

It was nearly 11.00 p.m. when Josef got to Lee's shabby, redbrick apartment block. He mounted the creaking stairs. The stairwell light wasn't working and the only illumination was from a streetlight filtering through the landing window. The gauzy light reminded him in an obscure way of some distant period in his life and he was briefly flooded with the disappointment peculiar to the consideration of time.

He paused on the landing with a hand on the worn banister and peered upwards into the darkness. Winter had settled into his bones over the past few years and he was aware now of an ache in his right knee. The apartment block hummed with unseen domestic activity, with the gurgle of water in pipes, the metallic swish of cutlery drawers opening and closing. The stairwell smelled of incense and boiled vegetables. Despite the late hour, someone was cooking curry. Probably bloody Pakistanis or Indians, up late on Bombay time or something. He tugged his jacket cuff down over his tattoo.

Lee's apartment was on the second floor. A box of ancient newspapers rested on the floor outside the door, the relic of an earlier tenant. Josef pressed an ear to the door but could hear nothing. No light seeped under it and there was no response when he knocked. Lee, he said. Are you in there? It's Josef.

He listened again, remaining utterly still, so that when at last he moved it was as if he were assembled from the darkness. Still nothing. He drew his gun, followed by his collection of skeleton keys. His bladder clenched. There were blokes who needed to shit in the midst of a crime and, in fact, he had once been involved in a robbery that was very nearly ruined by a young guy called Leon stopping to take a crap in an alley.

But for Josef, it was different. Without fail, even after all these years, the act of breaking into a house prompted in him the urge to piss. He tried the keys one by one, until the lock gave and he nudged the door open. He waited on the landing with his gun drawn for a full minute before stepping into the apartment. Immediately he could detect, by the bony silence, that the place was abandoned, an impression confirmed when he switched on the light. The furnishings were incomplete, heavy with transience. There was the television on the milk crate, a sagging couch and an ashtray on the windowsill, each stripped of any connection to whoever had used them. The place was chilly, unloved.

The tiny bedroom and kitchen offered no clues. The bathroom showerhead dripped into the stained bathtub with a soft, rhythmic *dunk dunk dunk*. In the bedroom, just a low wooden dresser and the mattress on the floor. What meaning, if any, could be harvested from these inanimate things? A bunch of rooms that offered nothing of the person who lived here. As he patrolled the apartment, Josef felt a sort of dry pity for Lee, a sense of having interrupted him weeping or reading pornography.

As a teenager, Josef would often break into houses alone. Of course he was searching for money or jewellery and other valuables to sell, but there were other satisfactions to be gained. He would sometimes spend an entire afternoon in a new house admiring the neat and ordered rooms, sitting primly at the kitchen table eating cheese or warming his cold hands among the clothes of strangers. He would doze on couches and wonder who would buy plastic place mats bearing the images of European cathedrals and bridges. He fondled letters from mothers and photographs of lovers. Broken toys. A small globe of the entire world. Even now, more than forty years later, he was unable to detect the scent of musk without being transported, almost bodily, back to the house on Mott Street where he first encountered it on the dressing table of a beautiful widow recently home from Africa; the thin afternoon light glinting on her glassware and the distant bark of a dog. More than once, it was only upon returning to his own house that he realised he had neglected to steal anything.

He often felt more at home in the houses of strangers, but there was nothing here in Lee's apartment; it was entirely too familiar. He stood in the bedroom with his gun still in hand. Clothes lay on the wooden floor in piles as if their owner had urgently disrobed before fleeing. The walls were grubby, dotted here and there with marks and smudges, like the thumbprints of ghosts. He was preparing to leave when the phone rang. Automatically, he raised his gun. As always, he expected the phone's plastic form to vibrate in accompaniment to the urgent trill and was slightly disappointed when it failed to do so. It rang about ten times before falling silent. Josef scratched his tattoo. He heard people walk past in the street below. A woman chuckled. He stood still.

The phone rang again. He crouched beside the mattress and lifted the receiver to his ear. Hello.

Lee, a woman said. Where on earth are you?

Josef stood up, phone in his left hand, gun in the other. No, he said after a pause. Lee's not here.

There was a brief silence. Sorry? Who's this, then?

I'm a friend.

More silence. He heard the woman transfer the phone from one hand to the other, the crumpling sound so close it might have been happening in the shell of his own ear. Strange that strangers could be so close. Josef knew that people would speak almost compulsively to fill silences. He hoped she would. It might be his only lead. She would speak or just hang up. He waited, tapping the gun against his thigh, and was surprised to detect a quickening of his heart. The woman said nothing.

Maybe I can help you? he said.

Well. Do you know where he is? She was curt, suspicious.

No. I was looking for him myself.

What are you doing in his house? What's your name?

I have a key, alright.

I see. Well, he was supposed to be here this afternoon and he hasn't turned up. I've been ringing all evening.

You were expecting him?

Yeah. I'm his sister. He's coming to stay with us for a while. Who are you?

His sister?

Yeah. Claire. Has he left yet, at least?

I thought . . .

What? Thought what?

You're his sister? Lee's sister?

Yes.

He told me his family were all killed in a car crash.

Oh, Jesus. Did he?

Yes.

The woman sighed. No. Not everyone.

There was a man's voice in the background and again the phone rustled. More muffled voices. He imagined the woman, this sister of Lee's, pressing the phone against her chest to relay their conversation to a man in a doorway.

Beside his own wan reflection, Josef could see that a large moth had attached itself to the outside of the bedroom window. Even from several feet away, Josef could discern its tiny wings, its rotating antennae and the furry bulk of its body. An aunt used to tell him that a moth attempting to enter a house was a harbinger of death and he wondered how such an apparently innocuous creature—this mute Labrador of the insect world—could signify such a thing. He always thought they looked like royalty outcast, their brown wings tattered robes fluttering about their bodies.

More rustling and it seemed the woman was back with him. He needed to force the conversation. And where are you?

So you don't know where he is?

Why don't you give me your telephone number and address and—

No. It's OK . . . I think I'll try later. He'll show up. He promised.

Wai—

The woman hung up. Shit. He'd blown it. Josef tossed the phone receiver onto the mattress. Shit. He shrugged inside his jacket. Again he looked around the bedroom and wondered at the sheer inevitability of a life that now found him standing in this apartment. It seemed he had not travelled very far since his adolescent break-ins. The moth still hung grimly onto the windowpane, its wings ruffling in the wind. He imagined it staring at him with its black eyes, but doubted moths could even see.

So. Lee had a sister. This was interesting.

He shoved his gun back inside his jacket, unzipped his trousers and fumbled until he stood ponderously with hips jutting forward, his cock between thumb and forefinger. A chill murmured through him like a current of polite applause. How painful that one's body eventually needed quiet urging to accomplish the most rudimentary tasks. Was old age merely an inability to complete those things that for so long have occurred naturally? He waited as his organs awakened somewhere in his abdomen and finally produced a hot, thin arc of piss. He aimed more or less at Lee's mattress and before long a sizzling pool formed within the folds of a dirty sheet.

He was unsure what to do when he had finished. He zipped himself up and waited while the rust-coloured puddle melted into the sheet and mattress. It didn't give him nearly as much satisfaction as he had hoped, but perhaps he had expected too much.

It was almost midnight. He needed a drink, but the only thing in the fridge was half a bottle of beer with a teaspoon dangling in its neck. He lifted the bottle out, shook it, then dropped it onto the linoleum floor. It landed with a thud but failed to break. Beer glugged out. Josef shook his head and smoothed his hair. He yawned and leaned against a bench to smoke a cigarette. The puddle of beer collected beneath the sink. His hands shook as he stroked the inside of his left wrist. He paused, stopped breathing. Yes. There it was. The hum, heard through his fingertips, of his tattoo.

7

Lee slumped against the passenger-side door with the gun in his lap. The lower half of his t-shirt and the waist of his jeans were heavy and warm with his own blood. His body was lighter, his mouth woolly with thirst. Although painful to do, every so often he swivelled in his seat to check the road behind. There was just asphalt unravelling into the darkness. Wild drove at an unthreatening pace but ever since the accident, as long as he could remember, Lee found himself pressing his foot to the floor in search of the brake whenever in a car. This despite never having learned to drive.

The car smelled of old takeaway food. Empty chip packets were jammed between the dashboard and windscreen. Soft-drink bottles lolled drunkenly about the floor. The back seat was covered in clothes and books. The door handle rattled beside him as if preparing to break loose and he moved to the middle of his seat, afraid the door would fly open under the barest pressure. The suitcase of money was on the floor. Now and again Lee tapped his foot against it, to ensure it was still there.

Without speaking, they drove through sprawling industrial suburbs, fenced in and broken. Smokestacks fingered into the sky, each topped with plumes of white steam or smoke. A girl waited alone in a bus shelter with her knees pressed together, a newspaper was flattened by the cold wind against a wire fence. The suburbs petered out as they fled. The buildings became lower and less frequent, giving way to open spaces until, finally, the city fell away altogether.

The countryside was dark, but occasionally Lee could make out an ancient shed listing in a field as if frozen mid-collapse or the bulky shapes of cows dumbly watching as they passed. There weren't many other cars. Lee didn't know where they were going, but was relieved to get away.

He turned to face Wild. You really a doctor? I mean, this car is pretty shitty.

Wild sighed and wiped his nose with a sleeve. Yes. More or less.

What does that mean?

Wild shrugged and stared straight ahead. His voice was ragged. It means that I studied medicine and that I worked as a doctor for a long time but that due to certain … Due to certain factors, I am what they call *suspended*. Meaning I'm not able to practise at the moment, if ever. So yes and no is the answer.

Lee waited for more information. He stared at Wild's craggy profile. What sort of factors?

He didn't answer. The road climbed and they rounded a bend. Ahead on the other side of the road, a car was parked facing away from them. The brakelights glowed red, but the car's exact colour and shape were oily in the forest gloom. Its boot was agape. They slowed and Lee recognised the car as the one that had departed the motel earlier in the afternoon. One of its headlights continued to burn, illuminating a crowd of trees. Wild wound down his window and Lee heard the sound of their tyres crunching on the gravel shoulder. They came to a complete halt. Cold air filled the interior.

Lee shivered and adjusted his position. The bandages Wild had applied earlier pressed awkwardly into his abdomen. What are you doing?

Wild waved the question away. Beyond the sound of the idling car, Lee heard the metallic *tick, tick* of a cooling engine. But there was something else, a hiss of air escaping. Lee peered more closely at the parked car and saw that, in fact, it had crashed. He grimaced. The car's front end was compacted into half its size and the windscreen was jigsawed and sagging. Liquid dripped onto the asphalt. It seemed a tableau just perfected, and Lee imagined those responsible scurrying into the shadows and crouching out of sight. Some elaborate joke.

This is how it was, a scene that might even have been assembled from his own memory. The moaning silence. The stillness. The *tick, tick, tick*.

It was only then, as he assembled the discrete elements, that he saw a face leering from the bottom corner of the passenger-side window like that of a drowned woman. Her bloodied mouth was slightly open and pressed against the moist glass. A wave of dark hair drifted like seaweed across one eye.

This is just how it was.

Panic spidered through him. Oh shit. Let's get out of here. Let's go.

Wild didn't move.

Lee poked him in the shoulder with the gun. I don't think this is a good idea. These people are dead. Let's go.

But still Wild made no move.

Don't make me shoot you.

Wild faced him. He breathed heavily. In the half-light, his face was a cliff of hollows and ridges. Wild blinked and ran a hand through his wayward fringe. He looked down. Let's not go through this again, he said. He sounded afraid, but didn't make a move.

Lee sat up to relieve the pressure on his wound, which had begun to throb. Please. Can we keep going? He paused. Please.

Wild scratched his neck and turned away. He appeared not to be even looking at the other car, but at nothing really, just staring straight ahead at God knows what. Something twitched in his jaw, some muscle working away beneath the skin as if attempting to surface. There was a sharp pop of exploding glass from the crashed car.

Lee jammed his gun into Wild's side, but it drew no response and Lee wondered if Wild had even felt it through his huge overcoat. He made another movement with the gun but again it elicited nothing.

Then, unbelievably, Wild grabbed his bag, got out of the car and walked across to the wrecked car. Just walked right over to the car.

Lee remained where he was. Fuck, he said under his breath. Fucking Wild. He shivered and tried to curl himself into some position of warmth, to no avail.

After a minute, he too stumbled from the car and followed, the gun still in his hand. Whatever pipe or valve was hissing, it began hissing even more as Lee approached, as if aware of him. His breath fogged in front of his face and he had the sensation of stepping into a dream.

Wild banged on the passenger-side window with the heel of his palm and might even have said something, some sort of doctor-style reassurance, but the woman's head just jounced against the glass. A smear of bloody drool bubbled near her broken lip and smashed teeth.

Through the rear window, Lee could see the driver slumped against the steering wheel. Wild walked around to the open driver's-side door. There was a smell of hot metal and singed plastic, the aroma of the machine age, of chaos and organisation. It was also, Lee knew, the smell of loss.

Lee looked around. His breathing was loud. The wreck's windscreen sagged with a damp crackle. He heard a low growl and remembered the dogs accompanying the couple when they left the motel. He stepped away, expecting them to leap from the wreckage, but the back seat of the car was empty. There was no sign of them. They had been killed or had run off into the forest. He imagined them bounding through the darkness with rolling eyes and pink tongues and wondered what would become of the poor things.

He wanted to get away from here. If he knew how, he could take Wild's car and drive off into the night. Or just set out walking into the woods, into the forest, into the darkness? Keep going until something happened, until he fell into a fucking hole or off a cliff or something. Anything would be better than standing on a country road in the middle of a cold, cold night. Instead he shuffled over to where Wild was leaning over the driver's-side door.

Again the low, strangled growl and the driver sat back in his seat. The man sighed deeply, unbuckled himself and stepped from the car with the demeanour of one who has recently completed an arduous journey. His face shone with blood and there was a deep horizontal wound along his forehead that bore the crenellated imprint of a steering wheel. The man swayed, and spat blood and matter from his broken mouth.

Lee's heart scrabbled in his chest. He felt sweat beneath his armpits, the itch of perspiration on his neck. He wanted to shit or sob, as if his entire body were attempting to abandon itself.

The car continued to emit high-pitched squawks of regret and sputterings of mechanical distress. Wild dropped his bag onto the ground and placed his hands on the driver's chest. Around them, beyond the penumbra of the headlights, the world dissolved into darkness. Lee licked his dry lips. His wound was sticky and painful beneath the bandages. This was bad. This was really fucking bad. The worst. Meanwhile, Wild was restraining the driver, saying: Wait. Hold it. You've been in an accident. Let's wait a minute.

But the driver peered over Wild's shoulder at Lee. A fringe of dark hair fell across his eyes, partly covering his wound. The driver stuck out his bottom jaw and then retracted it several times, as if testing the hinge. Then he appeared to finally notice Wild. He opened and closed his mouth. A ragged whisper: That was, uh . . . That was. What was that? Who are you, anyway? We were just . . .

The driver's wound was bleeding freely now and he wiped at it with both hands. His forehead was already bruised and swollen, the skin the colour of thunderclouds. Blood flooded his eyes. Wild continued to reassure the man, patting his chest with his palms, but the man brushed past Wild and shuffled towards Lee.

Resisting an urge to flee, Lee waited until the driver stood directly in front of him. He wanted to raise his gun, but instead held it against his thigh. He and the stranger watched each other, exchanging foggy breath.

The man inspected Lee as one might a newly discovered relative, as if he held an ancestral clue. You, the man said, and he emitted a belch and began to fold at the waist in a slow, architectural collapse. You again. And the driver coughed, exhaling a spray of blood and teeth before dropping to his knees.

Despite himself, Lee caught the man by the shoulder. The man was looking down at the ground, at the wet grass, moving inwards, breathing with effort. He was unshaven. His groans were weighty, crammed with sorrow. After a minute he stared Lee in the face. Lee could smell his breath, already growing cool.

You've killed me, the man said at last, crying now, adding tears to the wreckage of his face. You've killed us. And Lee and the man stayed like that for several long moments, a meeting of sorts, on a cold and lonely road. He wished that Wild would take this man away, but he just stood there. Lee knew there were many ways to die. The tarot of agonies. Regicide, fratricide, parricide, infanticide. Death by water or flame, by hanging and burial. Gunshot wounds. The random beating on a city street. In jail he met a man who had ground a broken bottle into a stranger's guts because he spilled his drink in a crowded bar. The unchecked bolt of an aeroplane wing springs free and slips thirty thousand feet into the ocean.

And, of course, of course, a man loses control of a car and slams into a tree in the middle of the night. Accidents and murder, disease and terror. The frailty of human beings, these sacks of blood and gristle. How was it possible to live to a ripe old age?

Lee might have known this, but he stared into the bloodied face of a dying stranger and something within him broke clear and fell away. What are you talking about? What are you talking about? We just got here. You crashed into the tree. It's not my fault—

You've blood on you, the man said. And then his gaze grew watery and began to drain away.

Lee could think of nothing to say. He was struck by the man's phrasing. *You've blood on you.* The precision. An unfamiliar flavour stained his mouth. He swallowed and nodded. Then at last in a dry voice: Yes, I've got blood on me.

You're hurt. But it will be alright. And the driver became even heavier, crumpled from Lee's flimsy grasp and slumped to the ground.

Lee gasped. He wiped his hand, the one that had touched the stranger, and stepped back.

Finally, Wild approached and kneeled in the gravel beside the driver. From a safe distance, Lee watched him prise the man's eyelids apart and shine a little torch into his eyes, all the while muttering to himself like a priest.

OK. What we do now is . . . What we do is, uh . . . And Wild fiddled about in his bag. But he didn't really seem to know what he was doing.

Lee moved his palm across the heads of the overgrown grass beside the road. The sensation was slight, but pleasant, like being tickled by insects. He licked the dew from his skin. It was soft and tasted, or so he imagined, of clouds.

Shaking his head, Wild stood and wiped his hands on his overcoat. Jesus Christ. This is terrible. Just terrible. What a thing to happen. He scratched furiously at his thin beard. Bloody terrible.

Lee looked down at the man beside the road, whose head was thrown back at an awkward angle and whose blood was leaking out and pooling on the ground. The grass had been flattened where Wild had been squatting but was now already springing back to its original height. In an hour or so it would be as if they were never here. Again he wished they had not stopped. They should never have come this way. It was Wild's fault. Can't you do something?

Do what?

I don't know. Help him. You're the doctor. You wanted to stop here, remember?

Wild sighed. It's too late. They're dead.

Both of them?

Yes. We're too late.

What about the woman? Maybe you can help the woman. Help the woman, at least.

Wild shook his head.

Lee knew he sounded frantic and wanted to say something, but instead looked away. Moths and other insects flickered through the column of light in front of the ruined car. A breeze stirred the leaves of unseen trees. Otherwise, the silence was immense, a solid thing bearing down upon them. And still the foreign taste upon his tongue, like metal filings. Perhaps it was panic, he thought, and spat clumsily into the darkness. The flavour of panic or despair.

What was he saying to you? Wild said. Did you know him?

No. No.

He seemed to recognise you.

Lee shook his head quickly. No. Don't know. Guy was dying. Dying people will say anything. Maybe he recognised me from the motel. Lee paused. I saw them leave that place this afternoon, a few hours ago. With their dogs. They left with their dogs on the back seat.

Wild nodded, although he didn't appear convinced.

What about the dogs? Lee asked, to change the subject.

What?

Their dogs? They had dogs in the car. When they drove away today from the motel. Maybe we should do something? What will happen to them?

Wild shrugged and rubbed his nose. Who knows? They probably ran off into the forest. They'll be OK.

Really? They'll be OK?

Maybe. Yeah. They'll eat possums or something. Go feral. How many dogs?

Three, I think.

They stood in silence. Although he tried not to look at the dead man, Lee was aware of a dark shape at the periphery of his vision. He began to shiver. He needed clean, warm clothes and went to the open boot of the crashed car. It smelled of motor oil and mildew. Tools were scattered about, along with a dark-blue travel bag. The car-boot light was buttery and he was aware of Wild's questioning gaze behind him as he unzipped the travel bag and checked the contents. Sure enough, there was what appeared to be a weekend's worth of clothes and toiletries. He pocketed his gun and dragged the bag free with a grunt.

Then Wild was behind him. What are you doing? You can't just take that bag. I don't think this is a great idea, I really don't.

Lee gestured to his t-shirt and jeans, both patterned with dark smears of blood. I need some clothes.

They stood face-to-face in the middle of the empty road. Lee became aware of a small burring sound. It grew steadily louder. They stared at each other. Wild's face glowed like a coin in the gloom. His blue eyes widened.

Lee sensed a now-familiar panic swelling inside him. Shit, he said and his breath hovered on the air. He looked at Wild, wanting him to realise that this was all his fault.

It was the sound of an approaching car.

8

The car drew closer. Lee looked back the way they had come. He hugged his leather coat tighter around himself and the pain of his wound throbbed through him. There wasn't enough time to get back into the car and leave. Fucking Wild. Trapped. They stepped off the road. Lee held his gun out of sight against his thigh.

The first thing he saw was the searching beam of headlights throwing the trees beside the road into sharp relief. Then the car came around the bend, as they had done ten minutes earlier. A roar and a blast of light. Unable to raise his arm to shield his eyes, he turned his face away.

The car skidded and slowed, coming to a halt on the shoulder of the road. Dust billowed and there was the warm, underwater sound of music. The music was switched off after a few seconds, followed by the engine. Again the dense, forest silence was interrupted only by the twitterings and sighs of a cooling engine. Lee stroked his gun with his thumb. He waited.

Eventually the sound of a car door opening. Shoes crunched on gravel, some indistinct muttering. Little, human sounds. Lee peered into the fierce light, but could make out nothing through the glare. He was aware of the dead man on the ground beside him.

Are you OK? A young woman's voice, followed by the sound of the other car door opening. More shoes crackling on the gravel.

Lee flinched as Wild stepped forward with an arm raised against the light and indicated the car behind them. There's been an accident, he was saying.

Two shapes emerged from the light. A man and a woman. They were young and eager, like deer. Jeans and baggy hair. University students. At least it wasn't the police. The woman squinted at Wild, then slowly across to Lee, with a kind of intense inspection. Lee watched her gaze move through the darkness and sensed her trying to understand the scene.

She mouthed something, then gasped and held a hand to her red mouth. Oh my God!

Then the boyfriend was beside her, grabbing at her arm. Shit. What happened here?

Before Lee could say or do anything, Wild explained how they had just arrived and that he was a doctor but there was nothing he could do, so they might as well keep driving while he and Lee waited for the police. It sounded plausible. It was even sort of true. Wild made shooing motions with his hands.

The couple observed the dead man with tight faces, curious and appalled. Lee nodded as Wild told the story but he began to feel faint, insubstantial. All this death, he thought. All this death.

The girl frowned. She broke away from her boyfriend and approached Lee. But are you OK? Were you in the crash too? She was looking down to where Lee was clutching his coat around him with one bloody hand. Did you crash?

Lee was inexplicably moved by the girl's concern and would have liked to squat by the road for a minute until satisfied everything was finished here, that it was all over, but he just said in a small voice: I'm fine.

Wild moved forward again. Lee watched several stray hairs waving about from the side of his head. They glowed in the white beam of the car headlights.

We just got here ourselves, Wild was saying. The car spun off the road, but there's nothing we can do now. The people have . . . passed away. We'll tell someone in the next town. We'll tell the cop—the police, I mean. We'll tell the police. Don't worry.

The boy nodded, but the girl walked over and kneeled beside the dead man with a hand still clasped over her mouth. Although several feet away, Lee could smell the apple scent of her shampoo and feel the warmth of her body. He tried not to look at her.

Wait a minute, the boy said. What's going on here? You're not going through their stuff, are you? Why is the boot open? What's that bag there?

The girl stiffened and turned on her heel. Lee swore softly and was possessed of the now-familiar sensation of things sliding out of control. In a gesture he began to regret even as it was happening, he strode forward and put the barrel of the gun to the girl's head. I told you. I *said* we'd be OK.

Wild groaned. The girl appeared not to realise what was happening for a second, then let out a low moan. Her friend took one step forward with his mouth open. The girl attempted to stand but then lowered herself into a half-crouch with her head retracted into her shoulders, as if trying to disappear. Her hands were waving about in front of her, appealing to the darkness.

Lee observed all this from somewhere outside himself. The whole thing, he thought, was just like another car accident: that slowing of time and thick liquidity of action before impact. You know it's coming, and yet it's always a surprise. He felt enormous, inflated, a giant astride this puny road. He imagined he would be able, should he try, to observe each leaf on every tree for miles around, to smell wood smoke from ancient fires and to hear, beneath the breeze and this girl's dry wail and the thuddering of his own heart, the sound of a witchetty grub chewing at a leaf, the very snicker of its tiny jaws.

Then Wild was flailing about in the middle of the road. Lee, he was saying. Whoa. Whoa. What are you doing? This is crazy. He walked backwards, hands up in some gesture to inform the boy to back off, until he stood beside Lee. The girl was sobbing and making tiny, inarticulate sounds. Her body trembled. Lee, Wild said softly. Don't do this. This is stupid. Really stupid. He stepped closer. Think about it. We'll have cops *all over us*.

Lee watched Wild's mouth opening and closing. Why was it, he wondered, that men's beards change colour and tended to be darker around the mouth? Like a nicotine stain, even on people like Wild, who didn't smoke?

The boy just stood there with his mouth open. He had placed one hand palm-down on his head, as if preparing to screw himself into the earth. His face shone with tears.

Wild continued to plead with Lee. Come on. Come on. This isn't the right thing to do. Please. Lee?

Then the girl turned her head slightly, just enough for Lee to see her luminous face. Her skin was stretched tight across her skull and she looked up at him through wet lashes. Blue eyes. Please, she murmured. Please, mister. Have mercy. Please don't shoot me. Please don't kill me. I'll do anything. Please.

Lee stared down at the girl. He could hear Wild's breathing at his other shoulder. His leather coat creaked and again he felt like weeping, unsure whether for himself or the girl. Why?

Please, the girl went on, her voice growing in volume and pitch as if suddenly certain this approach was the key to her survival. Please. Please.

Why? Why did you have to stop? Why did you even come this way? This is an old road, not even the highway. This is nothing, not even *scenic*. A piece-of-shit road. Look what you're making me do. Look at me! We told you to go away.

The boy spoke up. We were going home.

What?

We were going home. That's all.

Home?

To see our parents.

Lee's breath fish-hooked in his throat. You're what, brother and sister?

The boy nodded. A tremble passed from the girl through the gun, along Lee's arm, through the root of his shoulder and deep into his body. He looked into her moist and shining eyes. It was an inevitable intimacy. At that moment a person is unlike at any other time in their life; their noises, the flash of their eyes, the darknesses they must be prepared to betray. He believed her when she said she would do anything to save herself.

Lee thought quickly and tilted his chin to address the boy. Come here. Give me your driver's licence. The boy did as he was told. Lee inspected it. What you need to do, he said at last in what he hoped was a calm voice, is to get back into the car and drive back the way you came. You need to do this quickly. Straight away. You have to get as far away from here as possible, OK? This is no place for you. But I find out you told anyone and . . . I'll come after you. He thought of the worst threat he could make. I'll find your parents and kill them, do you understand me? This is no place. No place for you.

The boy nodded eagerly and Lee removed the gun from the girl's blonde head. She stayed crouching where she was for several seconds before scrambling to her feet and running to her brother. She was sobbing loudly now and they both vanished behind the glare of headlights. The car rumbled to life, skidded on the gravel skirt and sped away. Lee listened to the car recede until they were enveloped in silence once more.

Lee could feel Wild looking at him but ignored him. He turned to one side and spat before picking up the bag he'd taken from the car and staggering across the road with it banging against his calf. He flung the bag into the back seat of Wild's car and lowered himself into the passenger seat. Automatically, he reached down to check the suitcase hadn't been disturbed. The money. The money. His body was leaden with pain.

Wild returned and sat behind the wheel. Can't take you anywhere, can we? He sounded disappointed. Lee stared straight ahead. Wild paused with both hands on the steering wheel before starting the engine and easing out onto the tarmac, but braked almost immediately. There on the road in front of them, hovering at about knee height, were six shining points embedded into thick, dark bodies.

The dogs were immobile, watching. Their growl was almost beyond hearing, a low monotone of a pitch equal to the car engine. Despite the car, they didn't move. Their malevolence didn't seem to be personal but was perhaps of a more indiscriminate nature. Wild edged the car towards them. Their fur shone silvery in the headlight glare. They stayed firm. The car crept forward and the bumper nudged one of their solid bodies.

Only then did they surrender the road, allowing barely room enough for the car. Lee averted his gaze as they edged past.

They left the dogs unmoving on their stretch of road among the whispering trees. Lee lit a cigarette with trembling hands and resisted the urge to look back and see if the dogs were pursuing them. Instead he stared ahead at the roadside markers and at the white lines being sucked beneath the car. He held a hand to his nose and inhaled its bloody scent.

They drove through the night, with no hint of what the countryside around them was like, or what lay beyond the narrow periphery of the headlights. There were few other cars. Occasionally a truck swung past, decked with lights, like a lumbering carnival. They didn't speak and before long were utterly absorbed into the night.

At around dawn, a small town sprung from the darkness. Like any other town on the plains, it consisted of low, flat-roofed houses, a primary school and a few slabs of struggling grass. A wide and desolate main street with a newsagency, a fish-and-chip shop, a chemist and a motel.

Wild pulled into a motel opposite the railway station and checked them into a room while Lee slumped in the car. He was exhausted and in great pain. It was cold and the town was blurry and indistinct through the frosted windows. When Wild returned, he was stuffing the last of a muffin into his beard. His overcoat was flecked with crumbs. Lee listened as Wild chewed and breathed, chewed and breathed.

He turned to face Wild. Am I dying?

Preoccupied with a lump of muffin embedded between his teeth, Wild didn't answer. Finally, he licked his fingers, started the car and turned to face him. He burped and Lee could smell the food on his breath. Blueberry. Muffins were always blueberry.

Hate to tell you this, Wild said, but we're all dying. This Ishould know. I'm a doctor, remember? Albeit suspended.

Lee rolled his eyes. But why are you helping me? It seemed suddenly important.

Wild picked some crumbs from his lap and popped them into his mouth. He chewed and appeared to consider the question. Let's just say that we both could use a little assistance right now. I'm hardly what you would refer to as an upstanding citizen at this point in time, you know what I mean? Let's say we both have our reasons for disappearing.

Lee thought about this. But why should I trust you? I don't even know you.

And you trust the people you *do* know?

Although it hurt, Lee laughed. The old guy had a point. A bird cawed and swooped like a stone from a powerline to the road, where it cracked a snail against the asphalt. I don't understand how all this happened.

Wild didn't say anything, merely shrugged and guided the car into the parking space. He cut the engine and wiped his nose with a dirty sleeve. He was outsized in the interior of this tiny car; the top of his head brushed the cloth ceiling. Beside him, Lee felt like he was shrinking, draining slowly away, becoming even thinner.

Where are we going, again? Lee asked, but Wild had already stepped from the car and unlocked the motel room. Lee grabbed his suitcase of money and followed.

The room smelled of old cigarettes and cheap carpet cleaner. It was the foreign smell of strangers. When he was a boy, people brought food for him and Claire after their parents died, ordinary meals like casseroles or pies, but they always tasted somehow wrong, not at all like his mother's versions of the same dishes. And he and Claire would stare at the pie dishes on the kitchen bench, sometimes as many as five or six, unable to eat them. That difference, infinitesimal, just enough to matter.

The main concern with your bullet, Wild was saying, is infection. As far as I can tell, no major organs were hit, but we need to clean you up a bit.

Lee didn't like the reference to *your bullet* and had a brief vision of the mangled lump making itself at home somewhere below his right ribcage, shouldering things aside. Settling in. You've got to get this thing out of me.

Wild closed the door and slid the chain across. He tested the door, then turned and looked at Lee. He opened his mouth to say something, then stopped. We'll get you somewhere, he said at last. I know where we're going. To see an old friend of mine. He's the best. You'll be fine.

Can't you do it?

Wild shook his head. No. And don't ask me to.

Lee placed the suitcase onto one of the two low, narrow beds and sat next to it. The bed emitted a birdlike squawk. I got to change my clothes. I'm covered in blood. Gingerly he removed his leather coat and wiped his hands on already filthy jeans. His t-shirt crackled with dried blood. He sniffed at his hands and exhaled, embarrassed. And I don't even know whose it is.

Wild scratched his face and cleared his throat before throwing out a hand and saying in a booming voice: *I am in blood so far steeped that I should—No, wait. Should I . . . wade no more, to go back would be . . . as tedious as going over.* Or something.

What?

Shakespeare old chap. The *bard*.

Lee nodded absently. He was fading. He tried to focus on his surrounds. There was a radio on the sideboard alongside a metal jug of water. The edge of the laminated bedside table was scored with thin, black scorch marks from forgotten cigarettes. A truck pulled into the car park with a mechanical snuffle. Outside, morning was taking hold and light trickled into the room like weak, milky tea. He thought of the bullet inside him, this fragment of the world he now carried. He was exhausted. The ceiling light fizzled. What did all this mean, if anything? Everything. Nothing. He opened the suitcase. The money, all there. His money. He thought of his sister, of his childhood self pulled against her stomach, the cold smell of their kitchen. Still clothed, he arranged himself around the suitcase and passed into a thick and dreamless sleep.

9

Josef wormed through the traffic and arrived at Stella's apartment block early in the morning. It was a quiet street; hardly any people walked by, a few cars. He parked opposite the grey, three-storey block and checked his gun. He rolled a cigarette and smoked it inside the car, keeping an eye out for anyone going in or out. Nothing. Leaves gathered in the doorway, corralled by the wind. Josef checked himself in the rear-view mirror. He had barely slept the night before, just lay in the dark wondering what to do. He ran a hand over his face and patted his black hair into place. After twenty minutes, he crossed the road.

The stairwell was dim and quiet. A woman answered when he knocked. Strange. All his information was that Stella lived alone, that he had no family or friends in the city. I'm sorry. I think I have the wrong address. I was expecting someone else. . . .

The woman rested her weight on one foot. She was young, maybe thirty-five, with short, blonde hair. Her face was halved lengthwise by the partly open door. Well. That makes two of us.

Josef stammered. He looked around the musty landing and tugged at his sleeve. Perhaps it was the next apartment? Sorry. I was looking for a Mr. Stella.

There was a dim murmur of domestic activity emanating from somewhere in the back of the apartment, a smell of food cooking. The woman tilted her head a fraction. Oh yeah?

Josef wondered if he could jam his foot into the door before the woman closed it. Does he live here?

The woman sniffed and looked Josef up and down slowly. She checked the hallway behind her before leaning in towards him. Look, she said in a low voice. You've got what you want, now piss off.

Josef sucked his tooth. He tried to see past the woman down the dark hallway but could make out nothing. I'm not here to see you, missy. I'm here for Stella, alright. Now is he here? I need that money back.

You can't see him, mate.

So he does live here?

You can't see him, the woman repeated and began to close the door.

Josef reached into his jacket for his gun, simultaneously stepping forward to press his foot against the door. This fucking bitch, he thought, is going to get it.

The woman pressed a pistol into Josef's abdomen. Don't move. I already shot the other cunt and I'll do it to you as well, old man. You're not getting in here.

You shot Lee?

The woman shrugged. That his name? Yeah. Sort of an accident, but you'll get it too if you're not careful. I'm not as afraid of you as you think, mate.

Did you kill him?

She shrugged. Doubt it. Maybe.

Josef had to stoop to see her face. Green eyes, a tiny glob of mascara on her eyelashes. It was early to be cooking, he thought. A roast perhaps, with vegetables and wine and the good cutlery. A family lunch, the clatter of plates. He froze with his foot between the door and the jamb.

We don't want your type around here, the woman went on in a quiet voice, obviously ensuring no one else in the apartment heard. You caused enough trouble here, lending money to a man like my dad, who only pisses it away at the track. Vultures.

Josef wondered if she would really shoot him. His own gun was half raised, not quite ready. He was too old to be shot and doubted he could squeeze off a shot before she fired. He could feel his blood running close to the surface, just beneath his skin. The tattoo at his wrist felt as though it were attempting to wriggle free. Despite his predicament, he was relieved to know an injury was the reason for Lee's absence, rather than his own poor judgement.

What about the money? Just give me the money. That was a loan. Not a gift. It won't go away. What he does with it is none of my business.

The woman shook her head and kicked at Josef's foot to dislodge it from the doorway. You're not listening. We gave the money back. With your little friend. Dropped him off somewhere with it.

What? Where?

On the outskirts. Some place my dad knew. Sylvia's. And she smiled, displaying two rows of neat and perfect teeth. Rolled him out the car with a suitcase of cash.

Why the hell would you do that?

Look. Stay away from us. You got what you want, now leave us alone. Leave us alone. You got what you need.

You dumped him with the money?

Yes.

Then another voice and the shape of a man emerged from the shadows of the hallway behind the woman. What's going on, is that Carlo at last?

Go back inside, Dad, the woman said, not taking her eyes off Josef.

Oh no, Stella said, pressing his palms to his cheeks.

Go back inside. This man was *just leaving*. I'm sorting this out.

Stella swore in some foreign language and threw his hands up like an old woman. Fucking Jew. There was a high-pitched squeal from the depths of the apartment and a toddler ran into the entrance hall. Stella cut it off and hoisted it into his arms.

A light came on. Then the silhouette of an older woman stepped into the hallway and enquired after the child. She favoured one leg as she walked. A flash flood of domesticity. Curious glances, whispers. Who's at the door?

Josef was unsure where to look. I should take my chances, he thought. Just shoot this blonde bitch. Get off a shot and run. For being smart. Shoot her in the face. Although he was looking past her, he knew her eyes were on him.

Her throat bobbed as she swallowed. You'll never get away with it if you shoot me here, she said in a whisper.

And as if on cue, there came the sounds of a group of people entering the apartment block and mounting the stairs. There was the rustle of shopping bags and laughter.

Josef paused for long enough to let this bitch know that he could still do it just for the hell of it, that she was lucky, that he might come back for her later. He lowered his gun and removed his foot. The woman winked at him and slammed the door. He heard the sharp scrabble of the chain slotting across. In a futile gesture, he kicked at the door before spinning on his heel and stalking down the stairs into the windy street.

Outside, he walked quickly, smoking furiously. Crisp, brown autumn leaves eddied in the air and crunched beneath his feet like the skeletons of birds. Standing in a phone box, he located Sylvia's phone number in his notebook and dialled. At least she would be able to help him. If that blonde was telling the truth, Lee would be there. The money would be there.

But there was nothing. Just the dull tone of a broken line. His coins were not refunded. He threw his cigarette onto the floor and crushed it beneath his heel. The phone box stank of stale piss and wintry metal. He redialled, with the same result. Nothing. Nothing was working. Nothing was fucking working. And that fucking woman, winking. *Winking* at him.

With the phone in one hand, he braced himself and smashed the black plastic receiver repeatedly into the bulk of the mounted phone, against the cradle and circle of numbers that made a useless *ching* under each blow—against the rounded corners and metal phone-book rack until all that was left was a mess of wires and shards of plastic in his fist. A couple hurrying past, hunched against the cold, averted their eyes. Josef tried to rip the phone wires free, but they were as tough as sinew. As a young man, he could lift great weights, knock out men in higher weight divisions, extract almost anything from almost anyone. When he was a boy, he hefted a rose bush clear from the reluctant earth with just one hand, a feat that earned him the extravagant applause of his father. But now, in the tiny phone box, he gave the wires a final useless yank before shouldering out the door. Enough fooling around.

10

J osef parked across the road from Sylvia's. *Parkview Motel. Formally the Cabana Inn. Cheap rates clean Tv in most rooms v cancy.* Nothing about the fact that there was no park and no view, unless you counted the road out front and the empty lot at the back.

The Parkview was like prison: most people he knew passed through at some stage of their careers. Although called a motel, the function of Sylvia's was altogether more oblique; part halfway house, part detox, part brothel. Stray members of the general public who turned up in search of a room were likely to be turned away with a surly *Sorry, no vacant rooms today.* It was for their own good as much as anything.

He scratched at his chin and picked fluff from his shabby suit. He wondered if Lee was really trying to get away, like Marcel seemed to think. He had thought about it himself once upon a time; contemplated what it would be like to get a real job, pay taxes, listen to the football on the radio. Be upstanding, write cheques and remember to collect the dry-cleaning on a Friday evening. But what would he *do*? Live one kind of life for long enough and it becomes a sort of destiny, where the future is just a version of the past. It was too late for him and he didn't see why that little prick Lee should get away. He wondered idly if he would have to kill Lee. His heart squirmed at the prospect.

He sucked at his capped tooth and observed an ambulance moving silently through the traffic, like a shark. He touched a button on his coat, a sort of genuflection, to ensure he wouldn't be the next person to travel in it—another superstition inherited from his aunt.

Josef met Lee just a few months ago. The kid was fresh out of jail. Josef had heard about him through the grapevine. Someone always heard something about someone. But he seemed a good kid, capable. Had killed a bloke in jail over something or other but was never fingered. Josef set about luring the kid. He poured good liquor and put him at ease, painted a version of life involving large sums of cash, working outside the system, not being like every other dickhead out in the suburbs. *Can always use a bloke like that*, Marcel had said when Josef mentioned him. It wasn't only that Lee had killed someone, but how he did it. *We can always use a bloke like that.*

And so Josef, sure that Lee was up to it, took him around to meet Marcel, who laid a hand upon the kid's knee and said he might have something, like he was granting a wish. It was always the same routine and there had been a part of him that wanted to bundle the kid out, tell him to get a real job and forget all this ever happened. But Lee had shrugged in acquiescence and that was it—a career determined by indifference.

So Marcel gave Lee things to do, small things, collecting trivial amounts of money and running errands. Nothing complicated. The Stella thing was supposed to be simple: an old man living alone, a bag of money stashed somewhere. Not so much; this was the kid's first real job, after all. Maybe rough up the old Jew a little, just to make sure he didn't squeal. Josef did the legwork, checked things out. Lee was now his charge and he had a certain stake in him working out. Surely he couldn't have got it so badly wrong? But if he thought he could get away, then the kid was sorely mistaken.

The motel reception stank of old air freshener. A plant drooped in one corner. From a room somewhere behind the counter came a television's low burble and an accompanying grey flicker. Canned laughter. There was a path worn into the orange carpet between the front door and the reception counter. As he made the short trip, Josef thought of all the shoes that had made these exact same footfalls, how he himself was contributing to the history of the old dump. He tapped the bell on the counter and there was an intimation of movement from out the back. A muttering.

Sylvia surfaced like a pale fish from the gloom. Her eyes were at a permanent squint and her mouth set tight, sealing the tomb of her face. She approached and placed her wiry hands palm-down on the laminated counter. Her breath smelled of talc and her voice was thick with suspicion. Yes?

Sylvia. It's Josef.

Sylvia peered at Josef for a second before her features softened, but only slightly. She pushed a stray curl of bleached hair from her forehead. Josef? Jesus. Haven't seen you in about a hundred years. Should have recognised you straight away, you're still wearing the same suit. You got old. Where have you been?

Oh, you know. Just walking around. Up and down.

Everything alright, you old gypsy?

Yeah. I'm fine. How are you?

Oh, you know. Can't complain. Well I could but, you know, who'd listen?

Josef leaned in conspiratorially. He didn't have time to play these tired games with Sylvia, but she sometimes needed a little softening up before she talked. Besides, it was a relief after dealing with that bitch at Stella's place. He attempted a smile. I'd listen.

Yeah, right. But would you care?

Josef straightened to his full height. Probably not. But it might make you feel better.

Since when the hell are *you* in the business of making people feel better?

A lot can happen in a hundred years.

It can. But it doesn't. Not in this life, anyway. Maybe another time. People like us, we don't change. We go through the motions, that's all.

Their eyes met briefly before they looked away, embarrassed at sharing this shred of truth. Sylvia coughed wetly and dabbed at her lipstick with the clump of damp tissue always balled in her claw. She looked down at Josef's feet. Anyway, what can I do for you? You got no luggage.

I'm looking for someone.

Oh yes.

Young guy called Lee.

Sylvia nodded and slowly lit a cigarette. Too slowly. Her entire body seemed to swell with smoke when she inhaled. He tried to remain calm. You seen him? Is he here?

What's he look like?

He tried to sound offhand. Young. Dark hair. Skinny. Wounded maybe.

Oh.

You know him? Which room? He's got something of mine.

Nah. He's gone. Checked out last night.

Gone? What? Where?

Dunno. Him and that fella he was with. Sylvia waggled her cigarette in the air and spat out a scrap of tobacco. She coughed into her fist and patted her measly chest before serving up a half-lit smile. Her bearing shifted; she knew something more.

Was he bleeding? Hurt?

Sylvia took another drag of her cigarette and made a don't-know-if-I-can-remember face.

Who was the other man?

Don't know. Big guy. Sort of like a bear, he was. Might have been, you know, that quack—

What quack?

Another elaborate shrug. Dunno. Can't think of his name right now. Been in the papers for skipping bail. Dope fiend.

Josef ran the back of one hand over his lips, inhaling the small smell of himself. Checked out last night? What time? Any idea where they were headed? Anything?

Sylvia shook her head sadly. Can't remember. Maybe you could read some coffee grounds or something? And she brought her cigarette to her lips and sucked on it hard.

And he didn't say where they were headed?

I don't ask these things.

In a car?

Yeah. Think so. The doctor's car. Piece of shit.

To hospital maybe?

I doubt it somehow.

Josef worried at the cuff of his jacket. What was it with women, always in the fucking way? He turned and looked behind him at the jazz of traffic in the street outside. Two men in expensive-looking suits were talking beside a new, blue car. The shorter man was touching the other man's arm to make a point. They looked like estate agents or something. White-collar dickheads. He wondered what men like that spoke about. Perhaps they were friends?

Sylvia spoke again in her husky rasp. Tell you what, though. Your friend didn't look too good. And she mashed her cigarette butt into the overflowing ashtray, where it smouldered stubbornly with the pale and crooked bodies of others. She smoothed the front of her faded floral dress and jewellery clattered up and down her arm.

Josef faced her. He sighed and set about rolling a cigarette to buy some time. He was suddenly very tired. This day was not going well. He needed something and Sylvia was his only lead so far. Come on, Sylvia. We've known each other a long time, alright. We go back a long way, you and me. We've been around forever, too long to fall for this old routine. I don't want to have to put the frighteners on you—

Hah! You don't scare me, Josef. Not now.

Josef lit his cigarette, concentrated on it, wondered if the estate agents were still outside on the street.

Sylvia drew breath to speak. She fiddled with a diamond ring, ran a comb of fingers through her crackling hair. Hair you could use as insulation when she died, Marcel had once said. Or stuff it in a cushion. She smiled suddenly, revealing rows of chainsaw teeth. You remember Sammy? That night with Sammy . . . and that bozo, whatever his name was. Larry? Lionel? Something?

Leon.

Yeah. Leon. Thought we were gone then. Who would have thought.

Josef sighed. Who would have thought.

Scared the hell out of me, that one. Body in the boot for God knows how long.

Two weeks.

Two weeks, was it? Jeez.

According to the papers.

Yeah, well. Stunk like I-don't-know-what.

Stunk like a man been dead two weeks.

In a boot.

In a car boot. Yes.

Sylvia shook her head. In summer. Jesus, but that was close. Really thought that was the end of this old place. Not that it would have been a tragedy but, you know . . . What happened to him, anyway?

Leon?

Yeah. They execute him?

We don't execute people in this country, Sylvia.

Oh, yeah. Course not. Too civilised.

But I heard he died. Sammy too, I think.

Sylvia inspected the back of one hand, webbed with thick blue veins. Dead or in jail, I guess.

Yes. Dead or in jail.

They stood in silence for a minute. Josef scratched at his tattoo and wondered what his next move could be. Sylvia was rubbing at her chest, around the place her heart should be, her hand like an implement, pressing at herself. She looked like she was working up to something. Finally she withdrew her hand and ran it slowly across the laminated counter in front of her. Why don't you just let him go? Give him a chance?

Josef adjusted the cuff of his jacket. It was cold. A butt in the ashtray had begun to burn and now the whole pile gave off a junkyard smell. He sighed. We already gave him a chance. Gave him a chance and the little bastard has run off with something that don't belong to him. And if I don't get it back I'm in as much trouble as he is. I can't afford screw-ups at my age, Sylvia. I'm sure you know what it's like. Josef considered the sly old thing for a moment. He leaned in over the counter until their faces were only inches apart. He didn't offer you anything? He didn't give you any money, did he? Because that isn't his money to give.

No. Sylvia sniffed. Course not. It's nothing like that. He's young, that's all.

Josef smoothed a wing of his hair. You appealing to—what?—my sense of *integrity* or something?

Sylvia sighed. They checked out last night. Late. Don't know where they were going, you know what it's like around here. Lee was just dumped here the night before. Found him with his suitcase out front—

A suitcase?

Yeah.

Of what?

I don't know. Clothes, I expect. Anyway. He was in rough shape. Had to throw the linen out, there was that much blood. Something I don't appreciate, by the way. Been shot in the guts. Had a guy stabbed in the stomach in here once before who bled like that. You know what it's like, right? Anyway. That was that, see you later, *but* . . . Thing might interest you, couple came in here real late last night looking for a room. Woman all over the place, crying and carrying on . . .

Sylvia paused. Josef watched her as she plucked a menthol cigarette from the packet, slotted it between her greasy lips, lit up, inhaled, waited for the hit, shook out the match and tossed it into the ashtray.

Seems they had stopped out on the highway at a car crash, she went on at last, obviously enjoying herself now, back to her old self after the sympathetic detour. An accident or something. Two blokes there on the road and one of them sticks a pistol into the girl's head and tells her he's going to kill her unless they get in the car and come back the way they came. Back this way. And not to breathe a word. Dead guy on the road already, some crazy thing, Lee and Wild by the sound.

Wild? That the quack's name?

Oh. Yeah. *That's* it. Wild.

They here now?

The couple? No. Course not. What do you think this is, a motel or something? And she wheezed right through to a gurgling cough.

And where exactly was this?

Christ. Reflux. About thirty miles up the road I think. Heading west.

The plains?

Maybe.

But that's it?

Yeah. That's it. All I know. Everything. She patted her chest again. What's the deal? What's he got?

Money.

You sure?

Josef paused. Yeah.

Well. If he had money, I don't know what he was doing staying here. Might have been better off somewhere cleaner and safer if you ask me. And, like a machine, she exhaled a long, thin stream of cigarette smoke.

Josef turned to survey the empty motel car park and the road beyond the glass. There seemed a pause in the traffic and it was very quiet. The two men had disappeared. He couldn't think what day it was, or even if it mattered. There was that discouraging smell of a midweek afternoon. The time when people should be returning to their families, to their cosy houses and roast chickens and the perfume of freshly bathed infants.

Sylvia shrugged and licked her lips. Well, she said with a toss of her head, I'd better get back. It was nice seeing you, Josef. I guess. Take care, old man. And she shuffled down the gloomy hallway towards the sound of the television and its chemical flicker.

Josef watched the road and the car park a little longer, aware of something surfacing within him. Sylvia had to be lying about something. It was her custom. He waited another minute before following her.

The back room smelled as he imagined it would: of cigarettes, fried foods and ancient make-up. The place was filthy, slatternly. Sylvia had her back to him, crouching at the television fiddling with the dials. When she resumed her place on the soggy sofa, she barely glanced at him. There's no point hanging around here. I don't know anything else. I'm tired, Josef. I got nothing else to say.

Josef remained in the doorway. His hands dangled at his sides. Sylvia sat on her green sofa with both stockinged legs tucked beneath her. On a side table was a well-thumbed television guide, an ashtray and a red lamp. The base of the lamp looked as if it were made of something heavy and solid, like brass. It offered a dull, fish-eyed reflection of the room.

A game show on the television. People jumped around and hooted. A bank of coloured lights flashed on and off and on again. Sylvia stabbed at the remote control. Grainy images of a bomb blast, a burning church, men in military fatigues hurrying civilians across a road. A burning tank, a crying infant. Some war or other. Bang. Another game show with a woman in evening wear astride a car bonnet.

Sylvia picked at a red fingernail and looked up at him. Her moist eyelashes closed and then opened ponderously, like sea anemone. Despite the raucous noise of the television Josef could hear her breathing. He stepped into the room.

When he thought about it later, Josef was unsure why he killed Sylvia. It was inevitable. Even she seemed to expect it. And when he was finished with her, he stood in the darkened room, gasping for air. Thin sweat covered his forehead. The room trembled and jerked with the grey television light. The lamp was in his hand. Its cord whipped uselessly across the floor. He was right; it was made of brass.

His mouth flooded with bile as he staggered back into the hallway with a hand clasped across his lips. He rested against the wall and retched dryly onto the linoleum floor. A soft but determined army of exhaustion trooped through him as he crouched on the floor for several minutes with his hands splayed across his thighs.

He thought suddenly of something his mother used to say—what was it? *Tremblement de terre.* What did that mean? Many years ago, when he was a boy. *Tremblement de terre.* Memory was such a strange beast, surfacing at random, from unexpected depths.

Beneath the dappled shade of an apple tree. The smell of grass and river water.

Josef held his coat back with one hand, wiped his mouth and stood up. He coughed and spat and waited a few seconds before patting his hair into place and straightening his clothes. Eventually he composed himself and strolled back through the reception, into the cold street and lowered himself into his car. He smoked a cigarette to rid his mouth of the tart flavour of vomit before edging out into the traffic.

Earthquake. That was it. *Earthquake.* With his family in the backyard one day, there had been an earthquake, a tremor, the only time he had ever experienced such a thing. The sleepy rumble of the planet. He must have been only ten years old. Twelve at the most. Before all this. What an amazing thing! To look at the ground with brand new eyes, his mother almost drowning in laughter while his father collected apples loosened from the tree and held them to his nose. And the leaves, shaken free from their branches, falling around them, onto their shoulders and heads, onto their laughing, upturned faces.

11

Lee stands in the yard smoking a cigarette. He is afraid, but that is nothing new; he has been afraid since his sentence began a month ago. Beneath the blue all-weather overalls, sweat moistens his armpits. At 10.00 a.m. it is already hot. The sky is pale, any colour burned out by the high summer sun.

The yard is a large, dusty rectangle dotted with struggling clumps of grass, like an impoverished primary school's. The ground slopes down to one side. Apart from a small group throwing a basketball into a rattling hoop, there are about thirty men standing around smoking and talking in low voices. Many are shirtless. Everyone is inert, stopped in their tracks. Almost without exception their skin is the colour of clotted cream, bruised here and there with tattoos.

Lee spends quite a bit of time wondering how it all happened. There was the routine questioning, the court date and then suddenly he was here. The first few times he was nicked, they assigned him a social worker who talked about opportunity and socioeconomics and neglect and stuff. The social worker tried to blame Claire for what she had or hadn't done, and asked him if he was getting enough to eat. The social worker asked about their guardian, about the accident and the death of his parents and about life with his sister. He said it was OK to feel whatever he was feeling. They wanted something from him, an expression or reaction perhaps, but he was unsure what it was.

Adjacent to the main yard is another smaller yard which is fenced off for the kiddy fiddlers and granny bashers. A beefy man called Fowler is the only prisoner in there at the moment. Simmo and Greene, each with a face as sharp as a razor blade, lean casually against the wire in the main yard and spit and swear in Fowler's direction. Only occasionally, borne by a favourable breeze and a suitable heft, does it reach the hapless Fowler, and when it does, Simmo and Greene cheer joylessly as he wipes the dull coin of spit away with a bunched sleeve. Even at night, whispered threats stalk the tier: *Hey Fowler, I wouldn't eat your porridge tomorrow. We're getting bleach put in. Hey Fowler, your soup taste like piss today?* Even if Simmo and Greene grow tired of it, which they never seem to, there would be others to take up the slack. There's plenty of people and plenty of time.

Lee tries not to look but finds it hard not to. It's like watching a disaster in slow motion. Fowler stands in the corner furthest from the main yard with the fingers of one hand hooked through the wire. He looks resolute but presumably he knows what's in store for him. He just doesn't know if it will be a sharpened toothbrush in his neck, a slashed throat or a good, old-fashioned bashing.

The guards in the two surrounding towers are armed with rifles, even though this is supposed to be pretty minimum security, only thieves and fraudsters and junkies. The high-security boys hardly even get out of their cells these days; it's only sleep, TV and porn for them. From the highest point of the grassy yard, Lee can just see over the wire fences and high brick wall. There are orange-tiled roofs of houses about a mile away, and the curve of a nearby service road. He's not even sure what suburb or town it is. Now and then there is a flash of sun on a windscreen as a car drives past. It seems an incredible thing, a signal from another planet, but it's just people going about their business, driving the kids to school or doing the shopping or something. Driving to get a fucking video. It's cruel to build a prison so close to regular people.

He wonders if the people driving by ever look over to where he's standing, not that they would be able to see him from that distance, but the thought of someone—anyone—glancing up is reassuring. He imagines the round face of a child, partly obscured by a frosting of breath on the glass, pressed to a back-seat window.

There is loud celebration from the basketballers. Pats on backs. All these men. What happens to men without women or children? An entire world in here with its own ecosystem, churning away like those places on maps he used to pore over as a boy. The Amazon Jungle. The Sahara. The fucking Congo.

A heat haze trembles in the air around the razor wire atop the fences and hovers over the distant rooftops. It reminds him of water. Is he anywhere near the coast? If he were to escape from here, he would go to the sea, walk right into it, out to the breakers, past the salty smash of surf. He remembers his mother wearing large sunglasses, dislodging a strand of hair with the heel of her hand, and Claire marching with a yellow bucket, leaving perfectly formed footprints in the wet sand. The aching sun, a golden flare of light beneath a red beach umbrella.

A bloke called Morris comes up and stands beside Lee. Morris doesn't say anything but Lee can feel his crackling presence, like a powerline. Morris is bald and nuggety. He wears a faded blue singlet, as if he's just a plumber having a smoko, the top half of his overalls rolled down so the shoulder straps dangle around his thighs. Morris has meaty hands and speaks from the side of his mouth. He is a chronic gambler who cooked up a credit-card scam that netted him more than fifty grand until he was caught. That's what Morris says, anyway. Morris will bet on anything, given half a chance. *He'd bet on two flies walking up a wall.* That's what they say about him. Morris hates a lot of things but he hates losing a bet more than anything. They say it took four coppers to subdue him after he lost ten grand on a dead cert at Flemington a few years ago and nearly smashed up the members' bar. Lee has already been warned about Morris.

Lee doesn't really acknowledge Morris, but nor does he ignore him. He just throws across a nod, so slight there is no way it can be misinterpreted, and gazes out over the horizon. In another place, on a mountain top or something, it might be a companionable silence, but there is no such thing in prison; there's always something else going on. Morris sniffs, takes out a crumpled packet of White Ox and rolls a cigarette expertly, jamming the packet into the waistband of his rolled-down overalls as he does so. The raw smell blows past Lee when it is lit. One of the dark smells of prison, like piss and disinfectant and concrete.

They stand in silence for several minutes before Morris indicates a cluster of low houses. See those houses over there?

The day seems to have become hotter in the past ten minutes and the fierce glare makes it difficult to discern the houses in question. Exercise period must almost be finished for the day. Lee wipes his forehead with the back of one hand and nods anyway. Yeah.

That's where me mum and dad live.

Unsure exactly what's expected of him, Lee nods again and makes a noncommittal sound. He still doesn't look at Morris. He feels like a cigarette himself but doesn't move to light one. He just wants Morris to go away. He wishes someone would approach and short-circuit this conversation. Where's Simon, his cellmate, his only friend in here? People seem to leave Simon alone, which is what Lee wants for himself.

Thought I might buy 'em a telescope for Christmas, Morris goes on. That way, they'll be able to check in on me every day. Keep an eye out, you know? Make sure I'm not getting into any *mischief*. And he laughs in a monotone way. Not that you can get up to anything here. This is prison, after all. Nothing but . . . rehabilitation. He says *rehabilitation* carefully, giving each syllable plenty of room, like he's only recently learned to say it or he's talking with a child or something. Like they can turn us back into what we used to be, before it all went wrong. You reckon that's possible, you think we can get back to where we used to be?

Lee shrugs.

Morris flicks his head to one side and there is a damp plop of a bone or joint cracking into place. Oh, he murmurs. That's better. Me neck's all out 'cause of these fucking bunks or something. You have that problem?

Lee shakes his head and looks around. A young guy called Carl is slumped sideways against the wire fence nearby. Carl seems to be having trouble standing and the fence balloons outwards with his weight. Carl always has a fresh wound of some sort and today his right eye is swollen shut. The front of his blue overalls is patterned with blood. Repeatedly he leans and spits. Carl is on his own. Carl is always on his own. Nobody will associate with someone so obviously doomed. Prison remakes people, the screws told Lee when he first arrived, but never into anything of their own choosing. Lee looks away and busies himself with a cigarette.

Morris still watches him, as if gauging his response to Carl's plight. Doesn't look too good that bloke. I reckon, not that I'm a doctor or anything. I'm no expert and I don't know who that guy is, but I reckon he's on his way out. He sniffs and flicks his cigarette butt into the dirt. I guess some blokes aren't cut out for things in here, you know?

Lee takes a drag on his cigarette. It's like inhaling an entire desert. There is a shout of jubilation from the basketballers and another desultory round of abuse from Simmo and Greene. Lee sort of nods, as if he's digesting the importance of what Morris has been saying, and stares past the shimmering fences to the wall beyond. A guard comes out of his post and strolls along the walkway. His belt buckle glints in the sunlight but otherwise he's an insubstantial shape, the antenna of his rifle jutting from his back.

It's Lee, right? Morris says.

Yeah.

Morris.

And Morris sticks out his hand so Lee is forced to turn to face him. Morris's grip is solid, meaningful.

How'd you end up in here, Lee?

Oh, they drove me in a van, you know . . .

Morris laughs loudly and other prisoners turn to look at them. Nah mate. What did you *do*? To get slotted?

Lee flushes with embarrassment and hitches his baggy overalls to buy some time. The overalls material is still thick and stiff; it's like wearing a tent. He knows Morris is waiting for his response, can feel him staring at the side of his face. All crims lie about themselves, it's part of the whole game. They make their crimes more spectacular for other crims and tone them down for the general population. But here, where status is everything, the lies take on a mythic quality. If Lee believed everyone, all pickpockets would be fearsome muggers, all thieves armed robbers and every two-bit junkie the Mr. Big of the entire class-A drug world. Crime, like any pursuit, thrives and falters on ambition.

Although, Morris goes on as he rolls another cigarette, we're all innocent here, aren't we?

Lee chuckles and hoists his overalls again. Sweat trickles down his ribs. He knows the truth won't do and wishes the whistle would sound for them to return to the block. His crimes are of carelessness as much as anything. Small-time stunts: burgs and stolen cars, vandalism, the sort of thing any bored kid gets up to in a country town.

But he has a story for himself, prepared well in advance. Breaking and entering, he says at last in what he hopes is a nonchalant tone. Aggravated assault. Went into a place in the middle of the day and a woman was home. He sucks the last from his cigarette and grinds it underfoot.

Morris waves a fly from his face. Damn. That's a bit rough. Nice boy like you. Who would have thought.

The low whistle sounds and the men in the yard begin moving like cattle towards the gate that leads back to the main block. Relieved, Lee turns to join them, but Morris leans in close, shoulder to shoulder, not quite preventing him from leaving but almost. Lee can detect the sweet barber-shop smell of hair oil or shaving cream. Cheap prison soap.

Morris smirks before grabbing at his own crotch, rolling his eyes and growling in a parody of pleasure. Did you give her a little something? You know, give the bitch a little something to remember you by? Hey, Lee. You know what I mean, right? I always give them a little something. Got to take what you can get, right?

Lee stops and looks at Morris. He needs to pull this off. By now they are standing so close he is aware of the heat of Morris's thick body. Course, he says at last. What you think I'm fucking doing here?

Morris doesn't move, maintains contact. He jams a stubby forefinger into one ear and waggles it back and forth a few times. Smile gone now, he inspects Lee before removing the finger and wiping whatever he's gathered there on his singlet. He nods, ever so slowly, as if he's been told something unlikely. Right, he says. I see.

Lee senses the other prisoners watching them and scuffs at the dirt with the toe of one shoe. Morris still waits, even though most of the other prisoners have been checked off and have filed out of the exercise yard. Lee doesn't want to walk inside with him but Morris just stands there with his hands in his pockets until they are hurried along by the screws. In the end they pass together through the corral made by three wire fences and along a corridor beneath caged fluorescent lights.

It's later that day that Simon again warns Lee about Morris. The cell they share is small and sparse. The walls are unevenly textured with grey institutional paint layered across rough brickwork over many years, worn thin and grimy at shoulder height. The paint is easy to peel off and comes away like ancient toenails. Photos are arranged haphazardly across the walls. Some are of Simon's family and others have been left behind by previous inhabitants. Just people, gazing out from the walls. A boy of about two standing beside a car with his mum, the pair of them squinting into the sunlight. Strangers, some of the photos probably been there for years, long before Lee's time. Pages torn from porn magazines, signs and markings, a selection of crude limericks. There are sketches of naked women reduced to curves and fierce scratches of hair, just the parts that matter. In one corner is a washbasin and a dull steel toilet with no seat. There are no removable parts anywhere. A desk cluttered with empty cigarette packets and Simon's notebooks.

The hot air in the cell is laced with the smell of lighter fluid as Simon painstakingly fills his lighter. The fluid is forbidden, of course, but the screws turn a blind eye, as they do to so many things. Lying on his side on the lower bunk, Lee watches Simon's cropped head bent to his task at the desk. He doesn't know what Simon is inside for but imagines it to be something ingenious—fraud or safecracking. Simon is full of ideas and often leaps up in the middle of the night to scrawl notes down in his books. Simon jokes about the other prisoners and has an old man's laugh, even though he is probably only forty.

You seen that guy Carl? Simon asks without looking up. Out in the yard?

Yeah. Course.

Well. He's one of Morris's.

Morris did him over?

Simon makes a face and twitches one foot as he concentrates. He is always jiggling his foot or drumming his fingers, ever since he gave up drugs a month ago. Is, he says. *Is* doing him over. Most days. If you've got a couple of pals like Simmo and Greene to hold someone down, you can do pretty much anything to a bloke. People will always be as cruel as they're allowed to be, and in *here*, well . . .

Simon reassembles his lighter and thumbs the wheel to produce a long, wavering flame. He clinks it shut and blinks at Lee through grubby glasses. You could call it an initiation, I suppose. That might be a good word for it.

But why him?

Simon shrugs. No reason. Got to be someone. That's how it works.

Lee rolls onto his back and picks at the intestinal-coloured wadding poking through the rusting springs of Simon's bunk above. Sweaty hair sticks to his forehead. When he thinks of Morris, all he can see are the hairs bristling from each of his nostrils, like there's a mob of spiders living up there. He is trying, really trying, to hide the panic stalking his body. Instinctively he knows he must keep everything to himself. No light can escape. Be as secretive as an oyster. It's a futile task. He coughs and pulls a handful of wadding away. It's kind of hard to avoid people in here, he says.

Simon lights a cigarette with trembling hands. Yes. Well, that's the thing. The way I see it, you got three choices: stay so low that nobody ever knows who you are; be scary so nobody comes near you; or make yourself useful so people are happy to have you around.

Which are you?

Simon pauses. Well. I used to be useful, when I was getting dope for people and stuff. But now? Now I'm just scary.

Lee laughs. With his notebooks and glasses, it's impossible to imagine Simon scaring anyone. But Simon doesn't laugh, just picks up a glass of water and drinks deeply from it.

There is a slamming sound from the walkway outside, followed by the blunt laughter of two or three men. Lee and Simon remain silent for some time. Lee lies back and closes his eyes, tries to imagine himself away from here, to imagine what might otherwise have become of him. What other, better selves might there be out in the world? It is an old game, one he has played with himself for years. He feels a hand pressed to his chest. He tries to jerk upright but is held down. Shit, he thinks. Is this it already? But it's only Simon leaning over him. The door is closed.

Listen, Simon says in a low voice. I'm going to tell you something I shouldn't, because you helped me with that dope thing, so I owe you a favour. What I heard was, Morris bet Rocco two hundred bucks that he'd have you on your knees sucking his cock by Sunday. And every day after that. Simon takes his hand away and clambers into his own bunk. And you know how Morris hates to lose a bet.

Lee sits up so fast he almost bangs his head against the upper bunk. His heart grinds in his chest. Shit. You sure?

He swings around and sits on the side of his bed. He lights a cigarette, which burns unsteadily, damp from his sweaty fingers. Someone sings in the tier below. *Oh, my daaaaarling Clementine.*

Then Simon speaks from his bunk above, as if he's read Lee's thoughts: Today's Thursday.

Part Two

12

Lee woke in the semi-darkness of late afternoon and instinctively searched it for intimations of light. His tongue lay in his mouth, heavily, as if just placed there. If not for the absence of noise, he might have assumed he was in prison still. Even the machinery of his own body, with its myriad grumbles and burrs, was silent.

After some time the world came back to him, apportioned sense by sense: a shaft of pale light; the electrical hum of powerlines directly outside; the smell of a cold afternoon; the dull weight of pain across his body. He remembered he was in a motel somewhere, but this didn't make him feel any better. After all, he was in a motel somewhere earlier today. Or was that yesterday?

Gasping with pain, he wrenched himself into a sitting position. The suitcase was beside him on the bed. He opened it and checked the contents. The money, his money, all there. He closed the warped lid, patted it and lurched into the bathroom. The fluorescent light hummed. After pissing, he stared at his reflection in the cracked mirror on the wall, leaning on the basin's cold rim for support. He splashed water into his eyes. He prodded his cheeks, ran a palm over his features, heard the soft crackle of his boyish whiskers. The man in the mirror did the same, a visual echo. Again he ran a palm over his face. The small sound of skin upon skin is like no other, has no equivalent in nature or art. His reflected selves regarded each other with interest and envy. Men fear other men in a way women never could, because they alone know what they are capable of.

Lee looked old, as if time had crept up on him while he slept and committed secret acts. He was unshaven and his eyes were red and rimmed with moisture. Water dripped from his chin. A sudden, unwelcome thought: he was looking at the face that, for one man, had been the final human landscape he ever saw. What would it be like to carry an image of that face—his face—across that particular distance?

He became aware of a dim, human burbling and held his breath to listen. Low, furry voices from the neighbouring room. A man and woman, perhaps. A gasp of laughter, a woman's throaty laugh. He thought of that expression—what was it?—that his mother used to say: *Laughed like a drain.* The woman laughed like a drain. He pressed his ear closer to the wall.

He listened some more and, by his twilight divination, conjured an image of her: the brown and curling hair, always with a rebel strand dangling across one eye; thin lips; the dark cream of her throat; the habit of putting a hand to her mouth when she laughed, usually at one of her own jokes. The elements that constitute a person, the trail of a thousand crumbs. The way she sat on the couch with bare legs folded beneath and her cheek resting on the cushion of her upper arm, how she rubbed at an eyebrow when she was thinking. *Hey, Tom. Grab me a drink will you, honey?*

Unconsciously, Lee leaned in as if aboard a listing vessel, until the soft shell of his ear was flush with the wall. Although he was unable to make out actual words, some primal human seismograph enabled him to discern the rhythm of narrative through intonation alone. He closed his eyes. The man was telling a story, perhaps recounting the time he fell asleep on a park bench on New Year's Day, or else mimicking his mother-in-law. The woman's laughter grew louder, unravelled from her red mouth, and Lee found himself, as the story corkscrewed to its conclusion, smiling along with her, inhaling the intimacies of strangers. He imagined the tangle of their limbs in bed, probably only a few feet away, on the other side of this flimsy wall. Strange that people could be so close and yet utterly unaware of him. He could tap on the wall, or cry out. A small act was all that was required, a small, dense and difficult act. A flexing of muscles, an explosion of air from his mouth. A signal from one human being to another.

After a while the next-door conversation petered out and silence took hold once more. Lee was unsure how long he stayed with his ear to the wall, but soon enough the pain across his torso reminded him of himself. His body demanded attention.

It was only when he returned to the bedroom that he realised Wild was gone. The other bed had been slept on, but otherwise there was no trace of him. Bastard. The bastard's run off. And there was no sign of that bag he carried, his doctor's bag or whatever it was. Lee checked the suitcase of money again. It was all there. He still had the money. That was the main thing. With money, he could at least get to Claire's and she would help him.

He opened the door as far as he dared to peer outside. Wild's car was still where he'd parked it. He couldn't have gone far. Probably gone to get food. Hopefully just gone to get food. He looked again around the room. The car keys were on the dressing table but they were no good to him. Meanwhile, he needed to do something about his wound. The dressing Wild had applied earlier was sodden with blood and needed to be changed. He would just have to take care of it himself.

Slumping on the end of the bed, he removed his blood-heavy t-shirt and lay back to access the dressing, which tore away with a marshy sound. A dark and medieval pain muscled through him. His hands shuddered, his body shuddered and he held his breath and ground his teeth and eventually the shaking subsided, but not before it had run its course. He exhaled.

Lee switched on the old-fashioned box radio beside the bed. An announcer told of a distant war, an election, the sale of a painting, news familiar to any moment in history, a bulletin that could even be from some version of the future. The news segued into a ragtime tune. He listened to its nasal trombone and jittery rhythm, the soundtrack to a nervous breakdown.

The bullet hole itself was small, but very black, as if an opening to a much larger world. The bruising had faded but had been replaced by a soft, pink stain. The area immediately surrounding the entry wound was swollen and the skin had a tight, shiny quality, like a fleshy drum. He seemed to have stopped bleeding for now, although the stain of dried blood extended below the waist of his jeans. Blood even in his navel. Lee prodded the area with a grimace. It was tender and hot to the touch. He groaned and swore. Fuck. Where the hell was Wild?

He wanted this bullet, this vestige of his former life, gone. He swivelled his torso slowly back and forth to try to locate it within him. In prison he had seen a man sew up another man's partially severed throat with a guitar string. *Shut up, you cunt. Shut up.* He wondered if he could squeeze it from himself like a hard, black pimple. Just press his thumbs together really tight. When talking about splinters or insect stings, his dad used to say *It will work itself out*, as if the body could force out such a thing, like villagers rounding on an invader. He doubted the same was true for a bullet, although you heard of old soldiers carrying portions of shrapnel around in their bodies for years because it was safer than an operation. He didn't want that. He certainly didn't want that. He wanted this piece of fucking metal gone.

Lacking anything more suitable, he moistened shards of toilet paper and attempted to clean some of the skin surrounding the actual wound. Again that foghorn of pain sounded through him. Blinking back tears, he dabbed at himself, taking his time between each foray to catch his breath. He cleaned blood from the wiry hair on his stomach and stuck a wad of paper to the wound as best he could. It was better than nothing. Where in hell was Wild?

He stayed on the edge of the bed for several minutes, catching his breath before riffling through the bag he'd taken from the crash for fresh clothes. Awkwardly, unable to raise his left arm much higher than his sternum, he changed into a white shirt and dark-blue suit, leaving his own bloodied clothes in a pile on the floor. It took some time. He noted with dismay that his underpants were soaked with blood. His blood was everywhere. There was even a patch of it on his thigh, God knows how, in the shape of a country, a dark-red country.

The suit smelled of mothballs, of special occasions laid to rest. It possessed another smell—indefinable—of another man, but was a comfortable fit. As a boy he had often worn hand-me-downs donated from around the town and had enjoyed the illusion of slipping, if only for a moment, into someone else's self, like a disguise. Then, as now, it was a visceral relief, almost a holiday.

He shrugged within his new suit and looked at his bare toes wriggling on the mustard-coloured carpet. A new man, he thought. A new man. Ready to go. Dressed for a wedding. He stood for a moment in the room, slightly bent at the waist as if preparing to fold in half, before crossing to the window and looking out into the street. The day had slunk away. It was almost dark. A streetlight fluttered to life. An elderly man locked the newsagency opposite, tested the door with a tug and walked away with his hands thrust into his pockets. His fading footfalls were audible as he strolled past the darkened chemist and closed-for-the-night fish-and-chip shop. The radio played some sort of dirge, complete with wailing bagpipes.

A car cruised past, then returned. Shit. A police car. It slowed and parked opposite the motel. Two dark shapes conferred inside the car and, after a couple of minutes, two cops stepped from it. They swaggered across the road towards the motel, looking around, their hands hovering about their holsters. Lee squatted down and lowered the blind until he had the barest space to see through. The cops stopped at Wild's beaten-up old car. One of them checked the licence number against a notebook, then peered into the car with his hands cupped around his eyes. Lee licked his lips and crouched down further. The cops spoke again and nodded. One of them indicated the motel with a jab of his young chin. He swore and shrugged away from the window. The radio tune faded out, followed by the announcer's toffy voice. *Ah, what a marvellous tune. That was—let me see if I can find the record here—ah*, Loch Lomond.

Lee scrabbled in the stolen bag, located a pair of shoes and pulled them on. He grabbed the suitcase and stepped into the cold air. He didn't know where Wild was but he had a fair idea.

13

Wild breathed heavily. Pebbles of sweat leaked from his armpits. His body had become foreign and unlikable, at odds with itself, the skin swarming with life of its own. He scratched his neck and face, then raised and lowered the sleeve of his coat, which had become heavy and abrasive. His teeth brawled in his mouth and a clump of pale hair stood out from the side of his head. His body was fraying at the edges.

He crossed the road and sneaked to the rear of the row of shops lining the main street. The afternoon was drawing to a close; it was already nearly dark. His body was absorbed into the shadows. The lone page of a newspaper crabbed across the asphalt and flattened itself against a redbrick wall. An empty beer bottle rolled to and fro, as if fraught with indecision. He paused to listen.

He had woken in the motel room and realised with panic that his bag was missing. The bag contained many things: instruments, personal papers, a packet of biscuits. But these were just things. With the sensation of a wave breaking through him, he had realised that the bag also contained his morphine and his other backup drugs. He had rummaged frantically through the room, even, idiotically, through the drawers of the bedside table. Nothing useful, just a Bible. Meanwhile, curled slightly on his narrow bed, Lee had slept on. People and their sleep. Wild had watched him enviously for a moment before lurching out to the car to make sure it wasn't in the boot, or back seat. Damn. He must have left it by the road at the crash. Lee had been right; they should never have stopped. Damn, damn, damn. Standing in the car park, Wild had hefted the small crowbar he kept in the boot for such moments. He had hoped he wouldn't ever have to do this again.

Now he took the crowbar from beneath his coat and applied it to the thick iron of the chemist shop's rear door. A loose fan of calling cards from a security firm was stuck in the jamb. A balloon of urgency swelled within him. His nose and eyes were running and his hands were moist and sensitive. It was as if his body were dissolving into some former evolutionary state. He edged the clawed end between the door and the jamb and leaned with his body until he heard the mournful crack of the physical world giving way.

Even in the dim, angular light, locating the storeroom was routine. A brickwork of pale cartons and bags on low metal shelves. The dry smell of chalk and bleach. Gloves and powders, the stuff of quiet salvation. It didn't take long to locate what he wanted.

The once-tender crook of his left arm was clouded with bruises and fresh needle marks where he'd been striking at his ever-reliable median cubital vein for so long. With pursed lips, he regarded the wreckage in the shallow light, deciding where to try first. By now the desire or need had become something else entirely: a vast, unfed tenant pressing against his interior, pounding at the walls of his body.

Wild knew about veins, venules and arteries; about the systems that carried his blood, about their layers, how veins had valves but arteries didn't. About the hepatic portal system that ferried blood from the spleen to the liver. Basic stuff, really, first-year medicine, but it still managed to amaze and frighten him. He knew the map of the human circulatory system from *Gray's Anatomy*, the illustration like that of a leafless tree.

He had studied the body and its workings for years, but it was still largely a mystery to him. Like remote African tribes, his organs went about their business regardless of his knowledge of them. The *why* was always elusive. In Renaissance Europe, theatres of anatomy were established in the belief that such visceral exploration had a moral imperative, like colonising savage lands. The body as a map of God's very own making. Anatomists were not dissimilar to priests, interpreting the divine as they found it in human form. The title-page woodcut of Andreas Vesalius's sixteenth-century *De Humani Corporis Fabrica* features a crowd of men, a hundred or more, jostling for a better view of one such examination. The men are bearded and robed, their mouths agape with wonder at the sight of the organs of the unfortunate woman on the table, whose skin is folded back like a curtain. One can imagine the collective inhalation of breath, the murmurs of incredulity and horror. And in the centre of the crowd is Vesalius himself, gesturing serenely towards the cadaver's inner world. The same year, whatever year it was, Copernicus published his treatise on the solar system. All this artful investigation, of worlds inner and outer, to no great end.

Wild decided to try an entry point elsewhere, and tapped at the vein curling from his elbow across his wrist. The radial vein, closer to the surface. He flexed his fingers until the blueish worm swelled, vaguely erotic. He felt sorry for it as he angled the needle in low under the skin until, striking the vein, a thread of blood blossomed into the liquid. *Hypo* means under. *Dermis* means skin. Holding his breath, he depressed the plunger until the full amount had vanished. In this fashion he ushered portions of the world into himself.

With his back against the cold wall of the chemist storeroom he monitored the drug's rapid progress through his body, warming first his heart then flooding outwards until the medicinal flavour stung the back of his throat a second or two later. His frame sagged and his bones softened as the opiate exerted its primary effects on his central nervous system. His cough reflex was suppressed and he imagined he could feel his pupils contracting to the size of pinpricks. He didn't really feel much. After all, that was the whole point. He cast the plastic syringe aside. His breathing became long and deep, and his body became loose and habitable again, a place to set up home.

Addiction is a concentrated form of futility; it was always almost worth it, never quite so. A former friend used to say with a mocking laugh: *Why do we like beating our heads against a wall? Because it feels so good when we stop.* Wild exhaled and ran a hand through his hair. He rolled the empty morphine ampoule between thumb and forefinger, detecting writing on its otherwise smooth surface; tiny words, possessing secret meanings. *Morphine. 120mg/2mL Btch 24060G.* Isolated in the early nineteenth century by a German pharmacist with a long and complicated name—Friedrich something or other—and named after Morpheus, the Greek god of dreams. Chemical formula $C_{17}H_{19}NO_3$. The only thing between himself and oblivion.

Wild stretched out his long legs and concentrated on shucking off his humanness. One of his shoelaces was undone. Later. He would fix it later. It was dangerous to stay here longer than absolutely necessary, but he resolved to do so for a little while at least. He stared at the tiled floor and imagined it would be strangely pleasurable to run the nail of his little finger along the grouting. It looked perfect for such an action, and the combination of the rough grout and the smooth tile would certainly be pleasing. He was tempted to lean forward and try it, to see if he had been right, but was reluctant to disturb his newly established balance. There would be time for that later.

He thought about his life, the remains of which were a long way away, many continents from here. His house, the bony winter jasmine clutching at flaking weatherboard, how the slab of sunlight fell upon the carpet each morning. What he felt was something akin to nostalgia, not for the past but for an unlived version of his present, the life he could have led. It was a condition of his exile, this feeling.

He sat for some time preoccupied with himself. On the storeroom floor beside him was a cardboard box of morphine ampoules and another box of syringes. He rubbed his nose with a palm. The empty ampoule tumbled to the floor where it jangled and rolled until it came to a halt against the wall. It seemed a meaningless thing, remote, like the bark of a neighbour's dog.

He wasn't sure how long he'd been sitting there when he heard the back door being shoved open. Metal squawked on wood, followed by silence. Strange how one could sense the small shift in the quality of the air that suggested a person listening. Wild struggled to his feet in stages, like a camel, and turned off the light. Everything was slow and unwieldy. Too late. The silhouette of a figure appeared in the doorway, standing awkwardly, a suitcase in one hand. Wild stayed still, just breathing, flat against a shelf, willing himself invisible. The figure was wearing a suit, like a detective. He reached about for his crowbar. A stupid thought. As if he'd do anything like that.

A whispered voice. Wild?

Wild paused. Lee? Is that you? You scared the hell out of me. What are you doing? How did you find me?

We have to get out of here.

What are you wearing? A *suit*?

Yeah.

Very nice. You look very nice. But I got to say, you scared the hell out of me. Please don't do that. I thought you were the police.

The sudden movement had unsettled Wild and he stood and steadied himself against the wall. Bile rose in his throat and he assumed a vomiting stance, hands braced against his knees. His skin was cool and slick with sweat.

Lee indicated the boxes shipwrecked on the linoleum floor. Take your dope and let's go, he said. The jacks are outside.

Wild jerked to attention. The police? They're here? Oh no. Damn. We've got to get out of here. He gathered his boxes and followed Lee into the alleyway. He made to return in the direction of the motel, but Lee grabbed at his arm. The cardboard side of one of the boxes came loose and a handful of ampoules clattered to the cobbled ground. He squatted and began scooping them up.

We need to go another way, Lee whispered. His face had a lunar shine in the alleyway light.

But the car?

They know the car. That's how they found us. Those kids from the crash must have told the cops. They seemed to know the licence number and everything. I should have … I don't know, but it was a mistake.

Wild stood up and adjusted his hold on the boxes. His thoughts were cumbersome, not suited to comprehension. Even things happening immediately around him seemed to be a long way away, the sounds and implications taking some time to reach him. He looked at Lee and when he spoke his breath smudged the damp night air. They didn't follow you, did they? The police?

No.

You sure?

Lee nodded. Yeah, I'm sure.

It had begun to rain, a thin drizzle visible as a halo around the streetlight at the alleyway corner. Tiny drops trembled on Lee's eyelashes and jewelled in his hair.

Anyway, Lee said at last. Let's go. We got to go. We got to move somewhere.

Wild stood where he was and gathered his boxes to his chest. They were awkward to handle, like small, squirming animals. He looked about. We can't go on foot.

Lee slumped against a crumpled corrugated-iron fence. He grimaced and pulled his collar about his throat. Well. What are we going to do, then? How are we going to get out of here?

Wild could detect the thick stink of blood on Lee. It reminded him of surgery. At this rate the boy wasn't going to last much longer. Water overflowed from a nearby gutter and spattered onto the ground. It looked almost beautiful in the low light. A row of rubbish bins huddled against a wall. A train's whistle sounded. Then again, this time closer, accompanied by a chugging sound. The two men looked questioningly at each other. In silent agreement, they moved through the sodden air towards the railway yard.

14

L ee followed Wild across the railway tracks and the blockish sleepers. Everything shone with water. The silent shapes of train carriages were visible in the half-light and rainwater dripped from the carriages' metallic handles and the skeletal undercarriages. Lee moved in a half-crouch, his torso almost parallel to the ground, his left hand pressing against his left side. In his other hand, growing heavier, was the suitcase of money. It banged against his leg with each step. His jaw ached from gritting his teeth. Mindlessly, he tailed Wild, unsure of what else to do.

They kept close to a wire fence and picked their way among empty beer cans and food wrappers and shitty nappies and bottles. A hundred yards ahead were the lights and dark mass of the railway station. A man stood under the conical penumbra of the platform light and exhaled a pale plume of cigarette smoke.

They stopped some distance away and squatted in the shadows. The air stank of animal piss and wet metal. Wild struggled with the sodden boxes and turned to face him. What should we do?

I thought you had a plan?

Well, we can't just go up and buy a ticket.

The old guy was right.

Could we . . . jump on one?

On a train?

Yes.

Like bums?

Wild laughed. Yes. Like hobos. Then he looked around, placed his boxes on the wet ground and stood up. Wait here.

Lee panicked. What? Where are you going?

It's easier if I go alone first.

Lee paused and swallowed. That taste again. Will you come back? How do I know you'll come back? He sounded pathetic. He knew he sounded pathetic.

Wild put a hand on his shoulder and indicated the boxes on the ground. I'll be back in ten minutes. Don't worry. Wait here.

Only partly reassured, Lee watched Wild bob through the darkness with his coat flapping about his knees. He gripped his own new coat more tightly around himself and slumped with his chin on his knees. He wondered how he could possibly describe these past few days. What would he say to someone, to Claire? What could he say when he saw her? He imagined her rebuking him even as she pulled him to her, the way she would shake her head and wind a strand of hair behind one ear. Supposing he made it to her house at all. He didn't seem to be getting any closer. Would it be raining there, at the foot of the mountain range? Would the creek be full and plopping with bullfrogs? Would they be thinking of him, or would he already have been dismissed as screwing up again? He thought about lying down here and falling asleep, or dying, or whatever. Just to pass into some other place would be enough. Any other place.

A rat scrambled over some nearby stones. The creature paused and gave him a cool, appraising look before scurrying away, as if committing his whereabouts to memory, as if to say *I'll be back for you later when this rain has stopped.* This place of silent trains and silvery clouds, with its line of narrow trees. This jagged place, was this as far as he would come?

A whistle sounded and a train trundled past. From his vantage point by the fence, he could see passengers settling in for their journey, standing on tiptoes to stuff coats and bags into overhead racks. They grinned with expectation and shook out their umbrellas. The train looked warm and cosy. A round-faced boy gazed out a window like a patient moon, but if he happened to see Lee in the drizzling darkness, he gave no indication. Just some lucky boy being borne away.

Then Wild was back, breathing heavily. Give me three hundred dollars.

Lee was startled. What?

I need money to get us on a train. Hurry. It leaves in a few minutes.

Three hundred bucks?

Well, I'm not buying a ticket. I'm buying us a favour. Come on, Lee.

But I need it—

Give me the money. The sooner we get away from here, the better.

Lee watched the train sway away into the night, then stood and allowed Wild to rummage through the suitcase in search of suitable bills.

Then Wild grabbed his upper arm and picked up his boxes. Come on.

They stumbled across the damp tracks as silently as possible, keeping low until Wild broke ahead and approached a tall, uniformed man standing beside a freight carriage. They spoke in hushed tones and then the man slid open a carriage door and sauntered away counting his money.

Wild waved Lee over, tossed the boxes in, scrambled aboard and leaned down to help him.

Lee looked around. I don't know about this. This doesn't feel right.

For God's sake. We're on the run. Of *course* it doesn't feel right.

Lee stared up at Wild's grizzled face above him. The old guy seemed to be enjoying this. The floor of the train carriage was as high as Lee's chest. There was no toehold and he knew it would be excruciating getting himself on board. It was cold and he was afraid and his fear was of a new and unfamiliar sort. He looked around one final time before throwing his suitcase into the carriage and stretching out a hand for Wild to hoist him aboard. As Wild did so, a pain monstered through him. He feared he might actually break in two. He cried out. Shapes eddied in front of his eyes, pain made visible.

When he was inside at last, Lee rested on the floor on elbows and knees. He moaned and waited, holding his breath. He lost all sense of himself in the physical world, so absorbed was he by the immediacy of the pain through his body. The pain was bottomless, surely too vast to be accommodated in a body as slight as his? His stomach was sticky with blood.

Only after several minutes was he able to move at all and then only gently, afraid of each new jolt on his body. He gathered the pieces of himself and sat with his back against one of the hard carriage walls. There was a graveyard smell of earth and splintered wood.

Finally, he was able to speak. You think we'll be OK? You think the cops will find us?

Wild shook his head and made a face. He looked scared. They waited for the train to move. Fifteen, twenty minutes passed. The carriage floor was coated with a thin paste of mud. It was cold and their breath fogged in front of their faces. When it seemed as if nobody was coming to arrest them, Lee jammed a cigarette between his lips, lit up and watched the smoke snake upwards and disperse. A cigarette. Pure fucking bliss. He smoked in silence.

Lee was aware of movement from the opposite side of the carriage.

Wild sniffed and scratched at himself. Were you really going to kill that girl back there? On the road?

Lee took a lengthy drag of his cigarette and shrugged, a tiny gesture of the mouth as much as the shoulders. Water beaded on a lick of hair plastered to his forehead by rain or sweat. The bead swelled and broke free to find its way along the ridge of his angular nose and the curl of his mouth. He thought of the girl by the road with her face upturned like some pale flower and wondered how old she was. It already seemed a very long time ago. Was it yesterday? This morning?

He looked at Wild and shook his head. No. I'm not cut out for that kind of thing. Those people are animals.

Those people?

You know, Lee said, and he waved his hand to indicate some point in the distant past. Josef and them.

Wild said nothing. Lee could just make out the flicker of his eyes in the gloom, the soft shine of his rain-damp cheeks. He could smell potatoes stacked in crates beside his head and the earth from where they'd been plucked. It was a smell laden with possibility. He wanted to reach out and pick one up, just to feel its body in his hand and thumb the scabs of dirt from its surface. It would yield a small, tactile satisfaction. He could almost imagine eating one raw, just like that, with the dirt and everything. Experimentally he reached out and slid some fingers between the slats of the nearest crate, feeling like a blind man, by touch and smell.

He resettled himself to relieve the pressure on his ribs. Again he felt the warmth of his own blood beneath his shirt and pulled his jacket tight. Foolishly, he regretted the ruin of his new suit. He attempted to lie back to ease the pain but it seemed to be gaining momentum as if, having suckled on his body, the bullet within him had swollen and was taking up increasing amounts of space. Breathing was difficult. He placed a hand against the curve of his ribs and spat thickly onto the floor beside him. A strand of saliva looped from his lip and caught on his coat. He didn't bother to wipe it away, but instead waited for it to collapse under its own weight. It was a pathetic derro's act, something you'd scorn from the safety of a passing bus.

He had a sudden idea and pointed to the boxes beside Wild. Give me some morphine.

Wild jolted upright and reached out a hand protectively to the white boxes of paraphernalia arranged on the floor. Here? On the train?

Yes.

I'm not sure—

Just a bit, for God's sake. If it wasn't for me, you would have been pinched by now, back at the chemist.

Oh yes, and you'd be living it up in Monte Carlo, I suppose?

Come on, Wild. I've been fucking shot. I'm in actual pain here.

Aren't we all?

You won't miss it. How many you get in that bust?

It was difficult to see clearly through the gloom, but Wild sat up and flattened himself against the opposite wall as if attempting to engrain himself further into the darkness. It's not that, he said in a small voice.

Lee waited in silence—in pain—until Wild finally pushed a box across the floor with his shoe. Then the other box.

Syringes. There you go. Help yourself.

Lee peered through the silvery dark into one of the boxes. A stash of glass ampoules, packed like treasure. He picked one out and held it in front of his face. The ampoule was smooth, with tiny hieroglyphs embossed along its surface. It resembled a weightless, transparent bullet. The liquid moved sluggishly when he shook it. Then he tossed it back into the box with the others. I don't know what to do with this, he hissed. *You're* the fucking doctor.

Wild appeared to have fallen asleep. His head was thrown back and his hands rested limply across bent knees. His closed eyelids shone in the wedge of thin light coming through the barely open carriage door.

He reached forward and swiped at Wild's shoe. Come on. I don't know this stuff. This isn't my scene. I can hardly lift my fucking arm. And he sat back on his haunches. Emotion trembled in his throat. He could feel the curiously satisfying granular crunch of mud pressing into his knees through the material of his suit.

I'm not sure, Wild said, awake again.

Come on. This pain is killing me.

Wild closed his eyes once more. Then he grunted in assent and plucked a morphine vial from one of his boxes. Lee watched him crack it open, unwrap a syringe, draw in the morphine and flick a thumbnail against the plastic chamber.

OK. Take off your jacket.

Lee did as he was told. His entire body felt tender, like newly turned earth. Do you really know where we're going? Lee asked, partly to distract himself. Or are we just going off to God-knows-where?

Wild jammed the syringe lengthwise between his front teeth, like a buccaneer with his cutlass. He grabbed Lee's wrist with a clammy hand, pushed up his shirtsleeve and angled his arm in the meagre light. He turned Lee's arm this way and that. Wild was breathing laboriously, as if struggling with even these minor actions. Lee felt Wild's thumb stroke the inside of his elbow, luring a vein to the surface.

Don't worry, Wild mumbled. God doesn't have a clue where we're going.

Lee resisted the urge to withdraw his arm. He'd seen men in jail shoot each other up with sloe-eyed concentration and the brutal ritual—part medical, part sexual—always made him feel slightly queasy. But we'll get there, won't we? he asked. I mean, you know, we'll be alright? I'll be alright? I really have to call my sister. I was meant to be there today, or yesterday. I got to get away from here before Josef tracks me down. He'll fucking kill me.

Wild removed the syringe from between his teeth. He looked exhausted. Sure we will. We'll get you fixed up.

This guy will help me?

Yes. He'll help.

You sure?

I'm sure. He's a very decent man. Not at all like me.

What's his name? You never said his name.

Wild sighed. He's an old teacher of mine. Sherman. Had very high hopes for me in days gone by. We were great friends. When he moved to the country, about ten years ago, he and my wife Jane would collude and pack me off to his place to get me off dope. I spent a lot of time in that old house shivering. Wild held up a thumb. See that? Nearly sliced my finger clean off trying to break into his drug cabinet. I'd sneak off from the house in the middle of the night and break into chemists. Never worked, of course, or only for the weeks I was there. Just got stoned as soon as I got back to the city. And Wild shook his head. But I haven't seen him for a few years. He rubbed his nose and applied himself again to Lee's arm. Now just so you know, this might make you throw up.

Lee looked away. The light seemed suddenly too thin. Can you see what you're doing?

Don't worry. You do this long enough and you can smell where the blood is running. Like trout. It's a sort of divining.

Lee held his breath. These words hardly reassured him. Finally the intimate invasion of the needle puncturing skin and his body grew warm as the dull, narcotic glow seeped through him, limb by limb. The world receded, or he from the world. Indeed his entire body seemed to be borne away, as if out to sea. He was dimly aware, however, of Wild watching him for a minute before preparing another injection and turning away.

Lee resettled himself against the carriage wall and thought with distaste of the bullet snuggling against his ribs. He had seen pictures of bullets taken from bodies, the manner in which they change shape and crumple but always remain a bullet. He wondered how they were made. Was there a head-scarfed immigrant woman on a production line somewhere, scanning them through a machine to check for inconsistencies? Lee didn't know anything about ballistics other than vague terms: bullet, powder, primer, flash. Was there someone, somewhere, who squeezed the finished products thoughtfully between gloved fingers and held them to the light? Did they ever wonder, these people, in whose body these things ended up? A bullet was an object with a single purpose, would never have another.

Wild said something.

Lee heard the words from deep within the meat of his body. What? he asked after locating his tongue.

But you've done it, haven't you? Wild asked.

Lee wondered if they had been having a conversation he was unaware of. His head was woolly. He felt mildly seasick and contemplated whether they were perhaps on a ferry of some sort and not a train at all. Perhaps they had left the train. Done what? he asked.

Wild ran his tongue over his crippled teeth. You know. Killed people.

Lee flinched. He shrugged and closed his eyes. He breathed in the earthy smell of dirt and dry wood. What sounded like an animal scuffled in the rocks beneath the carriage. Probably that rat, he thought. Come back for me. He swallowed. His saliva was like glue. I never killed anyone for this money here, if that's what you're worried about.

Wild made no comment, barely seemed to register his words.

But yeah, I've done it.

How many times?

The pain of Lee's wound had dimmed, thanks to the morphine. He was able to move about more freely and cleared a space on the floor to lie on his uninjured side. He was warm, almost relaxed. Nearby was Wild's leisurely breath. Once. I killed a man once. That's all.

Killed deliberately?

Lee paused. What are you getting at?

I'm not getting at anything. Why did you do it?

Why?

It's OK. Forget it. And Wild wiped a sleeve across his nose.

Lee wasn't sure he liked this conversation but felt he couldn't leave it dangling. Self-defence. In prison it's always self-defence.

You were in jail? You killed someone in jail?

Yeah, I was in jail.

For what?

He remembered the last time he'd been asked this question. Nothing serious, he said at last. Burglaries, stealing cars. Kids' stuff, you know. Petty crime. Judge called me a petty criminal when I got pinched.

Wild sat forward. What's it like?

What?

Prison.

What's prison like?

Wild cocked his head. Yes.

You ask a lot of questions.

Well, I'm a curious person.

You don't want to know.

Yes I do. Were you afraid?

Lee closed his eyes, or rather he allowed them to succumb to gravity. All the time, he said.

Nobody had really asked him much about prison. It was space within him devoid of geography. From his childhood he remembered mock-ancient maps in books about whales and sailing adventures. Scorch marks and tea-stained corners, always a portion of the earth as yet unmapped. *There be monsters.* He moved his palm across the floor in a circular motion. He was resting on his right side, using his right forearm as a cushion. There was an unfamiliar scent to the suit, the warm olfactory ghost of another man's cologne. He wondered briefly if it wasn't, in fact, another man's arm he was resting on, that of the man they had left in the grass beside the road. How long until these clothes began to adopt his smell, until he began to inhabit this new self?

I didn't expect to be doing this shit, he said. I was doing odd jobs, you know, collecting money and stuff. Just bullshit. Running around. It was sort of . . . accidental. I came out of jail a few months ago and met these people—mainly Josef, I guess—and they offered me work. I didn't have anywhere else to go. He shrugged. His body was mountainous. Mute, dense, unfeeling.

So whose money is that? I take it it's not yours.

Lee looked at the battered suitcase. The darkness made it easier to speak. It is now. But I took it from an old guy called Stella. That was a job. Grab this coin from this old guy who owed money, that's all. Gambling debt or something. I was never going to take it back to them. Just fucking take it and get the hell out, but someone shot me. This blonde woman. A blonde woman shot me. I don't know what happened. But now I'm getting out of here. Going home. I know it's not a lot of money but . . . I don't need so much. Those people are, you know, *animals*. He sighed, embarrassed. I'm not cut out for it. I'm lucky to be alive.

Yes, you are.

The carriage jolted forward. Like a cripple, it stopped, lurched, stopped and finally moved again, each movement accompanied by a metallic groan. The train's whistle sounded across the oceanic dark. At last. They were moving at last. They were getting away. Lee saw the flash of Wild's grin and felt one of his own spread across his face.

The train gained speed and settled into its clattering rhythm. Lee had a sense of solitary farmhouses out there in the night, of swaying trees and the tinfoil eyes of small animals observing their passing. A cold wind fluttered through cracks in the floor.

I can see why you like this stuff, Lee said above the racket.

Like what?

This morphine, or whatever it is.

Wild snorted. *Like* is not a word I would use to describe my particular relationship with narcotics.

Love, then.

I wish.

Well. It takes away pain.

It's a trade-off, really—one form of pain for another. At least with this I have the illusion of control. And he corralled the boxes of syringes and drugs to his side, as if they were kittens roaming into danger. From a coat pocket, he produced a packet of jelly babies and proceeded to pop them into his mouth, one by one.

Lee watched him, still unsure why he should trust this man, whether he was a doctor at all. Relaxed but nauseous, he remained where he was on the floor, lulled by the sound and movement, happy to abandon himself to the rhythm. He imagined the blur of tracks and sleepers whizzing below.

Wild cleared his throat. Can I ask you a question?

I guess so.

How do you handle them—him? How do you handle him?

Josef? I don't plan to have to handle him at all—

There was the Gatling-gun rattle of a warning bell as they passed a railway crossing, a glimpse of red flashing light. Wild seemed suddenly shy. No. Not that.

Who then?

How do you handle the . . . dead?

Lee licked his dry and flaking lips. He felt untethered, miles from anywhere. What?

That person you killed, Wild yelled above the noise. They make demands. I was wondering how, you know . . .

Lee stared at Wild, uncomprehending. Was it a trick question? He recalled something Marcel had said to him when they first met six months ago. *You know what?* Marcel had said. *The way people like us survive is that nobody really believes we exist. They go to the movies or read something in the paper, but they don't really think it's the truth. Or maybe they do but only in the—what's the word?—abstract way. Not that the man on the bus is, you know, a hoodlum. Like a ghost. You got to be a bit like a ghost. Some people swear they seen one, there's stuff about them, books and what-have-you, but nobody knows for sure, right?*

And Lee recalled the low, orange light of the apartment, the way Marcel perched on the edge of his blue sofa in a grey cardigan and scuffed shoes. He remembered Marcel's grandfatherly smell of mothballs and hair tonic and the way Josef stood nearby sucking at his tooth. And Lee also remembered how, afterwards, on stepping into the damp street, he had stood by a redbrick wall and trembled with something utterly mysterious, a feeling he now recognised as a presentiment of regret, as if he knew more at the time than he allowed himself.

He watched Wild hunting through his bag of sweets. The guy was always eating. What would you know? Look at you, stuffing your face like a fucking kid. What would you know about anything? You don't know anything.

Wild looked up with unfocused eyes. He made a sound as if he intended to answer, but instead just muttered into his beard. His face sagged and he returned again to his lollies. Lee wanted to say something more, but failed to locate the words, or even the reason to utter them. He watched as Wild turned away and scrabbled among his boxes, probably preparing another hit. Great, he thought. The old guy is going to OD on me in the middle of nowhere. He sat up and pressed his eye to a crack in the carriage wall. The train rollicked through the vast night, taking them wherever it was taking them. Even in the darkness, he could see the passing countryside was flat, relieved only by shallow topographical bruises and the occasional scarecrow army of power poles striding across fields with their cables. Halfway to the horizon, the blurred lights of buildings clustered like punctuation marks adrift on the landscape. What did Wild say before? *God doesn't have a clue where we're going.*

~

15

Wild knew not all darknesses were the same. Some were more complete than others, more shapely, larger or denser or more complicated than they first appeared. Some darknesses were familiar and others not so easy to identify.

The train had come to a halt at some point during the night. He had been aware for a while that they were no longer moving and had been trying to ignore the cold that had seeped through his coat and trousers and riffled through his ageing bones. Finally, he could no longer pretend. He opened his eyes. His head felt as if it had been stuffed with things as he slept. The dope, he thought, as he rubbed grit from his cheek and sat up. His back hurt from having slept on the hard floor of the train carriage and he shook out one hand to relieve the blush of pins and needles. His face felt like an unmade bed. The door of the carriage was ajar and a sallow dawn glow spilled in. He could hear birds. It was a thinning darkness, then. Morning. A new day, in fact.

Lee was beginning to stir. At least he was still alive. Perhaps he was tougher than he gave him credit for. He wasn't sure if this was a good thing. Wild nodded. Good morning.

Lee grunted. He looked emptied of colour and bulk and the skin of his face was papery, as if mere wrapping for the real face beneath. A smudge of dried blood below one eye and his scarecrow hair. The suit he'd stolen from the crash gathered in bulky folds around his scrawny frame.

Wild crawled over to the part-open door and peered out, careful to remain hidden should there be anyone outside. He inhaled the crackling morning air and the sharp, watery smell of fog. The milky sky was lightening as the sun rose behind a stand of distant trees bordering the railway tracks.

Are we there? Lee asked. His voice was a croak.

Wild looked around for anything he might recognise. The railway yard was sort of familiar but it was hard to tell. He nodded anyway. How are you?

Lee shrugged and held his stomach. I feel like shit, he said and winced as he sat up.

Wild stuck his head out a little further. No signs of life, just train carriages and half-lit signal boxes. The shine of rainwater and the twitter of birds.

Lee brushed past him and sat on the lip of the carriage before lowering himself to the ground with a soft grunt. Can you watch my suitcase? I got to piss. And he staggered off behind a carriage before Wild could say anything.

Wild scratched his neck and rubbed at his nose. His skin always itchy because of the morphine. He could do with another hit, but he should wait until they got away from here. They might actually make it. Just need to stay alert for a little while longer. Beneath his clothes, his skin felt like cardboard. He crouched in the shadows and patted dust from his coat and trousers and combed his unruly hair with his fingers. His feet were blistered and cramped, still jammed into shoes without socks. There was water in his shoes and he knew that later his toes would resemble bruised sea sponges waggling uselessly at the ends of his feet. I'm like some bloody Dickensian bum, he thought. Gobspittle or Farnwarkle or something. All he needed to complete the picture was a grubby kerchief about his neck.

He wondered how Sherman would receive him after all this time and smiled at the thought of his old friend's unflappable mask almost dissolving in surprise before managing to reassemble itself. *Yes, ah . . . well, hello and what do we have here, if I need ask at all? There is nothing that can't be solved, although you seem bent on proving that one wrong. You know, Wild, I was just saying to Jane the other day . . .* The way he would clasp Wild above the elbow and divert him so blandly that Wild would be under the impression that in fact it was he who was leading; how he would encourage another mouthful of barley soup; his dry and tuneless hum, like leaves across a wooden floor.

It must be three years since he had visited Sherman. A few months before the 'incident'. As always that momentary certainty that this time it would all be different; the intention to get off drugs was always like a bet with his darker self. They had talked on the verandah late into the evening, batting moths and mosquitoes from their faces. Wild remembered the glint of Sherman's oval glasses and the way the old man sat forward slightly in his chair, never quite looking at you but concentrating nonetheless, hearing everything, waiting for his turn to speak. Grey-haired, patient, forgiving. And Jane's exhausted shrug earlier in the afternoon, how she had turned away at the moment of farewell so that when Wild had leaned in to kiss her, he caught instead the ridge of her ear across his lips. Cartilage, the soft straw of her hair, and she was gone down the dusty driveway.

Wild heard Lee outside crunching over stones and turned to face the glare of a torch. He stepped back, stumbled.

Right, said an unfamiliar voice. What we got here?

Wild shielded his eyes with one arm. What? The torch still bright in his face.

Step out of there, will you, sir?

What? Who are you?

Are you armed?

What? No. Who are you?

Step out of the carriage, sir. This is private property here. Come on, now. No need for a fuss.

Wild paused, then did as he was told. Once outside he could see that it was a doughy railway guard, squeezed into a grey uniform. At least it wasn't the real police. He blinked in the dawn light and the guard again flashed the torch in his face. Hey. Stop that, will you?

The guard had one hand hovering over his black belt hung with keys and various sinister-looking implements, even a gun. Now sir, the guard asked as he allowed the torch to play over the rest of Wild's body, are you armed?

The whole torch thing seemed a little unnecessary, considering the sun was almost up.

Armed? Don't be ridiculous.

The guard was in his twenties, with a pink and shiny face. Probably the chubby kid always picked last for the cricket team, getting his revenge at last. He told Wild to stand with his hands resting on the railway carriage, legs apart.

You want me to do what?

I told you, sir, just turn around.

Wild wondered if he could make a run for it. He wasn't in great shape but this guard didn't look too quick on his feet. He ran a hand through his hair.

As if gauging his thoughts, the guard reached for his holstered gun. Come on, sir. Don't make me use force here.

Wild threw up his hands and turned around to face the carriage. OK.

The metal carriage floor was cold in his palms. Where was Lee? Presumably he'd reappear any minute. Did he take his gun? Were there other guards? This was bad, really bad. And when he was so close.

The guard frisked him and told him to stay as he was, bent in half with his hands on the lip of the carriage floor. Wild could hear the guard's laboured breathing, as he played his torchlight through the dim carriage. If I were his doctor, Wild thought, I'd be telling him to lay off the doughnuts and fried eggs.

That your suitcase?

Wild stiffened. Um. Yes. But there's only clothes and things in it.

What kinds of things, sir?

Oh, you know, thousands of dollars in cash, diamonds, that sort of thing.

The guard wheezed. What about that other stuff? What is that, medical stuff?

Wild cleared his throat. I don't know. That was here when I got in.

Right. So you admit to travelling on railway property without a ticket? Trespassing?

Wild said nothing, just stared at the stones beneath his feet. He felt sick. Where the hell was Lee?

Right. What else? Potatoes, is it?

What? Yeah, I think so. Potatoes.

The guard peered again into the carriage, probing his torch beam into the corners and across the ceiling. You alone, then?

Yes. Of course.

Why, of course?

Wild shrugged.

Because in my experience, you blokes often travel in pairs. You're not covering for any buddies, are you? Because—

No.

You sure? Because if you are, you'll be in even more strife than now. And with that the guard stepped back. You stay there, sir, right where you are.

He listened as the guard crunched back and forth, poking his torch under the carriage and apparently making notes in a small book. Stay calm, he told himself. Stay calm, stay calm. Already he could feel addiction's great hidden engine kicking into gear; the low anxiety of withdrawal.

He wiggled his toes in his battered shoes to warm them. The guard then stopped behind him and fiddled with something on his belt. Where the *hell* was Lee?

Then the guard took one of Wild's arms, his right arm, swung it up his back, jerked him upright and took the other arm around the wrist. And it was like his body remembered something before his mind because his body clenched even as he was thinking: Why is this action so familiar, this discomfort, this thrashing heart?

And it was only upon feeling the shameful cinch and ratchet hiss that he knew. Handcuffs. He struggled and nearly lost his balance on the rocky ground as he swung around to face the fat guard. What the hell are you doing, you fool?

Always got to cuff vagrants, the guard said, noting something in his book before snapping it shut and jamming into a shirt pocket.

What?

Vagrants. Going to have to charge you with trespass. Can't just go around travelling for free, you know. And he produced a padlock and began to close the carriage door.

But what about my stuff? My . . . clothes? You can't lock them in there.

The guard hooked his torch onto his belt, where it jangled against a massive ring of keys, then put his hands on his hips. His nose whistled like a tiny kettle. Well, I *can*, actually. He stared at Wild for a second before reopening the carriage door and reaching in to retrieve the suitcase. A corner of it snagged on something. He had to jerk it loose before hugging it to his chest and securing the carriage with the padlock. He took Wild by the upper arm, the way they do. OK. Let's go.

Do we need the handcuffs? Come on, it's not like I really did anything wrong . . .

But the guard ignored his pleas and led him away, explaining the intricacies of the *Trespass Act* as they passed between other trains huddled in the thinning fog.

Wild walked mostly with his head down. With his hands cuffed behind him, it was difficult to balance and he stumbled on the uneven stones. His feet were like bricks.

After several minutes they arrived at a guardhouse perched amidst the knot of railway tracks and jumble of carriages and signal boxes. It was just a small, wooden cabin with smoke unravelling from its thin flue. A square window glowed.

At least it was warm inside. The guard sat Wild on a wooden chair while he slung the suitcase to the floor, removed his own coat and stamped water from his shoes. He shoved a piece of wood into a pot-bellied stove.

Is this really necessary? Wild asked.

Yep. We take this pretty serious, even if you don't. Always got to prosecute vagrants.

Oh, come on. Vagrants! What *is* this, the Depression? I'm a *doctor*, not a vagrant.

Yeah. You look like a doctor. Living the high life, riding on freight trains and that. Wearing such nice clothes. You must think I'm stupid or something. My uncle's a doctor, I meet a lot of doctors, I know what a doctor looks like. Not you. Not a bit like you. Now you got some ID? You got a wallet or something?

Wild shook his head and looked around the cabin. The place possessed an earthy smell of coffee and wood smoke and boredom. A narrow iron bed squatted behind the door. Several coy pin-ups were tacked to the wall immediately above, along with a postcard from a seaside resort. Tins of food and packets of rice.

But the fat guard wasn't to be put off and began going through Wild's pockets, despite his squirming, finally holding his wallet aloft like a trophy. OK. Now I'm going to check your identification here so we know who we're dealing with. I presume you got a driver's licence or something?

Wild said nothing as the guard fingered his wallet. He didn't know what he could possibly say. His bones were becoming soft and sagging under the weight of his body.

The guard produced a photograph. This your wife?

Show me.

The guard flipped the small square in his chubby fingers.

It was one they had taken in a photo booth in London, Jane sitting on his lap, bedraggled, all smiles, the romance of foreign cities. He didn't like the idea of her in this idiot's clammy grasp. Yes, he said. That's my wife.

Nice picture. Daughter?

Yes.

How old?

Alice. Fifteen.

The guard clomped about behind him but Wild ceased paying attention. His skin was singing and his nose was beginning to run. He sneezed. His coat was bunched in awkward places about his body; under one arm, at his neck. Behind him, the guard was making a phone call, talking softly and hmming to himself. Wild writhed sideways on the chair. He wondered if he could ram this fat guard, run at him or something and get away from here. Was he capable of that? Had he at last become that kind of man?

But then the guard was back, walking about the tiny cabin with a ridiculously proprietary air. Well. Seems you're a wanted man, but I guess I don't need to tell *you* that, do I?

And it felt to Wild that something clanged shut inside him, almost audible. He sneezed again and wiped his nose on his shoulder, leaving a shiny trail. The guard blinked, slowly, with his girlish lashes. Or is it *blunk*? Wild thought. Why isn't it *blunk* or *blank*? The guard *blunk*.

Anyway. Police'll be here soon and take you back to court or whatever.

Wild stared at the little prick. Fat little prick.

Yeah. They were quite interested, as a matter of fact.

How long?

What?

Until the police get here?

The guard shrugged and set about making coffee, placing a small pot on the cast-iron stove. He fetched two cups, milk and sugar, and cleared a newspaper from the table before sitting opposite. He picked up the bottle of milk and sniffed it. So, he asked with a particular concentration, who'd you kill?

Wild looked away and tried to maintain his composure. The fire crackled beside him. Suddenly hot, he wanted desperately to shed his heavy coat. Like a dead seal over him. Like a freshly killed seal, it was. Sweat ran down his face. The guard was enjoying this, making the most of the situation. Wild writhed and the chair barked on the wooden floor. But he said nothing.

The coffee came to the boil and the guard poured them each a cup and added milk and sugar.

Wild rattled his handcuffs behind him. How am I going to drink it?

Guess you'll have to improvise.

He slumped in the chair. Then he had an idea and leaned forward. He focused. I tell you what, he said, blinking moisture from one eye. Maybe we can do some sort of deal? A pause. What's your name?

Suspicious, the guard slurped his coffee. Carson's my name, not that it's any business of yours. What you getting at, Mr. Wild?

Well, Carson. I can get my hands on a large amount of money and you can let me go before the police get here. That kind of deal.

You can't even get your hands on that cup of coffee at the minute, so—

I'm serious.

Carson licked his lips and ran a hand over his bristly hair. That's called bribery, sir.

Call it whatever you want, but please, think about it. Wild took a breath. Manslaughter is not what it sounds like. I can't go to jail, I can't. Let me go and you can have . . . five thousand dollars. Cash. Let me go. Now. And he stood and turned his cuffed hands towards the guard called Carson. I won't say a word, he went on. I'll just be gone and you didn't know a thing. *Completely gone.* Please.

But Carson didn't move, just sat there drinking his coffee. Five grand, he said at last. If you had that much money, I don't think you'd be jumping freight trains to get around, Mr. Wild, I really don't. You're bullshitting. Just sit down and wait.

Wild turned around again. He had nothing to lose. Lee had evidently vanished or had himself been arrested. No, he said, trying to keep the tremor from his voice. You're making a big mistake. And he nodded at the suitcase on the floor behind the door. The money's right—

And then there was a thump, the sharp splinter of wood. The door was open and suddenly Lee was there, inside the tiny cabin. In one fluid movement he stepped across and put the gun to the back of Carson's head. Don't fucking move.

Carson whimpered and shrank in his chair, his eyes screwed up and his mouth askew. He looked ready to cry. Wild couldn't help himself. He leaped up, sending the chair clattering to the floor, and hopped from one foot to another. His cup of coffee tumbled to the floor. Lee, he said. The cavalry! Jesus Christ, this is great. Where were you? This is great. And he turned around to display his handcuffed hands. Let's get out of here. The key must be on his belt. Let's *go*.

It was just as well Carson couldn't actually see Lee, Wild thought, because if he could he might take his chances, gun notwithstanding.

Lee looked like he barely had the strength to even hold the gun. His face was drained of expression, as if his body were shutting off unnecessary functions to conserve resources. Even his eyes were a lighter brown. He was fading, and when he finally spoke, his words were shapeless and worn. You were going to give away my money?

Wild stopped dancing around. I thought you'd gone, been arrested. What choice did I have? Lee. Come on. I would have paid you back. Really.

I would have paid you back. The junkie's lament, Wild thought. It was hard to tell if Lee was even comprehending anything he was saying. His pale face registered no change. He stayed perfectly still, the gun still pressed to Carson's head. The guard continued to whimper and sniffle.

Wild persisted. The police are coming, Lee. This bastard called the police.

The police?

Yes.

Lee appeared to think about this. An expression skimmed across his face, like a breeze over water. His skinny throat bobbed as he swallowed.

Wild imagined police cars, sirens, journalists with their notebooks. He held his breath.

OK, Lee said at last.

Moving quickly now, Lee released Wild and they handcuffed the snivelling guard to the bed's metal frame. Wild took the circle of keys. Lee checked his money before yanking out the telephone cord and they stepped into a soft drizzle, their coats clutched tight about them. Wild drew in a lengthy breath. Cold air, beautiful in his lungs.

They stumbled through the empty railway yard, Wild half dragging Lee by one arm and congratulating him on his timely appearance. The kid was listless, barely able to walk.

I was almost a goner, Wild was saying. I thought it was all over for me. For us. That was magnificent. What an entrance. Like a bloody movie. Now we have to stop by the carriage before we get out of here. I think it's this one. Careful on the ground there. Watch that bit of train. No. Here. This one. Here, rest against this. Just there. Don't move.

Wild. We have to keep moving. The jacks. You said he called the jacks.

Wild picked through the keys and tried them one by one in the padlock. His hands were cold and unwieldy, like steaks. He breathed heavily, awkwardly, and his eyes were running. I know. I know, but I need to get something.

We don't have time.

I know. I don't like it as much as you don't like it. I'll be as quick as I can. Damn. Which *key* is this? How many do I have to try? *Damn*. Ah ha! Here we go.

And he slid the carriage door open and scrambled inside on his knees. With trembling hands and sudden focus, he prepared and administered a hit. He breathed. Then he collected the boxes of ampoules and syringes, several of which were sodden and falling to pieces, and clambered back down next to Lee. A box tumbled from his grasp and ampoules spilled onto the ground. Damn. He kneeled to pick them up, only to lose another box from his grasp, then another. He shovelled handfuls of ampoules into his coat pockets. The rocky ground was littered with them.

Lee offered him the suitcase. Here. Put them in here.

You sure?

Lee nodded. He seemed not to have the energy for anything more, propped as he was against the carriage. There was blood again all over his hands, fresh blood, presumably from where he had been clutching at himself.

Again Wild wondered about leaving him. He could give him some more morphine and leave him in one of these carriages. He flung open the suitcase and emptied ampoules and syringes into it. The blood-spattered money fluttered in the cold wind. Then he slammed the suitcase shut, took it in one hand and in the other grasped Lee, who was like a child in his grip, floppy and accommodating. Come on. Are you OK? Let's go. There's not far to go. Not far now.

They crossed the railway tracks and vanished into the fog. Morning spread out overhead, its light staining the low clouds. The contents of the suitcase clinked with every stride, as they stumbled over tracks, through a gate in the fence and out across a scrappy field dotted here and there with rubbish and clumps of grass.

16

They left the railway yard and walked along a dirt road with the trudge of a retreating army. Lee imagined an occasional dull clank, soft creakings of leather. The ghostly, panting step of hundreds. Drizzle had insinuated itself again into the air. They hadn't spoken, but somehow agreed on a direction. Occasionally, Wild looked over his shoulder and Lee sensed his impatience at their sluggish progress.

Come on, Wild urged every so often. We need to keep going. We need to get away from here.

Lee clasped his jacket about him. Where are we? he murmured, and then again, louder. Where are we? Dark hair was plastered to his forehead. He licked his lips. The tart, metallic flavour of his bullet wound had leached throughout his body into his mouth. He opened and closed his mouth idiotically, trying to isolate taste. Cordite, blood and metal, the flavours of violence. He spat until his throat was raw, but was unable to rid himself of it. It was embedded in his very teeth and jaw. He imagined Josef like a blunt force somewhere behind them.

Don't worry, Wild was saying. I'll take care of you.

Wild hoisted Lee with each step and was shocked at how light and frail he was. How weighty blood must be. He fancied he heard Lee's bones knocking together like the loose, wooden armatures of a puppet, but it was just the noise of the morphine vials clocking around in the suitcase when it banged against his leg. It was clear Lee was dying. He had that smell about him. He wondered what he could do. He recognised occasional portions of the countryside around them from the times he had spent at Sherman's house: the soft rise of a hill; the stand of pine trees next to a broken fence. Encouraged, he tried to walk faster.

They continued. Mostly, Lee walked with his head down, concentrating on the ground before him, but every so often he looked around. It was an alien place, another country altogether. The road was muddy and uneven. Occasionally, their shoes sunk with sucking noises. Waterlogged potholes reflected the low, grey sky. Across the horizon to their right a mountain range slumped like a herd of sleeping animals.

Apart from their breathing and the sound of their shoes on the road, the silence was vast and unearthly. Lee wondered, for a minute, if some massive natural disaster had occurred, or the world had moved away in the night. Surely the combined hubbub of millions of people stirring cups of tea, watching television or murmuring in halls made more sound than this, no matter how distant? They passed clusters of small, leafless trees; birds the size of a child's fist shivered upon their frail branches. It was dreamish, he thought. *Dreamish*? Was that even a word? Like a dream. It was like a dream.

They moved as one single, lumbering creature. The air was wintry and turbid. The few trees had the tangled architecture of lungs. It was like moving through a sparse forest of bronchia, Wild thought. Some strange, internal world. Beside him, Lee murmured to himself, just half-formed words, like the beginnings of language. Or, possibly, its end. They tottered and rolled on the road. Wild was forced to grab him tighter to prevent them both from falling to the ground. He murmured noises of encouragement and sympathy.

Then, bubbling up through the silence, Lee heard a low sound. A rumbling, perhaps some impossibly huge machine, accompanied by a faint, almost indiscernible vibration through the earth. He thought at first that it must have been the sound of a train passing nearby, or an airport. He stopped. What's that?

What?

That noise. The taste of his breath was bitter, like that of another man. He remembered reading that the flavour of garlic would infuse his mouth if he rubbed cloves of it on the soles of his feet. Was this what had happened? Had the sense of the man from whom he'd taken these clothes somehow passed into him, or was it just the bullet?

Again he spat, and was dismayed to notice swirls of blood in his spittle. He wanted to cry out, but no sound came. He imagined Wild and himself from a great distance, two tiny figures on a road in flat, featureless countryside. There was no sign of other people. Where had they gone? He listened for a long minute. The world was shrinking, becoming something frightening, something intimate.

Lee was aware of Wild at his side and was concerned, momentarily, at the prospect of bloodying Wild's coat. I'm sorry. I didn't mean to end up like this. I'm sorry.

Wild's voice was close by his ear. Come on, son. We're nearly there. Come along, now. Not much further.

He wished he could curl up and sleep in that warm, dark voice. He tried to turn and face Wild, but only succeeded in unbalancing them both.

It's OK, Wild was saying. We're nearly there. This looks familiar to me. We're nearly home.

They walked on. The afternoon drew breath, preparing for evening. The sound Lee had heard seemed not to come any closer, nor to grow fainter. It emanated from no particular point, but rather existed in the air around. He expected to see something appear from the murky distance: a tractor, or a truck of some sort. Perhaps it was the train they had travelled on?

But there was nothing. There was nothing.

He was overcome by fatigue, along with something else, an even heavier sensation that surfaced from some hidden part of him; despair and its terrible twin, hope. He detached himself from Wild's grip and, clutching at his side, lay on the ground, stage by stage. Despite the rain, the ground was hard and brittle. Pebbles and rocks dug into his hip and the palm of his hand, the places that bore his weight. He held a hand in front of him, gloved with blood, dark in the wan light. His own blood, abandoning the wreck of this body, seeping into the earth.

The hem of his trousers was damp and frayed. A pulse fluttered beside his mouth. The effort of his breathing swayed his body as he propped by the roadside, a clumsy fucking insect attempting something indecipherable. He groaned, but it made no impression on the silence. Even his senses were fleeing his body, leaving him in darkness, mute and unfeeling. He was aware, but only dimly, of weeping. He scrabbled through his pockets, located his gun and tossed it away. It clattered on the gravel.

Then Wild heard something. A horse-drawn cart rattled up behind them. Amazed, he squinted at it. The elderly man driving the contraption offered them a ride and waited patiently while Wild helped Lee onto the wooden bench.

The man had milky eyes and every so often his beggarly frame was racked by a barrage of coughing that sounded like cardboard shredding. Consumption, he said matter-of-factly, wiping flecks of spittle from his chin and lower lip with the back of his hand. Kept me out of the war, at least.

Wild looked at him. Which war?

The old man shrugged. Some damn war.

The man expressed faint surprise when Wild asked if he knew Doctor Sherman's place, but nodded and said he would take them there. The man asked them nothing about themselves and appeared not to notice Lee's bloodied condition.

Wild slumped on the hard bench, Lee against his thick shoulder. The nag pulling the cart halted every so often to catch its breath, whereupon the driver would coo until it pulled again. The cart rollicked on the uneven road like a boat upon angular waters.

Memories roamed the corridors of Lee's body like unruly children, searching for ways to surface, knocking here and there, clamouring for attention. There was the dry smell of his mother's hands. There was the dark silence of a childhood home. There were alleyways and cars.

He strode into a living room and a woman raised her head from a book. Her expression was as clear and open as a cloudless sky, just a tug at her eyebrow betraying any uncertainty at seeing a stranger in her house. She was reading the collected works of William Shakespeare. It was four in the afternoon. Her name was Mary. It was inscribed in the front of the book when it fell open on the floor. *Dear Mary, Happy Birthday and best wishes. With love, David.*

He played with the skin at Isobel's shoulder, squeezing it gently between thumb and forefinger. She watched him intently. There was the damp click of her eyelashes opening and closing. Her breath across his cheek. He loved that it was perfumed with her interior, with parts deep within her body. Unconsciously he had altered his breathing to inhale as she exhaled, to draw something of her into him. What's it made from?

What?

Skin. What is skin made from?

She continued to watch him. Her voice was plain and dry. It's just skin.

Skin is like no other thing?

Yes. Like no other thing.

Skin is just skin, then?

She shrugged. Just, you know, cells and whatever.

It seemed amazing, beyond possibility. Lee stayed with his head supported in the cupped palm of his left hand. Her body seemed to have a glow of its own. Even without any lights on, and with no illumination from outside, he could see the shine of her body, where her breasts collapsed to either side. The very rise and fall of her. Isobel wasn't even her real name, but he didn't really care.

She had a scar below her hipbone that peeked over the rim of her knickers. He showed her his own scar and explained that when he was a boy he was in a car accident in which his parents were killed. The girl didn't say anything and Lee wondered if she had heard him at all. He turned away, suddenly exhausted.

Wild adjusted his position on the cart's hard wooden bench. They passed through a small town or village, with low houses scattered about and a church on a hill. Creamy light spilled from the windows of houses. The valiant cry of a rooster. A pair of freckled children walking in the opposite direction stopped to watch them pass. They said nothing and offered no greeting or acknowledgement, even when he nodded and waved. One of them sucked thoughtfully on a length of grass.

Darkness and a swirl and blur. In the headlights the tree trunks look soft. A woman's short cry, like that of a bird. Squalling tyres and the crunch of metal. A boy on the back seat, in silence, now an orphan.

A girl of sixteen makes sandwiches for her little brother's lunch, careful not to destroy the bread with the force of her buttering. Her dark hair is worn in a ponytail and the tip of her tongue protrudes from compressed lips as she concentrates. Her brother watches from the kitchen doorway. They are both silent. Now they are always silent. After all, what can they say?

A phone rings in an empty apartment.

Two kids, one of them ten years old, the other a few years older, hold a spitting competition beneath a cathedral of trees in the backyard, sniffing and hawking at an empty paint tin.

They left the village and about a mile the other side turned through a high hedge onto a rutted driveway. Wild glimpsed segments of Sherman's weatherboard house through brief partings in the heavily overgrown garden. The crumbling staircase with stone urns on either side leading up to the front door. Looping tendrils of vine clung to the cast-iron latticework and embroidered the verandah. He grinned. They had actually made it. Water dripped from a rusted gutter and pooled on the gravel path. Although it had always been somewhat chaotic, the garden was more overgrown than he remembered.

The cart clattered to a halt in front of the house. The horse snorted and tossed its head. Wild helped Lee from the cart and shouldered him to a stone bench beneath a tangled arbor where he managed to prop him with his chin upon his chest, his upper body rolling as if trying to detach from the waist. Wild's hands and the front of his coat glistened with blood. He looked around, hoping to see someone, some assistant or nurse or something. Perhaps even old Sherman himself. Just someone to take over. He imagined a flutter of capable hands, the comforting sounds of busyness. Again his face broke into a grin. They'd made it. They'd made it.

The old man in the cart coughed wetly and leaned over the side of his cart to squeeze a pendulous glob of spit from his thin lips. Course, you know Sherman's gone.

Wild wheeled around. What? Where?

Gone. Dead six months. Look around at the garden and the house. Rack and bloody ruin, if you ask me. Nobody to look after the place.

The man clucked his tongue at his horse, turned and left. Dumbstruck, Wild stood and watched until the sound of the cart shrank and was finally absorbed by the silence. Sherman dead? The suitcase filled with drugs and money was at his feet. Lee groaned and spluttered. Wild was suddenly filled with hatred for him, and watched as he fell sideways onto the bench. This little bloody crim. This dying punk. What was he going to do *now*? Should just let him die. He gnawed at his thumb and spat out a hard sliver of nail. His eyes roamed in their sockets, searching for something on which to alight. Parked here and there in the garden were ancient cars huddling beneath green canvas tarpaulins. Three that he could see. A rusted wheel in long grass. An entire engine, like the greasy ribcage of an alien creature. Clouds of insects buzzed through the air. Rack and bloody ruin.

But still that sound. The low hum. The sound of the world turning in space; a terrible, dumb machine. Revolving.

A billion years from anywhere.

But there were other things, too. Lee remembered other things.

17

Not yet comfortable with his new prison swagger, Lee enters the visitors' room clutching a plastic bottle of water. He sees Claire before she is even aware of him. She is sitting with her knees pressed together, knocking the toe of one black shoe against the other. She looks fearful. When people talk about Claire they say she is a good woman and gently nod. Lee knows what they really mean is that she's had her work cut out for her looking after her little brother since their parents died. She even dresses like a social worker, just the fashionable side of dowdy.

The visitors' room has walls of thick glass on three sides and a linoleum floor. It has the rotten-fruit smell of a classroom. There is a vending machine for chocolate bars and chips. A couple of screws stand around the walls keeping an eye on things. Contact is limited to fervent hand-holding across the low tabletops. Almost everyone looks defeated and somehow embarrassed, except the children who are too young to have learned about such things. People talk about the football, about family, and about the future and the past. They know not to discuss their current lives because it's too difficult and foreign for loved ones to comprehend. The prisoners don't want to hear about the outside world. The women don't want to know what goes on in here.

Claire stands when Lee is several yards away and holds her arms out. He allows himself to be hugged and then inspected as Claire steps back with her head cocked. You alright?

Lee shrugs. Yeah. As well as can be expected, I suppose.

Sorry I haven't been down here to see you yet. Been flat out with the kids. Graeme's not keen on me coming down here—

Fucking Graeme.

Claire turns away with a lengthy sigh. Come on, she says. It's only been a couple of weeks—

Three weeks.

Claire looks around at the other people in the visitors' room. Lee knows that this is precisely what she feared for him and imagines that her disappointment is at least tempered with vindication. When he was fourteen, Claire sat him down with a local guy called Leonard—there being nobody else—who tried to impress upon him the risks of the kind of life he was beginning to lead, the stealing cars and shoplifting and whatever else he was up to. Leonard was Claire's expert witness: he'd done a few years inside and was tough in a minor way. Leonard's conversion to the straight and narrow failed to impress Lee, however. Unfortunately for Claire, there is no story quite so compelling to a teenager of a certain bent as the one that starts: *When I was doing time for* . . .

Claire tries again. So. You're alright? You need anything?

Another shrug. He hasn't a clue what to say. He is afraid he might actually cry. It is safer to rein in all emotion rather than risk any sort of leak.

It's only another eleven months. Can you hang on for that long?

Yeah, Lee says after taking a slug of water. *Only* eleven months. And regrets his rudeness.

Well, you just need to hang on. Stay out of trouble.

Yeah. Stay out of mischief.

He can feel her examining him now, possibly searching for signs of damage or violence. She sighs and looks around again. A little boy visiting his dad launches into a high-pitched wail, perhaps an imitation of a siren. The mother raises the back of a hand and the kid squirms away and sprawls on the floor in a knot of limbs. He's probably only ten years old but already has the angular prison haircut, like he's being groomed for a life inside.

God, Claire says in the kind of low voice she might have used years ago when commenting on a casserole a neighbour had left on the front porch in the weeks after the accident. What a dump.

You got that right.

And Lee looks at this woman, this remote being, and wonders if there is anything left for them to talk about. He feels the unwieldy burden of language, an implement he is unqualified to use. She has worked hard to fashion herself into something, smoothing away all edges, a woman of spit and polish. Twenty-eight years old, married to a respectable man, with two children. Probably owns an exercise bike. He can in fact imagine her pumping away in the sunroom, the room where their dad used to read the Saturday paper. Lee is amazed and appalled by her. He remembers her struggling with the can opener on the kitchen bench years ago, determined to break into that can of beans or soup or whatever, finally giving up and flinging the entire thing—opener and can locked together—through the kitchen window into the backyard. The crash of glass and outside sounds filtering into the house. How embarrassed she was, not just at what she had done, but at the fact that she had been observed. And Lee at the kitchen door picking sullenly at the paint on the jamb, always in a doorway in the months after the accident as if unwilling to commit to entering any room.

He thinks of something. Do you remember going to the beach?

Claire looks surprised, but nods.

With Mum and Dad. Mum was wearing sunglasses. You had a yellow bucket. Bright metal. *Really* hot.

Red.

What?

Red bucket.

Oh. Really?

I'm sure.

They sit in silence for a few moments more. Finally, Claire shakes her head. My God. You're in jail. In . . . *jail*.

Lee slouches over the table and lights a cigarette. He has always hated the way Claire leaves a meaningful space where a normal person would swear, like she wants to swear—really wants to—but is too civilised to go through with it.

He pouts to remove a shred of tobacco from his lower lip. You think I don't know that?

Claire rests her head in her hands, then recomposes herself. They talk haltingly of other, desultory things for several minutes, before she places a hand down carefully on the laminated table, as if playing a card. Anyway. What I wanted to tell you was . . . that if you want to . . . I think it might be a good idea to come and live with me again for a while when you get out, until we can get you some work and get you settled. What do you think?

With you? At our old place?

Yes. Of course.

What about Graeme?

Well. With me *and* Graeme, of course. He's OK with it.

Yeah, right.

He doesn't hate you, despite what you think. He just doesn't know you. Might be a chance for you two to get to know each other. Listen to me. Just for a few months. There's heaps of room. You can stay in the back room, where Mum used to have her sewing stuff. It's been repainted. The kids would love having their uncle there.

Lee doesn't say anything. He looks down, chips at the crappy table with a fingernail. He understands that expression—what is it?—about having your heart in your mouth. His own mouth is full to bursting. His lip trembles. Home seems an impossible idea.

Claire goes on. Think about it. It's a good idea. You might run out of chances one day.

It is a while before he is able to speak. I don't know.

What else are you going to do? You've got to get your life together, Lee.

He shrugs. A pathetic gesture. A shrug.

You need to make some new friends, maybe learn a trade or something. Mr. Ellroy is always looking for someone. Go back to school. Remember the lake? Fishing in the lake? She looks around at the smoking, mumbling crowd. This isn't for you. This is one of her favourite themes. Any second now she'll go on about the way she managed to pull herself up and how she didn't raise Lee in that damn house and keep him out of the clutches of the social workers for him to end up *here*.

Lee counters with a favourite theme of his own. What makes you so sure it's not for me?

Is that what you really think? That you belong here or something?

Maybe.

What does that mean? She lowers her voice. What does that *mean*, Lee?

Some of the other prisoners look up and smirk. A birdlike woman with a scrawny neck offers Claire a wry nod, a sort of *You think if we could tell these blokes anything, they'd be in here right now?*

He shakes his head. Nothing.

Please, Lee. Think about it. Please.

OK, OK. I'll think about it. I've got a few months to think. Jesus, you sound like someone's mother. And knows immediately this is the wrong thing to say. If he were a better person he might apologise right now.

Claire rolls her eyes and looks away, blinking. They sit in silence for a while and Lee smokes another cigarette, angling the burning end to a point against the tinfoil ashtray. Almost everyone in the room is puffing away on a cigarette and there is a grey slab of smoke at shoulder height. Nearby a woman with heavily made-up eyes is sobbing and saying *Why now?* over and over. She dabs at her face with a tissue and inspects it to see how much of herself is coming loose.

Claire scowls and waves cigarette smoke from her face. I thought I saw them the other day.

Lee senses a trapdoor has clanked open somewhere inside his chest. He licks his lips and toys with his cigarette. He doesn't want to, actively resists asking, but gives in. Where?

Actually, I see them quite often. It comes and goes. Sometimes not for a long time and other times I think I see them regularly. It's weird. Sometimes I think—this will sound crazy—but I think I *conjure* them from a crowd.

Lee raises his head to look at Claire and is met by her gaze, which seems calibrated somewhere between accusation and pity. He is mesmerised. He has seen them himself—on streets, in his dreams, always in the distance or on their way somewhere—but has always been afraid to tell anyone about it. He has been awoken by their murmuring night-time voices, by the feel of a hand on his brow and by the smell of his mother's occasional gold-tipped cigarettes. *They're good for my heart so* please *don't look at me like that, sweetie.*

I was on a tram, Claire goes on, and it was in the city. Crowded. Peak hour, you know, people everywhere, and it was raining hard, a real summer rain. Everyone was covering themselves with newspapers and umbrellas and coats and whatever. Trying to stay a little bit dry . . . People everywhere. And I was on the tram and the tram window is all foggy from people's breathing, you know how it gets like that? So it looks almost underwatery. So I wipe the window with my sleeve to look out and I see a man and a woman, about the right age, maybe early fifties. And the man is covering himself and the woman with his coat, a black coat, very . . . gallant, I suppose, and they're sort of crouched over, like you do when it's raining. Scurrying along. Just going around the corner of the Town Hall, where the benches are. And I swear to God . . . for a second I thought it was really them. Almost stood up to pull the cord. Crazy. And then they dropped something. The woman dropped something and they had to stop and turn around to pick it up. And I'm watching them real close, my eyes right on the glass and I could see that they were laughing. Really laughing. Like it was the funniest thing. You know how Mum and Dad used to do that? Just crack up like there was always some private joke going on. Especially Mum, that—what would you call it?—wisecracking. *A wisecracking dame,* Dad used to call her. Remember that? She was laughing like a drain. That must have been it. I thought it was them because of the laughter, the way they were laughing as they got soaked.

Lee draws the last from his cigarette and grinds the butt into the ashtray. In the weeks after the accident, Claire would talk incessantly of their parents, attempting to describe them back to life, as if speech might have had the power of resurrection. Tom and Jean, she called them now. She spent hours on the telephone with friends, going over their lives. She spoke with strangers on trains, at the cemetery, accosted old women in public toilets. At night she rang radio talk shows for the bereaved and broken-hearted, her voice out riding the airwaves, leaking into the homes of strangers. She even took up prayer for a while, as if conversing with mortals failed to satisfy her. A monstrous unravelling of language that frightened the ten-year-old Lee. He worried she would run out of words and, in fact, she seemed to have less and less left over for him. Increasingly they would sit in silence at the kitchen table after dinner, listening to the house creaking and sighing like a liner about to slip its moorings. At other times, Claire would make Lee tell her everything he remembered about the accident. *Everything*, which was very little, just the scream and crunch, just the scream and crunch. The scream and crunch and the smear of sudden darkness. The ticking of a cooling car engine.

So it wasn't them? Lee asks in a small voice, afraid of the question, afraid of the answer.

Claire looks at him, as if only now aware of his presence. Her glance is thick with pity. She loops a strand of blonde hair behind her ear. It wasn't your fault, you know, she says in an unconvincing voice.

There is an announcement over the loudspeaker that signals the end of visiting time and there is a commotion of people standing and talking. Chairs scrape on the floor. She smiles and reaches across the table to touch Lee's face but withdraws before making contact, perhaps remembering where they are and thinking it is forbidden.

Part Three

The house was more or less as Wild remembered it, dim and cluttered, a jumble of rooms, each awkwardly placed as if added as an afterthought. It possessed a sort of threadbare elegance. The hallway with red-and-gold wallpaper; a bathroom with a pink bathtub overlooking a damp, overgrown side garden; a library with books in teetering piles on the floor, so that moving among them was like walking through a miniature city with jagged buildings at waist height. A kitchen with two deep sinks, each with the rusty stains of dripping taps. At the rear of the house a sunroom with one entire wall of glass, and a shabby consulting room with a desk and wall-mounted medical certificates. He picked up a framed photograph of himself with Sherman and Jane, taken in the backyard, each of them squinting and giggling into the sun. He recalled the exact day it was taken, how the air sang with cicadas and heat, the bone of the old man's shoulder at his chest.

Everywhere he went, Wild expected to encounter an ancient person living amidst the rubble, to see some hunched and desiccated crone emerge from a shadow, perhaps even Sherman himself. But there was nobody: the only sign of life a pile of grey bird shit on the laundry floor and a pair of dirty dishes on the kitchen sink that had presumably been there since Sherman died. The kitchen cupboards were still stacked with plates and cups, and the pantry was piled with tins of food. Sherman had no family that Wild could remember and obviously no one had bothered to clean the place since the old man's death.

Fearful of the closing darkness, Wild had forced the front door, carried Lee in from the garden and laid him upon a wooden dining table in the main living room. The boy offered no resistance; it was like carrying a sack of bones. The electricity supply was apparently disconnected, but before nightfall he'd been able to scrounge a couple of gas lamps and several candles from a cupboard beneath a kitchen sink. Their light was skittish and infected everything with a kind of nervousness. Shadows jumped and rose, remained inert for a second before writhing away. It made it seem later than it really was.

Still wearing his tatty overcoat, Wild sat in one of several deep armchairs with rounded arms in the lounge room. Now in the house, he was bewildered by the thought of Sherman's death, ashamed he hadn't even known. How was it that age—that most absolute of inevitabilities—could be so unexpected? He thought of the times he'd come here seeking refuge through the years, Sherman's quiet but certain presence, the way he'd try to distract him from his suffering. Was there a greater melancholy than to sit in the abandoned house of a loved one long dead?

He had no real idea of what to do now and sat in silence, just breathing, hands steepled in front of his nose. He felt old, dense with meaning. Older than he had ever felt before. To travel is to age, he thought and raised his hands to his forehead to trace the contours of his skull with his fingertips. There was only the texture of skin stretched tight across his head. Frontal bone. The superciliary arch. Temporal bone. Parietal bone. Fingers traced down across his face. Zygomatic, masseter. An entire landscape of muscle and bone, sinew and gristle. The names were architectural, archaeological, like words lifted from strange texts, which, in a way, they were.

Like a cathedral, Sherman used to say of the human body. *Nothing complicated. Don't be afraid of it. When you know how it is held together and have its laws explained, it's not so remarkable. It's correct to feel awe at first, but important to inquire after that. And like a cathedral, he would add, you need to enter with delicacy and respect. Take care not to disturb the atmosphere. Like pilgrims. Enter a person's body like a pilgrim.*

As medical students, they laughed at ancient remedies and thought of themselves at the sharp end of progress. In days past, some terrible medieval century or other, people believed that in order to rid oneself of whooping cough one should stand on a beach and wait for the ebbing tide to drag their cough out to sea. Wild thought of this every time he visited a beach, imagined a line of tubercular people spluttering along the shore. They also believed diseases could be transferred from the living to the dead. A crowd of women at the scaffold pressing their swollen, bubonic children forward to touch the still-warm corpse of some poor bastard recently hanged.

He looked over at Lee, who lay on the table, his composure disturbed only occasionally by a quickening of his breath. Rub a piece of raw meat on a wart, bury the meat in the garden before dawn and within a week the wart will vanish. The thighbone's connected to the hipbone. His hands, now resting in his lap: more bones than any other part of the body. Twenty-seven or something. Scaphoid, trapezium, distal phalange. Flexor carpi. The hands were everything. Industry and destruction. Incredible things, the single most-useful instrument on earth. At medical school there was always the running joke, uttered in mock hysteria: *Not the hands! These are my future. Do what you like. Break anything, but not the hands.*

The lounge room was a junkyard of furniture and clutter. Several fleshy couches, low side tables. Piles of magazines and books, Persian rugs layered across the wooden floor. Black-and-white photographs in small, silver frames. Three cabinets, each crammed with objects: books, unusual rocks, fossils, jade boxes with intricately carved lids, a glass mortar and pestle, bottles, dried flowers, a dried seahorse, the skull of a bird, a bowl of marbles, a curved dagger in the shape of a crescent moon. The place smelled faintly sweet, of preserved things, of spices, like a museum or apothecary.

He went over to the bookcase and trailed a finger along the broken spines. Gardening books, texts on tropical diseases. Herb guides. Cookbooks. Philosophy. A predictable selection of regulars, such as *Huckleberry Finn* and Shakespeare, but also more obscure medical classics: *Journeys in Diverse Places*, written in the sixteenth century; *On the Motion of the Heart and Blood in Animals*; *A Morbid Anatomy of the Human Body*. A collection of Freud. The Bible, dense with sorrow, its Psalms alone enough to kill a man through sheer force of lamentation.

Standing there in near darkness, he allowed a well-thumbed *Gray's Anatomy* to fall open across his palm. Clumps of pages collapsed to one side and he breathed in the tome's exhalation of ink and paper, a whiff of mould. As ever, the drawings were breathtaking. Delicate and strong; almost impossibly human. More than a manual on human anatomy, they might have been the blueprints of God. Figure 1194, the anterolateral view of the head and neck. A man looking upwards and to his right, the pencil-drawn surface of his body marked and signposted. His head was tilted back slightly, revealing the triangular shadow of his jugular notch and the ledge of his left clavicle just beneath the skin. There is always so much happening in any living thing; they are never completely still. Wild inhaled again, deep and long. *The Masseter imparts fulness to the hinder part of the cheek; if firmly contracted, as when the teeth are clenched, its quadrilateral outline is plainly visible; the anterior border forms a prominent vertical ridge, behind which is a considerable fulness especially marked at the lower part of the muscle.*

Carrying a candle in one fist, Wild shambled across and inspected the boy. Lee's eyes were closed and his skin was waxen, as if all external functions were shutting down in favour of those required deeper in the caverns of his poor body. His lips were apart, revealing teeth and the dark throat beyond. A tiny thread of saliva. Lee's features were slight and angular, the facial topography as yet undetermined. We end up with the face we deserve, Wild thought, the accumulation of a lifetime's worth of good and bad decisions. This boy was yet to make those choices. Perhaps he really was an innocent, with a face in waiting, as yet undefined?

Lee's breathing was shallow. Patient. A patient. To be under medical care. To wait one's turn. From the Latin *patior*. To suffer. Beneath his jacket, Lee's white shirt was dark with blood and his hands were stained with it. There was even a smear of it on his face.

Wild thought of the suitcase full of money and dope. It didn't make him as happy as it should, considering it could get him a long way from here. He could perhaps even last for some months. But he would eventually exhaust any supplies and have to start all over again. Always the same fears—of running out, of finding himself bereft, of being abandoned to himself alone. Perhaps it was better to have nothing at all? It was a bleak thought. Just leave in the morning and go somewhere else. If not tonight, then Lee would certainly be dead soon. There was not enough food here, no way of reaching help. Not even a telephone that worked. They were miles from anywhere. Nobody would know that Wild had ever been here, let alone left Lee here to die. His escape could be accomplished without too much effort.

Attracted by the candlelight, a moth blurred from the darkness and was gone, leaving in its wake fine scales like snowflakes scattered in Lee's eyelashes and across his cheeks. The creature reappeared a few seconds later and landed ungracefully on Lee's face. Its wings were dark brown, a ruffle at the neck like a tatty stole. With antennae roaming above its blunt head, the moth moved in a drunken circle along Lee's cheek and stopped near his mouth. Perhaps it sensed the stubble there, or a change in temperature. Several times it lifted one furry leg and placed it down again. Its wings trembled in the breeze of Lee's exhalation. Lee displayed no awareness of the moth. Wild leaned in closer, fascinated, as if expecting the moth to say something. If this were a fairytale the creature might indeed speak, dispense advice in cultured tones, perhaps reveal itself to be a warlock or a king.

What people didn't realise was that death is a process rather than a single event. Brain cells begin to die after only a few minutes without oxygen, but muscle cells might last a few hours. Bone and skin cells can even stay alive for several days after the heart has stopped beating. The actual moment of death can be hard to pinpoint, but for legal and medical purposes it is considered to be the point of no return. The first time he saw a cadaver Wild was amazed at how much space it occupied, as if death had left mass in exchange for vitality. Almost impossible to believe the object that so resembled a person would never again stand or speak. In laboratories at medical school twenty-five years earlier, he had stood with a dozen other students and watched in disbelief as the dark-yellow flesh of a man's chest was peeled back like canvas to expose his sternum. It seemed so rude. The thick stench of chemicals settled on their clothes and skin. They shuffled and stared and whispered so as not to offend the man lying before them with his grey mouth agape. The inner world, so nearby. Right *there*. We forget the skeleton we carry with us at all times. Hard to believe, in many ways as distant as a Bombay slum. Under fizzing fluorescent lights they learned to handle the dead, to name the parts and know how they functioned. The grey lungs of a smoker and the swollen liver of a drinker. They were made to feel powerful and intelligent. Any dread of the inanimate was dispelled by the brutal matter-of-fact, before they were let loose on the living.

But Lee was not quite dead yet. Wild looked at him. Uncertainly, he held out a finger in front of the moth and waited until the creature stepped daintily onto the back of his hand, as if mounting a stage. Carrying the insect, he walked through the darkened house. He left the lounge room and moved down the hall to the front door, went outside onto the creaking verandah and raised his hand into the air above his head. The dark air was very cold and the trees and eaves drizzled with rainwater. He could feel the moth moving on his skin until it found the edge. It waited for another minute with antennae still rotating before blundering into the night.

Wild returned to where Lee lay on the dining table. A newly awoken urgency burned through him. *He who wishes to be a surgeon should go to war*, wrote Hippocrates. It is often in times of crisis that medicine is compelled to advance. The German wounded fared better than their French counterparts during the Franco-Prussian War thanks to a willingness to use Lister's ideas on antiseptics. Thus we progress.

As gently as he could, as if handling something newborn, he lifted Lee in his arms. Come on, son.

Wild was aware of Lee's shallow gaze upon him as he removed the young man's bloody jacket and shirt, laid him back down on the table and prepared to operate. The boy might even have tried to say something, but it was probably just an anguished groan; he was almost certainly beyond language.

19

Wild shook off his overcoat and arranged the things he would need on a low metal table he had retrieved from the consulting room: scalpels, needles, dressing, sutures, antiseptic. Forceps, with their long, serrated beaks. From Lee's torso he peeled away a soggy dressing of toilet paper and dropped the bloody mess to the floor. He waited, breathing heavily, inhaling the stink of blood and antiseptic.

He crouched closer until his face was only an inch or two from Lee's body, which emanated only the barest warmth. He considered the smattering of hair over Lee's chest, the visible outline of the pectoralis major. There was an older scar on the right side of Lee's waist, the opposite side to where he'd been shot. The body has its own dreaming of course, if only one knows how to read the marks and curves. It is possessed, like any geography, of entire histories, each bump and scar the result of some childhood accident or perhaps other, more sinister misadventures. The time during the holidays he fell from a tree in the neighbour's garden. The day he was hit by a car. Dog bite and knife fight.

Although the area immediately around Lee's bullet wound was inflamed, there didn't seem to be any sign of infection. The entry wound was small, its edges already rimmed by scabbing despite the dark blood seeping from it. Perhaps the bullet was not so deep, after all? Wild ran his hands across Lee's abdomen, searching for any sense of ballooning, for signs of internal bleeding. His fingers traced an arc above Lee's ninth and tenth ribs, feeling for any clue as to the bullet's exact location. Of course it might be anywhere, its trajectory having been altered from contact with muscle or bone. He thought of the abdomen, the body's largest cavity, glistening with viscera: liver, intestines, bladder, stomach, colon.

Lee showed little awareness of what was happening. Wild had arranged all the candles he could find around the lounge room and hung a kerosene lamp from the unpowered chandelier directly overhead. Lee's pale body stretched away in the uncertain light like a small, damp island. Never before had he been so afraid of another person. He was taut with fear, as if something were muscling for release against his drum of skin.

The air thickened with smoke from the candles and lamp. Wild dabbed at the wound again, holding the cotton wool like a knuckle of bread. He hadn't laid a hand on a patient since that terrible night, had barely even touched another human being. Physical contact was always the first thing to go. The world shrank from those it deemed unsuitable; even his wife avoided his touch afterwards. Not that he would have wanted to continue his medical duties, even if permitted. Two years in exile from a portion of himself. He wiped his hands dry on his shirt and wondered how on earth to begin.

Although Wild had never treated a bullet wound, he remembered some of the terminology. Yaw and tumble, velocity and pressure. A bullet doesn't enter a person's body smoothly, tip first, as people tend to think. The physics obscures the fact that it's just one thing thunking blindly into another. The bullet shatters and crumples. Damage to tissue is often caused less by the bullet itself than the shock waves it sends through the body, often creating a cavity ahead of where the bullet stops. Almost as if the body accommodates the object's anticipated trajectory and manufactures its very own injury. Then there are the problems of infection and blood loss. The point of impact is only the beginning.

Again Wild stared at Lee's face. He always suspected that the screen erected between the surgeon and patient before an operation was not for the patient's benefit but to partition the surgeon from the reality of slicing into another human being, who is objectified, whose skin is made yellow through antiseptic, whose signs of life are reduced to bleeps and numerical codes. In this way, medicine is the same as art; it's all about distance. Perhaps, he thought suddenly, that is part of what went wrong on that night. Good surgeons will never address a patient by their first name. An incision is made through a piece of some stranger's body. A girl with bucked teeth. Some middle-aged man with a wife. *Good morning, Mr. Jones. Please, call me Alfred. Well, Mr. Jones, the problem seems to be in the left . . .*

Wild prepared an injection of morphine and administered some to Lee. It was a risk, considering the boy's condition, but some sort of pain relief was necessary. Then he allowed himself the same. The drug moved through him like a dark and cumbersome tide, smoothing his edges, making him fluid and mathematical. He digested the sensation for a few minutes, inhaled deeply and rolled up both shirtsleeves. He placed two fingers against Lee's cool neck to gauge a pulse, but his watch seemed to have stopped sometime in the past day or so. Probably knocked it against something on that damn train. He suspected that the trouble caused by a bullet wound was mainly below the surface. If the bullet was lodged anywhere but in the half-inch or so of muscle and fat below the skin, then it would have to wait. At least there didn't seem to be any sort of rattle in the boy's breathing to indicate a perforated lung.

The house was utterly silent, as if moored to the bottom of the sea. It was unsettling. He worked his trembling hands into a pair of gloves and wondered about leaving the boy there and fleeing, but the idea was a mere cul-de-sac. After all, where would he go after that?

In desperation, Wild thought back to his studies. Back to the basics. Always let the patient know exactly what's going on. Take them through it. Talk to them, include them in the proceedings. The best doctors have relaxing voices. He thought of Sherman's refined whisper. He hummed anxiously for a minute, then cleared his throat and began to speak out loud, falteringly at first, just a mumble really, but with a rising momentum like a song discovering itself in the singing. As he did so, he began to work.

Well then, he said. What are we going to do with you? What we'll do is get this thing out of your body. A bullet. A bullet. We'll just . . . We'll see what we can do. With a bit of luck, it's more or less still in one piece because I don't think we can go digging around in there looking for bits and pieces. We'll be OK. We'll be alright.

I was a good doctor in my day, believe it or not. Before everything fell to pieces. Seems like a lifetime ago, now. Several lifetimes, actually. Incredible how quickly things can happen. Woman once came into my surgery with a two-inch nail jammed under her bloody *eye*. Walked in off the street into the waiting room like something from a horror movie. Incredible. Don't know how it happened, she was very cagey about it, but we managed to remove the thing. Eased it out from beneath the eyeball, patched her up and sent her on her way. She was drunk as a skunk, of course. Probably went on back to the pub or something. Drunks are lucky like that. Stupid, but lucky. Probably have their own damn saint. Irish, no doubt. Nobody celebrates their inadequacies like the Irish. Maybe I should have been a drunk. Nobody likes junkies. Not even junkies like other junkies.

He paused with the scalpel above Lee's body. It was straightforward. He would slice, the skin would peel back slightly at the edges, there would be blood. A bead of sweat trickled down his nose. *He would slice, the skin would peel back slightly at the edges, there would be blood.* Above him the kerosene lamp growled its throaty, monotone growl. He bent over, close enough to detect the smell of dried mud on Lee's neck, the uric waft of his own fear.

People sometimes forget that the patient is always the one in charge, he continued in what he hoped was a soothing tone. Directing the traffic, as it were. Everything revolves around the patient. Without him, we are nothing. *Respect the patient,* Sherman used to say. *Listen to what they have to tell you. Watch them and learn.* Fantastic man. Great doctor. The best. Of course the things people say are not always the heart of the matter. Good doctors know how to read the signs, to see beyond what people say, to read their body language and so on. Sherman could run his hands over someone's skin and detect cancers and blockages and organs not working properly; like reading Braille.

Wild lowered the scalpel to Lee's flesh and moved it horizontally at the point where the imaginary transpyloric and lateral sternal planes met. He was careful not to go too deeply. Nestled somewhere beneath was the colon and, a little further north, the gall bladder. It was possible

Lee's liver had been damaged, but there was nothing he could do about that here. He made a small incision, no more than an inch across.

Lee stiffened and groaned softly, little more than a sigh. He licked his lips, but his eyes remained closed and he made no other outward signs of discomfort, although he must have been in extreme pain. Fresh blood spurted from the incision, paused on the swollen lip of flesh and slunk over the ribs and coagulated on the table.

Still clutching the scalpel in his right hand, Wild stepped back. I'm not up to it, he thought. I can't do this. Apart from anything else, I'm not *allowed* to do this. He needed to mop up the blood. He needed to make another incision at a right angle to the first. He needed to find the bullet and remove it and then he had to stitch Lee up again. Damn. He looked around. The archaic domesticity of this house was suddenly rather pathetic: its faded rugs and dried flowers, the footstool beside the couch like an obedient dog. Damn.

Despite his anxiety—or perhaps because of it—he felt exhausted. What he wanted, what he really wanted, was to lie down, sink into the deep couch, curl up and sleep. When she was about two-and-a-half, his daughter, Alice, was convinced she could vanish if she herself couldn't see. They played hide-and-seek in the garden and when it was her turn to hide she would just stand there with her hands over her eyes, grinning like a mad person at the apparent genius of it. Her straight, dark hair and tiny fingernails. Then the pantomime of searching the bushes and undersides of the house followed by the extravagant surprise at finding her on the lawn in full view. She would be fifteen now, beyond the grip of innocence, although in many ways finally hidden from him, her father. After all these long years, it was he who'd vanished down the rabbit hole.

By now Wild's entire body was shaking, as if possessed by fever. Breath fluttered in his throat. He was aware of time passing, could sense its trembling movement. He'd spent two years outlawed from the possibility of being responsible for another's life—and now this? Unconsciously he raised a hand to his mouth to chew a thumbnail, only to realise what he was doing and stop himself.

Lee groaned and clutched at his left side. The pool of blood on the table swelled until it outgrew its thick meniscus and trickled onto the wooden floor. Another groan. What if he died? What if the boy died? What then? And he *was* dying, that much seemed obvious. Right in front of him. Dying right in front of him. Again.

What should I do? And Frank's round, unshaven face staring, disbelieving, staring at him. *What? You're the doctor.* Thinking that Frank probably should shave twice a day—maybe he usually does but missed today because of the fuss of the pregnancy and so on—and realising even at the time that it was an idiotic thought. And that silence and the feel of it in his hands, as good as dead, everyone waiting. The silence peculiar to tragedy. Everyone waiting.

Tears assembled in Wild's eyes. One thing at a time, he thought. One thing at a time. He stepped forward to test Lee's pulse again. Faint. The skin was still cool, but there didn't seem to be any immediate sign of arrhythmia. Ideally, Lee's knees should be bent but there was no means to keep him balanced in that position and it would make access even more difficult. He wished there were someone else present, just so he could ask: *What do you think we should do?* He wanted no more than that, only the companionship of a question.

But there was nobody. He inhaled deeply then mopped up the blood and drew the skin apart. Meditatively, he ran his hands over Lee's skin again, feeling for clues, for signs of swelling or rupture, all sense and feeling crammed into the tips of his fingers. Through his very hands, he breathed.

Let me tell you about the ribs, he murmured. There are usually twelve on either side but not necessarily. Sometimes more or fewer depending on the development of—what's it called?—a lumbar rib, I think. Something like that. The middle ones are of a certain shape and have particular characteristics—thin and flat with a groove for nerves and vessels—but the first two and the last three are different again. I suspect that your ninth or tenth ribs are broken, which may well have saved your life.

A long pause before he spoke again. Doctor Sherman was not too badly equipped, he said at last. Luckily for us. These forceps are perfect. Hold on, son. Hold on. Skin is amazing stuff. The stretch and the ability to repair itself. Strong and stretchy. Waterproof. Think of a pregnant woman. That stomach. Jane was huge when she was pregnant with Alice. Incredible. Big as a house she was, almost as wide as she was tall. I know a lot about the body. How it works and what goes where, but the idea of pregnancy still amazes me. That you can carry something alive within your own body, a version of yourself. And afterwards, it's almost as if nothing has happened. The day after Alice was born it was as if she had been with us all along, which maybe she had in some obscure way. The child you have is always the only one you ever could have had.

Wild stopped talking and looked up, realising this was an idiotic conversation. Tell that to Frank and Louise, he thought. People only believe in fate when the outcome is positive. It's in the face of disaster that we entertain other, multiple possibilities, when we imagine better alternatives. *What is* and *what might have been* stare longingly at each other but will never converse.

People look in all sorts of places for their proofs of God, he continued. But it's right here. You're walking around in it. All you need, under your nose. A vessel of wonders, sloshing about inside, perfectly arranged. Think of . . . well, think of just about anything to do with our bodies and you'll be amazed. In fact at this very moment certain cells are running around your blood looking for antigens so they can present them to the T-cells because they can't recognise them unless this happens and then the T-cell can get to work to repel the foreign body. So much work even in breathing. So much for the body to do to convert everything to useful stuff. No wonder we get so tired. No wonder our bodies wear down. Just to fight infection, which your body will be doing right now, as we speak. At the ends of science is God.

This light here is medieval. I feel like I'm in that Rembrandt painting. Don't know how I ended up here. There *are* other places, if you can imagine. Better places. Not everywhere is like this. I know because I've lived there. Once upon a time. Where it's light and there are clean surfaces and . . . I don't know, where there's a sense of possibility or something. *Women*. There's even a horizon.

Over Wild's head, the kerosene lamp's lean flame guttered, wavered and finally rallied. It was too late to back out now. Already his hands were smeared with blood. He'd located the bullet, could see its dark edge nestled within the red and yellow membranes of the deep fascia. This was a lucky break. He might be able to retrieve it. Lee remained utterly still.

Wild took a breath and kept talking. When we were first married, Jane and I went to London and stayed in a posh hotel. What was that? More than fifteen years ago. Our honeymoon. Now *that* is a city, people everywhere with their rubbish and bags and whatever. Just stuff. And quiet. I'd expected it to be really noisy, but people just moved through the streets in a gentle way, sort of whispering to each other, not because they were shy but because they were considerate of the people around, of not making too much noise. But the hotel. The hotel was the most modern thing I'd ever seen, shiny and neat and *ordered*. Even the flowers looked symmetrical. Amazing.

It was only later, much later, that Jane told me that she had cried on that holiday. One day when I was visiting a medical museum she'd sat by the window and wept because she knew it would never work out with us. And I wasn't even using drugs then, was actually a pretty respectable sort of catch. She told me this when she left, like it was something she'd been saving up for our entire marriage. Wild shook his head. For nearly twenty years she tended that scrap of information.

Strange thing is that I knew all along. I remember coming home in the early evening through the drizzle. It was cold and I knew she'd been crying and I knew exactly why, but I resisted asking her because I didn't want her to say it out loud. So when she finally told me it was like we decided to have the conversation we should have had years earlier, but by then it was too late. I didn't even know about this kind of world then, and now that I'm here I don't know that I can even remember what it was like in those other places. What it *is* like. Still going on out there somewhere, I suppose. One day you're a guy with a wife and kid and the next you're on the street, living like a bum.

And on this murmuring raft of language, Wild managed to bear himself and Lee through the darkness. Who knows how long it took? It seemed like an age that he crouched over that table, picking up and replacing things, wondering what to do, tapping his upper and lower teeth nervously against each other. He managed to imagine himself into another different, more capable person, so much so that he was almost disappointed to finally stitch Lee's wound and stand back, merely himself once again. Still talking, he carried Lee and laid him on a sagging bed in one of the bedrooms. He covered him with heavy quilts and waited until he seemed to be resting more or less comfortably. He made a fire in the dusty fireplace and it was only then he heard the rain spattering on the windowpane and, having rinsed himself of words, fell silent. Hands still sheathed in bloody gloves, he pressed a palm to the windowpane and allowed the darkness to pass into his hand and splinter through him. What a place to finish up.

20

Wild woke to find himself on the couch in the lounge room. The open fire had weakened throughout the night and his exhalations were visible in front of his face. He rebuilt the fire and staggered into the garden where the air was sharp and watery. It felt like late morning, although he couldn't be sure.

Sherman's house was set in about two acres of scruffy garden that might once have been contained but was now unravelling. The cloudy sky was only occasionally apparent through the low canopy of leaves glistening with rainwater. Bright-green moss coloured the underside of branches. Vines squirmed over the gutters and fingered any tears in the grey flywire over the windows and doors. He waded through the damp, knee-high grass, pushing aside overhanging branches. The place, as always, reminded him of an Edwardian children's book, a cross-hatched landscape for orphans and their melancholy guardians. He recalled his attempts at detoxing, sitting out here day after day with a rug across his shoulders, like some ancient being, shivering in the afternoon sun and wondering how bad one would have to feel before dying from it all.

He came across objects in unexpected places: a crumpled soccer ball on one of the tiny lawns; a stone birdbath overflowing with scummy water; a crippled wooden chair; a rocking horse in the grasp of a blackberry bush. Thorns and weeds caught at his coat, like anxious infants plucking at him. At the rear of the house behind the kitchen, two small sheds slumped against each other. When he peered inside, all he could see were boxes piled on shelves and a small army of dusty bottles on the floor, watched over by shapeless shadows of machinery.

The perimeter of the property was marked by a collapsing wooden fence. There were no neighbouring houses to be seen, just a grassy plain stretching for several hundred yards into thickening bushland that merged into a low bruise of clouds. It was difficult to discern where the earth ended and the sky began. The property seemed miles from anywhere, the only sound the susurrations of the wind through the trees and grass.

He turned his face skyward. His body felt even larger and denser than usual, as if swollen with the extra quantities of morphine he had taken in the past few days. Even his skin was thicker, a sort of hide. But it felt good to finally stop somewhere and not have to go on anytime soon. He felt like he had been on the move for a long time, longer even than the past few days with Lee. This was, he supposed, just a new version of what should by now be a familiar wilderness. At least out here the air had an unfamiliar bite. It was air that hadn't already been inhaled and exhaled a million times. It was somewhere else.

Wild strolled, gnawing at a thumbnail as he went. At the lower corner of the property he stumbled across a small, cleared patch overflowing with vegetables. The swollen heads of pumpkins, a tangle of green. A family of cabbages shouldered from the soil. He grinned and rubbed his hands together. Bingo! Just what we need. Food. Thank God. Perhaps we can survive here, after all.

He kneeled and set about extracting vegetables from the ground. He did it gently, almost regretfully, tugging at the bodies of these delicate things. Their bony crunch, the fragile grip of the earth and the scent of dirt as he shook soil from the fine webbing of roots. He would make soup, or a stew of some sort. It would be good for him, good for Lee.

Dirt smudged his broad hands. When Jane left, his gaze had fallen to her hands clasped in front of her. She had stepped back so quickly when he moved to take them that she almost tripped over a curling lip of carpet in the hallway. *Hey*, she'd said. *Stay away from me. Please, stay away. You've done enough.* She had paused. *I really think that maybe I should move out for a while. This is a strain on Alice, on all of us.* The words had come out in a rush, half garbled; it was obviously something she'd been wanting to say for some time.

He would never forget that wide-eyed look of hers. How she had pressed her hands to her chest as if fearful he would tear them from her, when all he wanted was to wash away the dirt that had collected beneath her fingernails from digging in their garden. The way she had gathered the silent Alice to her side and left, as if fleeing a strange and unpredictable animal.

Because I wanted to clean your hands?

How was it that love, when it has nowhere to live, becomes something else entirely? It was three months since she'd left. She said she was going to stay with her sister, but isn't that just what women say? Isn't that just the line that emerges under pressure? He remembered the older sister Carol, with her immaculate children that always seemed primed for a formal photograph.

He ran his tongue across teeth. He flattened his palms on the ground and tilted forward until their imprint was pressed into the soft soil. He inhaled the loamy smell. To think that Jane was actually somewhere on this very same earth, striding along in her practical way, blinking hair from her right eye, tapping a fingernail on the wineglass on the table before her. Alice in the background, rolling her eyes and twirling her hair, gazing at some point on the ceiling. He wondered if he might be able to intuit her whereabouts should he press his ear to the soil, perhaps detect an echo of laughter.

There was a soft thud from the bushes behind. Still kneeling, Wild turned but could see nothing. He was unsure from where the sound had come. He wiped a hand across his mouth. A bird, perhaps. A possum? Then a rustling, a shuddering of leaves, but closer this time. Rainwater spattered from leaves to the ground. Whatever it was, it was larger than a bird. More solid. Like a man. He waited. Nothing. Cautiously, he cleared his throat. Lee, he whispered, is that you?

He looked around and wiped his hands on his trousers before lumbering to his feet, leaving the pile of vegetables on the ground. Should he speak again, or just run? From his vantage point, he was unable to see the house through the thick foliage, but reckoned he could make a run for it. It was somewhere over to the right. He thought of the crumbling steps leading up to the large front door and the skeletal deck chair on the verandah. He clutched his coat around himself so it wouldn't catch on branches. He waited. But what if the house wasn't a good idea? The police. Perhaps it was the cops? Did the old bastard who drove them here in his cart say something to the police?

A shrub in front of him wobbled. Wild gasped. He stepped backwards and turned to run. His foot caught on something. He toppled partway to his knees with one hand outstretched to break his fall. His hand closed over a branch. A twig or thorn scratched his wrist. Suddenly in mid-fall, he felt ludicrous. To come all this way. Crashing around in some dilapidated garden. After all that had happened. To have come all this way for this—whatever the hell *this* was going to be.

Some sort of animal skittered, twitching and flickering, from the undergrowth. Black with pointy ears. Like a large, angular dog. The creature's face was long and bearded, with yolky eyes and fence-post teeth. What on earth? He tensed, indecisive, his muscles charged with adrenaline. *What on earth?* The creature shook its head and rolled its unhinged eyes. He released his grip on the branch and tumbled the rest of the way to the soft ground. By the time he crash-landed and felt the lumpy soil against his cheek and the nudge of a carrot in his ribs, laughter had tickled right through him and completely taken hold. With his face against the soil he laughed in huge, wheezing bursts, sending up puffs of dirt. He supported his weight on his elbows. Still more he laughed. His shoulders heaved and his lips became gritty. It must have been decades since he had laughed so much.

21

L ee stood at the window, slumping slightly to accommodate the dull pain through his side. He felt like an intruder in this strange room. On the pane of glass in front of him was a ghostly red handprint. A dream of faint laughter had woken him. The remnants of a fire smouldered in the fireplace and the room was woolly with heat. Wearing only trousers, his body was frail and bony, reduced to just the necessities. A milky throat, and nipples like thumbtacks pressed into his chest. The suitcase of money was on the floor beside him. He had checked it upon waking—his hand reaching out for it—while still anchored within his dreams.

A bulky dressing was taped to his torso below his ribs. He raised his left arm like a wing to gauge his freedom of movement, but his entire side was still tender and he was unable to lift his hand higher than his shoulder. Pain still gnawed on his lower ribs, but not as fiercely as he remembered. Perhaps the bullet had been removed. He gasped and lowered his arm, but smiled a slow smile anyway, a smile that had been biding its time. He'd made it. Gotten away with the money and nobody knew where the hell he was. How could they? He didn't even know himself. He allowed himself a small laugh.

He wondered what day it was. How much time had passed since all this had begun? Two days? Three? A lifetime. Perhaps it had been like this forever? He thought of his old apartment and felt a stab of pity for his former self still sitting on the windowsill staring down into the street, wondering what to do.

When he was eighteen, Lee had visited a brothel. Sex was a mysterious and complicated land; once, he'd snaked a damp hand beneath a girl's blouse at the back of a pub, but that was about as far as he'd ventured. Surprisingly, the brothel had a slightly domestic quality. There was a mug of half-drunk coffee on the arm of a chair in the lounge, a paperback face down on the floor and the radio was tuned to talk-back. The women who worked there were a soft and fleshy tribe sauntering half-naked through their kingdom.

Once he'd selected his girl, he sat on the edge of the bed, still fully dressed, playing with the zip of his jacket. The girl wore pink underwear and had a tiny roll of skin at her belly. The room smelled of talc and laundry and cheap incense. He was aware of the girl's hot thigh next to his own and had wanted something to happen but didn't know what.

The girl coughed into her hand and said her name was Isobel. Trying to be polite, Lee had asked her something about herself, to which the girl said: *Only thing you need to know is that I'm good at my job. Let's just say I don't plan to be doing this forever, mate. Now, shall we get those silly clothes off?* From the street outside had come the rumble of a truck followed by the sharp hissing release of air brakes. A woman had laughed next door or perhaps in the thickly carpeted hall outside the room. A throaty, wide-mouthed laugh. A hooker's laugh.

He shook away the memory, then imagined Claire currently going out of her mind, ringing his house and rolling her eyes. *I knew it. I knew it!* Graeme would say nothing. After all, *I told you so* doesn't always need actual words. He'd show the little prick. Appear with a suitcase filled with money. Hunker down and get a job. Stay out of trouble. Maybe learn a trade, become an electrician or something. A mechanic. Pick apples at McClaren's orchard. Do regular stuff.

Let's just say I don't plan to be doing this forever, mate.

He knew their house of course, had grown up there. A large place near a lake plopping with frogs. The air was oily with eucalyptus and in summer he swam into the darkest part of the lake and dived down to scoop handfuls of silky mud that would drain away by the time he surfaced. The hum of cicadas, morning frost on the laundry hung out overnight to dry.

Outside, the thin branches of a tree scratched against the window. There came a sound from a nearby room, like something scrabbling for purchase. It sounded like a group of small people. Children. The sudden slap of a screen door. Local teenagers or something. Whoever they were, they were inside the house. He shoved the suitcase of money under the bed with his foot. Then the sound of Wild grumbling and muttering. Shit. Lee looked around for his jacket, for his gun, but remembered— *Shit*—that he'd thrown it away back on that road, and before he could think what to do, Wild burst into the room with arms flailing and face halved by a huge grin. His hair was damp with rain and the front of his overcoat was stained with dirt. Frayed rope was looped around a fist.

Look what I found! And tumbling in stubbornly behind him was a skinny, black goat secured around its neck by a length of rope. The goat had a melancholy look. It was a boiled-down thing, the up-and-down action of its shanks apparent when it moved, so its haunches resembled a black sack of knives. The creature bleated sadly, looked around with its crazed eyes and shook its head as if expressing severe disapproval.

Wild was raving. Damn thing nearly scared me to death. An attack goat. A guard goat. Can you believe it? Vegetables. We can live here for ages. Chickens out the back as well. A whole menagerie.

A what?

A . . . Forget it.

Lee winced. Did you get it out?

What?

The bullet. Is it gone?

Wild nodded. Yes.

In the evening they sat on either side of a small wooden table in the dingy kitchen. Inside it was warm. Although there was no gas for the stove, a wood-fired plate in the fireplace still functioned, on which a pot of vegetable stew now bubbled. Steam softened the windows and obscured the outside world. It felt almost hearty. Not quite.

Lee was wearing a dark shirt he'd found hanging in a wardrobe. It had presumably belonged to Doctor Sherman. It was too large for him and the sleeves flapped uncomfortably around his wrists. Still, at least it was warm. He tried to sit straight-backed, but kept having to alter his position for comfort.

He had inspected the wound earlier in the afternoon when changing his dressing. It looked a brutal thing. His skin was folded like doughy bread and stitched together with thick, black thread. A crust of dried blood. Bizarre to see such a new addition to one's own body. What are you going to do now? he asked.

Wild looked perplexed. Now? Probably just sit here. Try and stay warm and dry. That's all I plan to do.

I don't mean right now. I mean in general.

That's what I'm talking about. Just sit right here in this kitchen for a few months. Lie low. See what happens. In this very chair.

Lee looked at the old guy, but could detect no sign of a joke. You can't stay here.

Why not?

What about . . .? I don't know. What about your family? Alice?

Wild looked up. What?

Isn't that your daughter's name?

I know who Alice is. How do *you* know who she is?

You talked about her.

I *talked* about her?

Lee pointed to his torso. When you were operating . . . You know, getting the bullet out. The other night, whenever it was. About when she was born or something.

And you remember?

I remember everything.

I thought you were—

I was conscious. More or less.

But you barely moved.

Lee shrugged and lit a cigarette. He shuddered at the thought of Wild's finger probing beneath the meat of his body. I was tired.

Tired? Lee, you were dying. I was *cutting into you*.

Lee didn't respond.

You heard everything? Wild chewed on a thumbnail and rearranged himself within the folds of his overcoat. He wore that dirty coat all the time now, as if expecting to have to leave at short notice. In combination with his rangy beard and wayward hair, he resembled some explorer just returned from a polar expedition. Alice is gone, he said at last. Well, I mean . . . Jane left me. My wife, that is. Took Alice as well, of course. So there's not much to go back to in that department, so perhaps I'll just stay here.

Why?

Only someone as young as you would ask that question. People leave each other all the time. It's what happens. As for my *career*. That is—how should I put it?—I'm not allowed to be a doctor anymore. Probably never will be. In fact, I'd be in all sorts of bother if anyone found out I'd operated on you. Although, of course, I'm already in all sorts of bother, so . . . Wild chuckled unconvincingly and looked out the window.

Despite the bulky clothing, he looked frail, as if he'd become less substantial in the past few days. If indeed he did stay here in this strange house, Lee thought he might whittle away to nothing, that coat across his shoulders like a corpse.

Lee shifted in his seat. Was it true, that story about the woman and the nail? The woman who came into your office or whatever with a nail in her eye?

Wild's eyes were wide and round, like two dark and shining stones in the pale putty of his face. Of course it was true. He scratched at his throat. What else did I say?

Lee thought. Just stuff. You never answered my question, anyway. What are you going to do now? Really.

I told you. Stay here. Eat vegetable stew. *Really.*

Right. And take morphine or whatever that stuff is.

Yes. Eat stew and take bloody morphine. Life of Riley, old chum. The life of Riley.

Won't it run out?

Wild winked and gestured expansively towards the back door. There's a lot of garden out there. A lot of vegetables. I'm planning an entire crop. A lifetime's supply of stew if we want it. Kill a few of those chickens. Raise some goats or something. There's one already. We could live here happily ever after. You and me. Get all self-sufficient.

Maybe you should give up?

Oh. I have given up, my boy. I have.

You know what I mean.

Do I?

Lee took a breath. I knew a guy in prison. He was using a fair bit of that shit. Smack, I guess. We cuffed him to the bunk for four days, by his hands. We shared a cell so I happened to be around when he wanted to try and stop taking it. So we cuffed him to the metal frame, you know, of the bed. Nearly dragged the whole thing off the tier when he tried to go and find some drugs. Begged us. Tried to snap his own wrists to get free. Thought he might be able to slip away. Yelled out at night, calling out to one of the dealers. Crying and groaning. Said he was dying. But he—

Why are you telling me this?

Lee shrugged.

You trying to *help* me?

I don't know. Just felt like I owed you, that's all. You did save my life. But, you know, forget it.

They sat in an embarrassed silence for several minutes. Wild drummed his fingers on his knee and got up and stoked the small stove. His face was shiny and orange in the fire's light.

Listen, he said when he sat down again. Don't worry about me. I've been doing this for a long time now. Ten years or more. It's all I got left. My old man was the same, had the same . . . compulsions, just a different way of going about it. A drunk. Dead at sixty. Runs in the family, this kind of thing. Genetics. Dopamine receptors and all that. Some would say that I'm predisposed to addiction. You could even say that it's destiny. Or that I'm spending my inheritance, I suppose. That might be one way to put it. I've given up on giving up. It's my destiny.

Fuck destiny.

Wild studied him for several seconds. You really believe that, don't you?

Lee ignored the question and rearranged himself on the hard wooden chair.

It'll get you in the end. Try as you might.

Lee met Wild's blue-eyed gaze. I'm already out.

You're an idealist, then?

Lee blushed under the accusation. Anyway, is that why you're not allowed to be a doctor? Because of taking dope?

Wild hesitated, as if deciding whether to allow this change of subject to pass. More or less. I can't go back. I jumped bail, actually. I couldn't face it. Can't face jail.

You jumped bail? Really? For what? You rob the hospital cupboard or something?

Wild sat forward with his elbows on his knees as if trying to fold himself into an even smaller shape. A flop of greying hair unfurled across his eyes. Something sizzled on the stovetop. I wish that was all, he said at last in a small voice, and then in an even smaller one: Manslaughter. Criminal negligence.

Manslaughter? You? You're kidding, right?

Oh yeah. Great joke.

What do you mean? You kill someone?

Wild nodded without looking up. Just the very outline of his profile was discernible, a flame-hued thread from his high forehead down to his curling nose and throat. A sound like a moan, but darker still.

Lee sat back in his chair and regarded Wild anew. His lips pursed to whistle, although no sound came out. Well. That explains a lot.

Maybe to you it does.

That guard, I mean. Back at the railway yard. The fat guard.

Wild got to his feet and went to the stove. He doled out two portions of a shapeless stew from the saucepan into bowls. Yes, he said when he had placed the meals on the table. I'm a wanted man, believe it or not.

The chipped bowls of steaming food sat between them. Although it smelled edible, the uncertain colour and consistency reminded Lee of prison food. He felt slightly ill. He was never hungry anymore. The idea of food was foreign to him. Eating was something other people did.

I'm not hungry.

Wild gestured to the food. You should eat. Good for you after all that's happened. Help you heal. Keep you strong.

When Lee didn't answer, Wild sat back and rubbed his hands together. I was supposed to be in court a week ago. Answering my charges, but I couldn't face it. It wasn't looking very good for me, so I made a run for it. The thought of jail is . . . I just couldn't face the whole thing. Cowardly, really. Everyone had left me. My wife, friends. A disaster.

Wild coughed into his fist, then reached out with a wetted thumb to rub dirt from the scuffed toe of one black shoe. There was a long and restless pause. I was a GP. In practice a long time. Just the usual stuff in the suburbs. Kids with broken arms and vaccinations and women with arthritis. It's a good life for the most part. Good money, but sort of boring. I started taking a bit of morphine, for the thrill, you know? Just to see what it would be like, and one thing led to another, and there comes the day when you realise it's completely out of your hands. Doesn't take long. A couple of weeks and you wake up sniffling and aching and jangling and it's almost impossible to get off. It's always just there. Wild dug at the palm of his left hand with the thumb of his right. This is all by the by, really.

Anyway. I got called out to a woman having a baby very suddenly. Unexpectedly. Early, you know? They were actually friends of ours, of my wife and I. A young couple, Louise and Frank. Although I didn't have much to do with her pregnancy, there was a sudden complication. She began going into labour very prematurely, middle of the night. Contractions and all, just pre-labour. But Louise was anxious and they called me out as a precaution more than anything. I think I was there as a sort of calming influence or something. Just to tell them that everything was alright and not to worry and go back to sleep. And I was stoned of course, and everything was sort of happening very quickly, as it sometimes does. The husband was panicking and the woman was struggling. I think the husband called an ambulance, but it became clear that we had to deliver the baby right there and then, on the damn bedroom floor. Prematurely. The whole thing was just not right. This was in their house, about two years ago. Three a.m. or something. I was completely out of it. Away with the fairies. In fact when they'd called me I was in my study in darkness, *staring*. Totally absorbed in the darkness. Completely irresponsible, but sometimes, in the midst of a binge, you feel so . . . I don't know.

Anyway. There's a drug which is used in childbirth. It causes the muscles of the womb to contract very strongly. Wild rubbed again at his shoe and fingered a crust of mud at the hem of his trousers. And it's administered when the baby is nearly born and it helps with the delivery of the placenta, but this particular night I administered the drug too soon, when the child's head wasn't crowned properly yet, when . . . the head wasn't out enough. Wild held his large hands out in front of himself as if cradling some small, invisible thing. His breathing was shallow and he sat up straighter in his chair.

And what happens if you do that?

Wild brought his hands together slowly with a soft, hollow clap. His gaze was fixed on some point on the wooden table. What happens? What happens is that the child—the *boy*—is crushed in the contraction. Suffocates. And dies.

Shit.

Right there in the bedroom. Everyone is crying at this stage, can you imagine? Frank with a hand across his mouth. And I say to him, to Frank, this young man of—I don't know—twenty-eight or something, maybe even younger, I say: *What should I do?* The baby is in my hands like a wet kitten. The ambulance comes and these guys take over. Just shove me out of the way and . . . But the boy is dead. It's terrible. *What should I do?* Still can't believe I said that. Really can't believe it.

A dead baby is the worst possible thing. Their first child, can you imagine? Couple didn't survive after all that. Broke up. Takes it out of you, that kind of thing. Sometimes a death in the family is like a bomb. Everyone gets caught up. The family is ruined. All that love gone to waste. The kid would be walking now if it wasn't for me. An entirely new person—what should have been the best thing in their lives. Actually, I think I'm more afraid of seeing Louise and Frank again than I am of jail. I assume they would have come. To court, I mean. They would have come to court and sat there chewing over that terrible night.

Lee felt sorry for Wild. If he was expected to offer some sort of consolation, however, he didn't know what on earth it could be. What are you looking at?

What?

In jail.

Wild laughed humourlessly. I suspect it doesn't matter. One year, ten years. A hundred. Any time in jail is too much for someone like me. I can't do it. Not to mention the fact that I'll never work again.

And you got nowhere else to go?

Wild picked up a spoon and folded it through the stew several times. No. Nowhere. Left my own house the day before I was meant to be in court. Just packed and got in the car and drove away. So, you see, staying here is about as good an option as I have at the moment, at least for the time being. Stay out of sight. Wait for something to happen. God knows what.

Wild began to eat without enthusiasm and for some time the only sound was of his chewing. What are *you* going to do? he asked when he had almost finished his meal.

Lee shrugged. Stick with the plan, I guess. Take the money and go to my sister's place. Stay with her for a while. Get a job. Try and go straight. Get away from here. It was strange to hear himself saying it out loud and he almost wished he hadn't spoken at all. It seemed stark.

Won't they come after you? Wild asked. After their precious money?

He preferred not to talk about Josef. I don't see how they can find me.

Won't they just look for your sister or your parents? Track you down?

Lee shook his head. They don't know anything about me. Probably think everyone is dead.

Why would they think that?

No reason.

Wild nodded slowly. I see. When exactly are you thinking of leaving?

In a few days, I guess. Soon as I'm up to moving again.

There's probably still bullet shards in you.

Lee grimaced. Really?

You'll have to get yourself checked out as soon as you can. Watch those ribs, as well. You need to be careful. You're not out of the woods yet, as they say. Keep the dressing fresh and clean.

OK. I'll remember that. Thanks.

Yes. Apparently you remember everything.

It's true, I do have a great memory.

Well. You haven't lived very long. You've got less to remember than some of us.

Lee thought with distaste of the pieces of the world he now carried within him. He had a sudden thought. Why don't you come with me?

Go with you?

Yeah.

To live with your *sister*?

Well. For a while, at least. Could be a good chance to get away. We can both lie low. Try and stay out of trouble. In the country. By the lake.

By the lake?

Yeah. By the lake. Where they live. It's beautiful there. Nobody would know we were there. It's perfect.

Wild said nothing, just crouched over the table and continued to eat, hurriedly, as if afraid his meal would soon try to escape.

The sound was barely audible, a small mewling somewhere nearby. It soaked into Wild's sleep like water into a sponge, deeper and deeper until he awoke. He shifted heavily and pulled the blankets over his head. The smell of his body was thick under their soft weight; the flavours of sweat, of warm skin and stale breath. Disgusting.

He had taken to sleeping on one of the couches in the lounge room, from where he could stare out the large bay windows throughout the insomniac night and observe the relentless progress of the stars, the rise and fall of the moon. In addition, there was the company of the open fire.

The crying sound sharpened, but became no louder, remained an aural mirage at the edge of hearing. Eventually, he flung back the blankets and sat on the corner of the couch. He raised his grizzled head to listen and stared into the gloom, completely still, listening with his entire body as if the sound might be detected by senses other than hearing. He passed a hand through his hair and ran his tongue about his muggy mouth. What time could it be? Early morning, before dawn. He couldn't be dreaming; he had long ago annihilated any capacity for dreaming. Again the small, despairing siren. It was, he realised, the raw, desperate sound of a baby. What kind of darkness was this?

He waited until he was able to make out the shapes of the surrounding furniture: the other couch, a side table, the gleam from an oil painting high on the wall, the imposing sideboard with its assortment of glassware and dried flowers. He stood unsteadily and pulled on his shirt and trousers. Like a ghost he moved through the house, along the narrow hall with its carpets underfoot. Things rattled as he passed. The crying was coming from the garden. He made his way to the kitchen and stood at the back door.

The air outside was fresh and cool. He peered into the garden gloom. When he was last here it was well maintained, with benches and chairs placed conveniently beneath luxuriant overhangs. Now, it resembled an abandoned city trapped beneath the fierce clutch of vines and weeds, with the smell peculiar to buildings reclaimed by nature. He could sense its chaos through the darkness, the constant rustling and creaking, the twitter of tiny things moving about.

Leaving the door open, Wild hugged himself and stepped out onto the slippery patio. His bare toes gripped the moist bricks; moss squelched beneath his feet. There was a smell of geraniums and the tang of ivy. His lungs filled with moist air. Again he listened, but there was nothing. The night had become still and quiet, the way the night is supposed to be. He was about to go back inside when he heard it again. There, that sharp bleat.

He scratched his nose and wondered if he should fetch Lee. He waited, not breathing. Just the whirr of his heart and the murmur of his blood. He angled his head to better determine from where the baby's cries were emanating. The garden sprawled drunkenly at the front of the old weatherboard house and along the entire eastern side. He followed the path down that side, grimly aware of the bugs being crushed beneath his feet and the occasional sticky drag of spider web across his face. An entire garden world, going about its business.

The baby's cries were still sporadic, devoid of any apparent human rhythm. He moved through the front garden, ducking beneath the low tree limbs he sensed rather than saw. Dry leaves snagged in his hair. He stood finally on a small patch of dew-soaked lawn but the sound had vanished. There was nothing here. The child—or whatever it was—was elsewhere.

After a minute or two, perhaps even longer, Wild made his way back along the side path to the rear of the house. The sound was clearer here, definitely coming from the back somewhere. He rubbed his palms together for warmth as he walked. The garden seemed aware of him. Thousands of small eyes blinked from cocoons and knotholes, from vantage points along the gutters and eaves. By now his feet were wet and unwieldy, growing numb with cold. He stopped breathing to listen. There it was, a small sound, a whimpering.

He edged towards the back of the property, where the garden was most overgrown. Sherman would be turning in his grave at the sight of this. He had loved nothing more than to potter about in what he called his *kingdom* on a Sunday afternoon, pulling at weeds and tying things back, murmuring softly to his more-favoured subjects. Leaves crunched like soggy toast beneath Wild's feet. The ground rose here at the back, became more even. There was a small mossy patio. When all this was finished, he thought, when things panned out whatever way they were going to, he would find and visit Sherman's grave. God knows what he could say to the old man, but he would go there and do whatever people do at gravesides, weep or pray or sit with him, perhaps forever, as Sherman had done for him on so many nights.

The sound was clear now, a sort of unbearable, plangent keening. Some teenager has abandoned her newborn baby in the back shed, he thought, and as this idea took root within him he moved quicker, pushing leaves and webs aside with his outstretched hands. Cold, flat leaves slapped against his face. His shirt snagged on a branch. He remembered reading of a schoolgirl who secretly gave birth over a sheet of newspaper in her parents' garden, one hand clutching a sapling for balance and the other cupped beneath her to gather her blood and offspring. It was not out of the question; the local teenagers probably knew Sherman's place was abandoned. Appallingly, the child was probably *conceived* here.

Panting with anxiety and exertion, he stopped at the shed's flimsy wooden door. He wondered what he would do if this were the case. What would he do with a girl in the dirt? Would that be the worst thing, the most horrifying scene? Should he return quickly to the house to fetch some medical equipment? That damn bag of his, probably in police hands by now. He imagined its crouching shape, the lustre of its black leather like that of a beetle's shell. Forget it.

The shed door was secured by a narrow bolt. He wriggled it back and forth. He yanked the door open to the smells of fertiliser and grass clippings, of rust and machine oil, the endlessly perpetuated perfume of country sheds. It was dark. Something scurried in a corner and slapped against the wooden wall before falling still or escaping into the garden. Then it was quiet.

Wild held his breath and listened. There was movement on the ground nearby, the blind and voiceless curling of something newborn. He lowered into a crouch with one hand crabbed on the dirt floor for balance. His eyes adjusted to the gloom and he could make out vague shapes. A bicycle. A trestle table. A sack of earth or manure. Blood roared through him.

He opened his mouth to whisper into the darkness but his voice turned to dust somewhere in his throat. What could he say? He closed his eyes and allowed his head to droop until his chin rested on his chest. His breathing was loud and deep. He stayed like that for some time.

Finally he stood, swaying a little, his body unstable as if preparing to buckle. His head felt vast and heavy, a labyrinth atop his shoulders. Water dripped somewhere nearby and there was a sigh of wind through the trees outside. Suddenly aware of the cold, the hairs on his body rose in pitiful defence. Of course there was no child. There never was.

23

The following morning, or the day after, or perhaps it was a different day altogether, Lee wandered into the lounge room expecting to find Wild still asleep but there was no sign of him apart from the crumpled dent in the couch where he'd slept. Logs smouldered in the fireplace and grey sunlight spilled through the windows and coated the furniture like ash.

The dining table had not been cleared of the debris from the operation. Scattered over its surface were scraps of bandages, empty glass ampoules, a strangely hooked needle and a tray of scalpels and long-beaked implements patterned with thumbprints of blood. On the floor a circle of blood, its wrinkled skin like that of cold gravy.

The lamp Wild had slung from the chandelier had leaked a small puddle of kerosene onto the table where Lee had lain. The stain of oil was a continent upon the polished surface, the smell of it layered and dark. Lee shuddered as he recalled the table's wooden surface pressed against his shoulder blades, Wild's whiskery voice circling like a crow far above him and the sensation of fingers digging beneath the layers of his skin.

In a kidney dish were bloodied wads of cotton and the bullet shard Wild had removed from him. The scrap of metal rattled around the dish when Lee shook it. He tipped the bullet into the centre of his palm and held it to his face, but it revealed nothing. Just a bloody blob, the size and shape of a rotten, snaggly tooth.

He heard footsteps and turned to see Wild standing on the far side of the room with a metal bucket in one hand and a length of chain in the other.

Lee dropped the bullet into his jacket pocket. What are you doing with those?

Wild's entire body tilted and his eyes were barely open. He resembled an abandoned building, flickeringly lit, perhaps someone moving around inside. Even from across the room, Lee could see the polish of sweat upon his forehead. Obviously, he'd been awake shooting morphine all night. He was crazy with it.

Is the offer still open?

What offer?

Again the thick silence. To come with you. To your sister's. I can't stay here by myself. I just can't.

Lee looped a length of chain several times around the metal frame of the bed and then around Wild's wrists, securing each end with a padlock. The loop wasn't large enough to slip over Wild's large hands but would have some play along the length of his forearm. He was unsure of this whole idea, but Wild seemed certain it was the only way.

Chain me up, he'd said. Chain me up.

At the moment, though, he seemed uninterested in what was happening until he looked up and said: God, I'm frightened.

Lee paused. Secretly, he hoped Wild would reconsider. Of what?

Wild lifted a handful of chain. It made a medieval clank. I'm afraid of everything. Of what might happen to me.

Lee looked at him but was silent.

The trouble is, Wild went on in his slurry voice, it never seems easier to give up drugs than when you're stoned out of your mind. Like now. *Anything* seems possible then. That's why you've got to strike while the iron's hot, so to speak. You sure you don't mind me coming with you?

Lee hesitated. No. It will be fine. They have a big house. Bigger than this one, even. Besides, we should stick together after all this.

And your sister won't mind? I am sort of, you know, on the run after all. I'm not exactly—

Don't worry about that. I'll sort that out with her. It's my house, too. Our parents left it to both of us.

I need a break, that's all. I need a fresh start so I can face everything.

Wild scratched his neck and Lee saw the marks of many other such scratchings.

I destroyed the rest of my dope, Wild said. Cracked the little bastards open and poured them down the drain. Nearly broke my heart. Cut my hands. Sometimes those ampoules are buggers to snap off. I should have quite a few hours though, before it all begins. Gorged myself. Probably won't feel the pinch until this evening or so. And he displayed the backs of his hands and the crooks of his arms smeared with bruising and blood from recent hits before he sagged and appeared to fall asleep, only to jerk upright again a moment later. What happened to your friend?

What friend?

The one in jail. The one you tied to the bed? Lee? Your friend.

Lee shook his head to give the impression that either he didn't know or it was so inconsequential it wasn't even worth discussing. He crouched down and laid wood in the fireplace, assembling it in a teepee shape like his father had taught him. You'll be OK. It's just a few days. Then we'll get out of here.

Was he OK? Your friend? Was he alright afterwards? After you helped him detox?

Lee stood and jammed a cigarette into his mouth. His fingers carried the smell of oil and rust from handling the chain. Wild was looking up at him expectantly, nodding as if trying to generate a positive answer by enthusiasm alone.

When he was a boy, Lee had been taken to a circus that had been set up in a local park. There was a crowd of lights, an elephant and the damp smell of hay. He had been inexplicably depressed at the sight of a bear galloping around the ring with a fez jammed upon its great brown head. The bear had appalled him and he focused on the other happenings around the ring—the trapeze artists and clowns—unwilling to look at the bear in the same way he was now reluctant to look at Wild.

He lit his cigarette and stooped to toss the still-burning match into the fireplace. The paper caught fire immediately and soon the kindling began to burn. He watched the flames curling and stretching. He nodded. Yeah. He was fine afterwards.

What was his name?

It doesn't matter what his name was, does it?

Curious, that's all.

Well, I can't remember.

I thought he was your friend?

He wasn't really a friend, I hardly knew the guy.

You said he was.

I just shared a cell with him.

What was his name?

Fuck. Simon, OK? Simon was his name.

Wild appeared satisfied with this scrap of information.

Lee smoked and the cigarette fizzled in the air. Outside it was raining again. He was fine. He was fine afterwards.

Wild nodded and stared into the fireplace where the fire had grown.

Lee doubted he had even heard what he said.

Lee retreated to the lounge room, which, with the fire blazing, was at least warm. He lay on the couch and stared at the ceiling or flicked through old copies of *National Geographic*. He was disturbed by the thought of Wild shackled to the bed and occasionally heard a low groan or sneeze, even snatches of conversations.

He wandered through the hallways and rooms of the house, ran his hands over the red wallpaper decorated with pale flowers. The entire place was damp, as if underground, an impression compounded by the murky light. Not only was the arrangement of the rooms idiosyncratic, but the items within them as well. Atop a cabinet in the ancient laundry was a glass jar containing the curled, restful shape of a baby possum in fluid with its tiny paws folded beneath its chin; romance novels were scattered over the examination room's vinyl couch; in one of the two bathrooms half-a-dozen plastic dolls sat in a puddle on the tiled floor, their smiles fixed as if hoping to avert some dreadful fate; a small, potted forest of withered ferns in the rear sunroom.

He passed through a dingy anteroom beside the kitchen and reeled at the sudden appearance of a shambling figure beside him. He swore, spun awkwardly and stood, face-to-face, with a man of his own height and age bent slightly at the waist. The stranger's eyes widened and he stepped back. He held a hand to his ribs and stared but even as Lee realised it was merely his own image reflected from a mirror, he was disbelieving. He laughed nervously. Himself. Of course.

The mirror was enormous, set within a thick, gold frame. It reached from floor to ceiling, like something you'd see in Europe. Lee considered himself and tried to stand straighter, but was restricted by the pain at his side. His borrowed and stolen clothes hung from his skinny frame and were stained with blood and dried mud. He looked a complete wreck.

Of course he'd inspected himself in mirrors before. He was aware of a small mole on his right cheek, that his left shoulder sloped slightly and that a hairline crack bisected a front tooth. He looked around. Shyly, in the quiet afternoon of a cold and derelict house, Lee allowed his hands to fall and rest at his sides. He stepped forward and brought his face so close that it frosted the glass when he breathed. So this was what people saw. He tried to imagine meeting this person for the first time. What would he think? A young man with a dark dusting of beard across his face and black, choppy hair perhaps more accustomed to being worn short. Dried and peeling lips. Dark eyes. And despite his leanness, the unmistakable doughy quality of youth. *He's just a kid*, Marcel had hissed when Josef brought him in. *No use to us. Just a fucking kid.* Was it possible not to be disappointed at such a sight? He swallowed and his Adam's apple lurched in his throat.

Did his father look like this at the same age? His grandfather? People used to say that he had his grandfather's chin, but he never knew what that meant and anyone who might have known was now dead. He tried to recall photos of him, but nothing definite came to mind. Perhaps a man wearing overalls and a white hat leaning against a weatherboard house, a shy bride and groom on some church steps, snapped in black-and-white with their eyes closing at the moment a handful of confetti rained over them.

Lee's father, Tom, worked in a printing workshop when he met Jean, the woman who would later be his wife and Lee's mother; there was a story of Lee's suspicious grandmother grabbing Tom's finger and comparing it with an inky print found on her daughter's skirt. Later, when the old woman was long dead, his father would mimic his mother-in-law, would dance around the kitchen squawking and hunching witchily: Is that Tom's thumb? Lee never knew her, couldn't even remember her name anymore. Already she had been consigned to history.

It seemed an act of forgiveness to imagine your ancestors at your own age, to think of them as painfully human as Lee felt right now. Could any of them ever have foreseen this moment, guessed that someday he, Lee, would stand before a mirror in a strange house and think of them, miss them, wish none that had happened had happened? He flinched inwardly. His father seemed too practical to have regrets, but what of his mother, frozen forever in his memory with arms crossed in front of her, a smile trembling at the side of her mouth?

When he was six or seven, Lee had been obsessed with the notion of becoming a sailor, of going to sea. His father had indulged him by buying several books with colourful drawings of ships pounding through waves as large as buildings and being menaced by a square-headed sperm whale. He dreamed of the Amazon River and the Suez Canal, and talked of clambering up masts to look for land. He would wear something stripy and have some sort of hat. There would be scaly monsters. They had visited an aquarium and seen roaming sharks, jellyfish and plankton floating in tanks like pollen.

What happened to all that? The thought of his childhood was so remote that Lee wondered if, in fact, he was trying to imagine a version of the future rather than recall a past. He inhaled and tried to stand taller but again was compelled to slouch. He placed a palm on the mirror, as if peering into some other place, and then his forehead on the glass. It was cold and smooth, entirely without smell.

24

Wild knew there were bombers flying somewhere over hairy, jungled continents and releasing their payloads into the sky. Could hear their low drone. Animals with fangs made of bamboo and steel, their snouts smeared with matter and blood. Machines that crunched chicken carcasses to pulp. Cancer with teeth and hair in an elderly man's lower back, crouching like a snickering homunculus.

The world was full of terrible things. It was armed, it curled and massed against him, like an enormous wave preparing to break. He could feel these things upon his skin, smell them through his teeth, almost taste them directly through his hands and feet. Indeed, he felt as though his skin were attempting to shuck itself free of him altogether. To be rid of this impossible body. He couldn't blame it. It's a terrible thing to be in horror of one's very self, to be aware of one's own stench.

How did that Psalm go? *I am a worm, and no man. A reproach of men, and despised by the people.* Something like that.

He scratched at himself, from arm to toe to thigh to ribs, seeking spot fires of discomfort and irritation that swarmed across his goosebumped skin. His bones were of ice, his eyeballs lumps of salt, his teeth like gravestones sunk into his gums. An itch in the back of his throat, the exact place impossible to locate: he would need to drill through at a point somewhere beneath his right ear to reach it. And then another, deep in the knuckles of his right hand. His nose and eyes streamed. Some dull explosion was taking place within but it would take a lifetime—incremental, interminable, an eternity—to be finished with him.

He lay on the bed, then sat on its edge and bounced lightly to hear the springs squawk. There was no position for his screaming body. His poor body, leaden with ache and keen as a blade. A sponge thickening with sorrow. I could live to be two hundred and never again feel like this, he thought. A thousand long, dry years. And he cried out at the thought of living so long.

Wild had tried to detox many times before, years ago, even before that terrible night at Louise and Frank's. When Jane had first found out he was using morphine, there had been the expected disbelief and anger. They discussed the matter around the kitchen table late into the night. This was when Alice was little, probably no more than six or seven years old, when she could be shielded from such things, when their marital sorrow could still be contained.

Jane had made whispered phone calls and driven him to a detox unit that smelled of disinfectant and loss in an outer suburb. It was like lifting a rock, an entire layer of the world of which he'd been hitherto unaware. Forms to fill out and blood tests and beds with rubber sheets, a place where everyone spoke from the side of their mouth and jiggled their feet. They asked him about his drug history and whether he'd shared syringes and how much he was using.

I use drugs to cope with the pain of using drugs, he'd volunteered later that night to a social worker opposite him in the waiting room, certain the wit of this would stand out among the dreary litany of abused childhoods and secret traumas. Actually, he went on, I blame Chet Baker. The worker said nothing, barely registered interest, but Wild had continued nonetheless. After all, he'd thought at the time, isn't that what we're here for? Some sort of therapeutic unravelling?

When I was about fourteen or fifteen, I stumbled upon a garage sale a few streets away from where I lived. There was the usual junk: old lamps, a blender, some clothes on a rack. But there was also a bunch of records in a box and they were different from anything I'd seen. They were these old jazz records. Some old buff must have died or something, I don't know, but there was a collection of Chet Baker and Billie and Miles Davis, you know, all the really good stuff from that era. The fifties, I guess. The real deal. Anyway. I bought a couple of these records, I don't know why. I think I just *knew* that they were something special, like they'd been put there for me, had been waiting for me to come along. And you know what? I was right.

From the first moment, I knew this was something. Those cracked voices and frail smiles. Chet Baker doing *My Funny Valentine*, you know that song? Unbelievable. Like he's so busted up he can barely bring himself to sing it, just sort of sighs through it, but beautifully. Only two minutes long. A love song, but what sort of love? I didn't know much about art or music or what was good or anything, but this was *something*. And the whole junk thing, you know? Billie being busted in a hospital room with hundreds of dollars stuffed into her stockings, Chet Baker jumping out a window in Amsterdam. All that romance of despair or something. In love with my own destruction. Not that I was ever a musician or anything, and actually didn't really start using drugs for a long time afterwards. I did my degree and carried on and got married and all that, so . . . maybe I'm wrong, but I still blame Chet. Course I don't have any of those records anymore. Lost or sold or broken.

And still the woman in the waiting room didn't say anything, just sat there and nodded absently. It was only when she wiped the back of her hand across her nose that Wild realised that she wasn't a social worker at all but just another damn junkie trying to get clean.

But he'd sat in the detox for an entire day and half the night watching television with other sweating creatures until he conspired with two other men to escape and score. He would supply the money if they could find some dope at this absurd hour. Win-win. At 3.00 a.m. they drove through bruise-dark streets in a rattling car until they finished up in some small, inner-city flat with a crowd of people huddled over bent and blackened spoons. Everyone was tattooed and smoked furiously, as if affronted by each and every cigarette. The men compared east-coast prisons. A fight broke out at one point and a toddler with a trail of shit down its leg wandered through the smoke haze eating potato chips.

They had watched television, the early-morning evangelical time-slot through to ancient American reruns and children's hour. Smiling people in bright jumpsuits, and stars made from red paper. On the way home, he had picked flowers from the local park for Jane, but she hadn't been at all pleased to see him stagger into the house a day after his shiny new beginning, and stared at him before turning away to drink her tea.

Now Wild thought of his wife. Poor Jane, for so long always on the verge of tears.

I am poured out like water and all my bones are out of joint.

25

Eventually Lee could rotate his torso a little better but was still compelled to crouch like a beggar when he walked. He changed the dressing on his wound and was pleased to see that the skin seemed to be gathering itself together, the stitches like black, spindly claws. The surrounding skin was pink and looked almost healthy. Wild had actually done a good job. With great effort, he was able to chop some wood and maintain the fire in the lounge room.

The rain became heavier throughout the afternoon and water leaked through the ceiling of one of the bathrooms so that its collection of dolls bobbled in the shallows. Lee opened a tin of something called borlotti beans and left them beside Wild, who, although awake, seemed unaware of his presence, so involved was he with whatever he was involved with.

He slept on the couch in front of the fire. The day diminished and later, when the night was at its deepest, Lee stood in the cold hallway and listened at the door to Wild's room. There was the clank of chain followed by a guttering cough. A groan. When he entered, Wild was sitting on the floor against the bed with his head on his knees. He didn't look up. The room was piled high with stench; of alcohol and shit and sweat, like an abattoir or asylum. The bottle of whiskey stood beside him with only a few fingers left in the bottom. The tin of beans was on its side under the bed with its pale entrails spilling onto the floor.

I'm dying. Wild sighed. I'm bloody dying.

What do you mean?

Wild raised his head but his gaze faltered, barely making the distance to where Lee stood. He wore just a shirt and trousers and his throat and forearms were patterned with bloody scratches. His beard was flecked with vomit or food or snot. Something terrible was obviously happening. He looked . . . what? Struck. Strucked? Stricken? Was that the word? *Stricken*. He looked stricken.

What time is it?

Lee hugged himself against the cold. Don't know. Feels like early in the morning, I think. Late at night. Maybe three or so. Don't you have a watch?

Broken.

Lee nodded. He loitered in the doorway.

Wild lowered his forehead again to his knees. His toes curled and uncurled against the linoleum and every few seconds his entire body jolted as if by an electrical current.

Still with his arms clasped around himself, Lee leaned on the doorjamb with his left hand pressed against the dressing on his wound. He wanted to say something, to offer some sort of encouragement, even opened his mouth to do so, but anything he could think of seemed pitiful. Such a small act, but everything seemed beyond him. What did people say at times like this? *You'll be OK. Everything will be fine. It will all work out.* The silence was interrupted only by the crackle of the log in the fireplace. How long will this take? he asked at last.

Wild grunted. He ran a hand through his hair and Lee saw that the skin at his wrists was bloodied from the chafing of the chain. Don't know. Few days. Long days. He paused. How long has it been?

Lee thought. Time seemed to have lost its hold on them out here. Since yesterday, he wondered out loud. Maybe . . . thirty hours? A day and a half.

Wild looked up again. Beneath his beard a nerve or muscle twitched in his cheek. Christ. Damn. Already feels like forever. Well, are you going to come in or what? Can you put some more wood on the fire? Do something useful.

Relieved to have something to do, Lee fetched more wood and coaxed the fire back to life. Then he made some tea and placed a chipped mug on the floor for Wild, who took uncertain sips of the black, steaming liquid as if expecting the worst from it. Outside, the wind prowled through the trees and fluted across the chimney top. Clumps of soot fell occasionally into the fire, sending up small spirals of sparks. It sounded as though the house were falling to pieces around them, sustaining damage from some ghostly assault.

Tell me about this sister of yours, Wild demanded.

What?

Your sister? Claire.

Claire?

Yes. Claire. I'd better know something about her if I'm going to be showing up there. Tell me something. Take my mind off myself.

Like what?

Anything, really. Anything. Just speak. Say something.

Lee scratched his chin and sat on a straight-backed chair by the fire. Really, he just wanted to go back into the lounge room and sleep on the couch. This entire scene disturbed him.

On the floor, Wild huddled with his arms again around his knees, the mug of tea cooling at his side. Is she beautiful, for instance?

I don't think so.

Is she tall?

He thought of Claire's sharp, practical face. How she walked with wildly swinging arms, enthusiastically, always heading somewhere. Her love carefully apportioned, as if fearful of running low herself. No, he said. Average height. Brown hair. Sort of pretty, I suppose, that might be a word for her. Pretty. Married for a few years to a guy named Graeme who's a scientist or something. A botanist. Into trees and leaves and stuff.

That why they live in the country?

Lee had never considered this. I guess so. Claire's always been into outdoor things as well. Liked horses when she was little. They've got two kids, as well. Boy and a girl. Sam and . . . can't remember the girl's name, Mary or something.

You can't remember your own niece's name? What about that world-class bloody memory of yours?

Lee blushed. Well, she's little. I've never seen her—I mean, just a photo once. Claire sent me some photos. She might even have been born when I was in jail.

Wild sighed, and when he spoke it was as if the words had been hauled from some great muddy depth. Did you and Claire get along as children?

What the fuck is this, Twenty Questions or something?

Just curious, that's all. Give me a break.

Lee bent down with a poker to rearrange the wood in the fire. He jabbed at a large log and moved some smaller pieces around. Every so often, he turned suddenly or began to raise a hand to his eye or push hair from his face, and pain detonated across his stomach and ribs. When this happened, he paused mid-action with a grimace, breath frozen, like now as he leaned heavily on the fireplace mantel and waited for it to subside. He reached for the nearly empty bottle of whiskey and wiped the mouthpiece on his shirt before drinking. The flavour was dark and muscular, like the air of an inner-city gym.

Begrudgingly, he sat in the flimsy wooden chair and considered what he could possibly say. Family was so obvious that it was often difficult to describe it in ways that others might understand, even if he wanted to. In prison they made him see a social worker who was always interested in his family, in the things that had happened to him. *Intrigued by the forces that shaped you*, is what the old guy would say. *Might be a few clues in there so we can make sure you don't end up back in here.*

She's a few years older than me, Lee said through his teeth. Six years older. When we were kids she told me that liquorice was made with rat's blood and I believed it for years. Even now, I can't eat it. That weird flavour.

Wild made no sign that he'd heard or understood, just stayed with his head resting upon his bent knees and hands clasped at his ankles. His breathing was deep and patient.

But *she'd* eat it. Run after me with a black tail of it hanging from the edge of her mouth. Her teeth smeared with black gunk, laughing out of her mind. Thought it was the funniest thing ever.

Wild remained quiet and still aside from curling his toes against the floor and the occasional shudder across his shoulders. Lee looked at the closed door and wondered if he could sneak away, but Wild finally grunted with acknowledgement or interest. Lee stared into the fire and felt the blush of heat across his right cheek.

What was that? Wild asked.

What? Liquorice.

Oh. Yes. And?

And what?

That's all there is about you?

Yeah. Pretty much. Just normal stuff, really. I told you about jail and—

Liquorice.

Yeah. Liquorice.

That all you ate? Jesus. What did your mother cook for you? What was your favourite food?

Now that the fire had been rebuilt, the room was warm. Ignoring Wild, Lee shifted back from the fireplace. OK then. Might leave you to it.

Wild looked up. His face was damp and streaked. He sniffled and ran the back of his hand under his nose. What do you mean?

Nothing. Just might go and sleep and—

No, don't. What are you talking about? Don't leave me. Please. A bit longer. What's the rush? Talk to me. Give me something.

Give you *what*? Why the hell do you want to know all this? What's it to you, anyway?

What are you so afraid of?

Lee attempted a shrug. I'm not afraid. It's late.

You look afraid. I was only trying to be friendly. To be a friend. Forget it then.

Lee listened to the drilling rain. If it kept up like this they would be flooded. He imagined the house being torn from its sodden stumps and borne across the fields, its ramshackle creak and sigh, snagging on fences and signs. The fire hissed and popped. He sat unwillingly back on the chair. I'm tired.

Wild scratched at his face and neck and ran his hands over his head, as if tormented by bugs. He grimaced and groaned and chewed at the air.

He muttered things to himself. After a minute or so, he settled and again hugged his knees to his chest. So? he said.

What?

Favourite meal. Best thing your mum cooked.

Lee stared into the fire. One of the larger logs was shaped like a dog's head, complete with two knots for ears and a small, sharp mouth. There was obviously no avoiding this fucking conversation. That smear of night. I don't really remember. My parents died when I was little.

How long ago?

Twelve years or so.

Or so?

OK. Twelve years. July 15.

Ides of July.

What?

Wild shook his head. Nothing.

They were both killed. In an accident, a car accident. Long time ago now.

And as soon as he said it, Lee wondered why he was telling Wild any of this, a sensation coupled to the fear of knowing that once he began, there seemed no way to stop. He was haunted, as always, by the insignificance of mere words. They could never be the thing; this was the great failure of language. *Killed. Years.* Such small and hollow sounds. *Accident.* That this word could mean both someone spilling their tea and what occurred to his parents on that night. The swerve of trees suddenly ahead. There must be better sounds than these. He lit a cigarette and considered its burning tip.

The car my dad was driving slid off the road into a tree. Just lost control, I think. No big thing. It was wet and raining and my parents were bickering. My mother occasionally picked on my dad. Sort of harassed him. I mean, she loved him, I'm sure she loved him, but, you know, people are strange. You never know what goes on between other people. She used to call him Lucky. *Here comes Lucky,* she'd say. *How'd you go today, Lucky?* Often with a little curl on the *L*, sort of drawing it out and raising an eyebrow. When she smoked a cigarette—which wasn't very often—the first time she put it into her mouth she would hold the very end of it, the end you light, and just hold it there on her bottom lip for the tiniest half a second before taking her hand away and lighting it. Like she was thinking about having the cigarette, *really* thinking about it, all in that little speck of time. Always seemed so exotic to me, so worldly or something. The lipstick on it.

Why Lucky?

Oh, because he used to love to bet at the track. That's what he wanted, really, to hang out with the guys in the yards and shoot the breeze and talk about horses. About who sired who and all that stuff. State of the track, which jockey was riding, you know . . . Not that he lost all our money or anything. We weren't poor. He worked in a printing place. Not sure what he did. We were OK, I think. But, you know, it's easy to have a go at someone like that. I think my mother had ambitions for us. High hopes. Like my sister. Wanted something bigger and better. Her mother never wanted her to marry Dad and, you know . . .

How do you know all this?

Lee drew on his cigarette and shrugged. His mind became arid. The tick of the cooling car engine. It was, you know, family knowledge.

Not that. About them fighting in the car and everything.

Lee coughed drily. How do I know? Because I was in the fucking car when it happened.

In the accident?

Yeah. Of course, in the accident.

And what happened to you?

Fractured my skull. Hit my head on the front seat and bounced back. Broke some ribs. Big cut down my side here. I was in hospital for a month or so.

But your parents died?

Yeah. They both died. And he paused. Right there on the front seat.

Wild wiped a hand across his nose and eyes. Jesus. That's incredible. I'm sorry.

Lee stood and poked again at the fire. His mother's voice, her hand clawing for his father's shoulder, her hand dark and slow in the car's interior, reaching across that space. Yes. It *was* terrible. He swallowed.

Inexplicably, his mouth tasted of chalk. He wiped his lips with the back of one hand. But that was a long time ago.

What were they fighting about?

Lee put another log on the fire. He licked his lips and looked at Wild. Those greedy blue eyes. Had he been listening like this the whole time?

They were fighting about me, Lee said at last. I'd run away, how you do when you're a kid. For a while I had this thing about this strange communication tower that I could see from the backyard and I was obsessed with getting to it. The thing was miles from our place. Anyway, I headed off towards it and was found by the parents of some kid at school and they rang my mum and dad and they drove around and collected me. In the rain. Freezing and windy. One of those real winter nights. They were mad as hell. And they were fighting about what to do with me, you know, how to punish me, I suppose. Whose fault it was that I'd done this thing. And Mum was saying how Dad had brought me up all wrong and carrying on, having a go at him and . . . Bang! Lee licked his dusty lips again, drew the last from his cigarette and tossed the butt into the fire. And that was that.

That smear of night, the swerve of tree, his mother's voice. *Tom!* The darkness rearranging itself around the crumpled car, accommodating them, the way darkness does. And that solitude, rendered more profound by its recent proximity to voices and noise.

I was in hospital for a few weeks, but when I got out me and my sister lived together. She was sixteen, I guess. Just carried on. Made our school lunches, tried to make me go to bed at a sensible hour. Nobody bothered us. We had an aunt in the same town who was supposed to take care of us. Be the guardian or something, but she didn't take much interest in things, probably sent my sister some money now and then. I dunno. People have their lives. Mostly people stayed away, like they were afraid of us or something. Like we might infect them. Like we were dangerous. Especially me. People looked at me funny. Whispered about me afterwards. Two kids on their own in a big house. Seems sort of strange, now I think about it, but at the time . . . Although, you know.

It was also great sometimes. We ran wild, did what we wanted. Swam all summer in the lake.

As always, the memory of his weeks in hospital conjured a particular colour. The ward's linoleum floor at night, dimly lit from the lamp at the nurses' station and the fluorescent light flickering in the hall. A faded, lozenge green that—even now, twelve years later—prompted a dull ache in the side of his head where he had smashed against the front seat of his father's car.

And the *tick, tick, tick* of the car engine cooling in the night air, then the sound of rain, which was itself just a variation of silence. And Lee on the back seat, an orphan, newly minted, the warmth of his own blood filling his mouth. Weeping.

26

He stood in a large wooden boat, an old-fashioned lifeboat, like something you'd see in a history book about old whaling methods. Despite the size of the boat, there was nobody else in it. There hadn't been for a long time. A kerosene lamp hung from a bracket at his side. It hissed and swung with the movement of the boat. He was in the rear, whatever that was called. The prow? The aft?

In his hands was a huge oar, but he was unable to gain purchase in the water. Each time he leaned forward and tried to angle it into the waves, the blade skidded away. Several times he almost lost his footing and tumbled. If he fell into the water it would be the end of him. Buckets and spades and coils of rope banged and rolled about in the bottom of the boat.

He had the sense he'd been here for a long time. His shoulders were dull with ache and his hands were frayed from handling the oar. He'd been on a voyage of some sort. The waves were large and so inky black they might have been made not of water but of something else entirely, something viscous and industrial. They assembled in gangs not far away, rose to their full height, and then charged the boat in groups of two or three. Icy water sprayed up over the sides.

It was impossible to see the limits of the ocean, perhaps a dim line of horizon in the distance, a slightly darker thread than the murky space stretching both above and below it. To be so far from land. To be so far from everything.

After some time, he made out a large shape in the distance and tried to steer towards it, willing his boat in that direction. Over the water drifted the sound of glasses clinking and a burble of voices. A firework of laughter in the night. He could make out an even line of circular toffee-coloured lights about halfway up the object's side. He peered through the gloom. They were portholes. It was a massive liner, as big and complicated as a city, edging through the water.

Suddenly he was beside the liner. It made no sound. He knew he had to get on board. Its bulk only served to remind him of how frail his little rowboat was. Surely something that size would never sink, would be able to carve through these waters? Through one of the portholes he could see cigar smoke and champagne glasses, hairstyles and jewellery. Pearls and bow ties. The waxy skin on a woman's neck. He had the sense they were people he knew, even though none were immediately recognisable. Surely they were people he knew. They would be excited to see him. They would cheer his entrance. They would care for him.

His rowboat banged against the side of the ship. Waves poured across him. He tried to raise himself but the thick sea grasped his foot. He was in silence now, in some place before sound. Again he reached out with one hand. Perhaps he saw something, a ledge or a toehold, but he was unable to feel it. His hands traced circles on the surface of the ship's hull, searching for something with which to hoist himself aboard. He was so close. The surface was scored and slick, not like wood at all. Whale skin. It was whale skin. The hull was made entirely of flesh, he realised. There was the smell of seaweed and porridge. The smell was on him. He wiped his hands on his trousers and shirt.

There was a statue of the Virgin, standing on a fridge, her plaster hands clasped at her chest in prayer. The statue fit snugly into his palm and was well handled. It was an old object, something smuggled in suitcases from other countries. He held it in one hand. The cut of her robes was grubby and worn almost smooth. The crucifix dangling over her right elbow was almost gone. Her nose was chipped off to reveal the white plaster beneath that pink skin. All this, but her brown-eyed gaze remained stoic, always looking past him, somewhere over his right shoulder.

He was knee-deep in tarry water, barely able to raise his legs to walk. He attempted to call out, but could not manufacture any sort of sound. Again he tried. A dry cough, little more than a whisper, just the scratch of air catching in his throat. The horizon had been absorbed by the sea, or perhaps it was the other way around. He opened his mouth. Like a dying fish he opened his great mouth. But there was nothing, not even silence.

And he woke and quickly sat up, gasping in the dark forest of night.

27

Josef pulled on a singlet and a pair of trousers. He crossed to the window, raised the blind and peered down into the empty street. A small and unremarkable place, just a mess of lines and shapes. His eye searched for movement, but there was none. Not even a lousy traffic light.

His reflection held a lunar shine, the skin dimpled and worn and thinly spread, making apparent the various ridges and planes beneath, the very shape of him. The sharp nose and high cheeks, his dark and drowsing eyes. In front of him, the window rattled in its frame as he brushed a lick of hair from his eyes.

His breath fogged the glass. He sucked at his gold tooth and curled his toes on the carpet. The cold didn't agree with him. There was an arthritic ache in his right knee. The tattoo on his forearm thrummed and he scratched at it, softly at first, but then harder.

He fetched a glass of water from the bathroom and returned to his vigil. The hotel room smelled of old wood polish and dust. The water from the bathroom tap tasted faintly of rust. It was still some time before dawn. There was no sign of life until a grey cat slunk across the bakery roof opposite, almost invisible against the tin. Not far above, the cloudy sky hovered like the pale belly of an even greater darkness.

Hunkered under night, the town appeared different from when he arrived yesterday afternoon. A blue thread of smoke curled from a chimney stack on a far hill. There was a very dim and distant light, perhaps from a house on the other side of town. He wondered if there was another person standing at a window just as he was, staring out over the darkness, listening out for cracks in the silence. Who else could be awake at this time, adrift in the night? Apart from animals in the undergrowth, only the very good or the very bad were awake at this hour. When he was a child his father would wake in the middle of the night and shuffle to the kitchen to drink tea and pray at the table beside the humming fridge. He wondered about the urge to pour oneself into the silence.

After a lifetime in the city, the prehistoric hush of places like this unnerved him. He was a thin man in a strange hotel room, his movements slow and careful, like those of a mantis. He smoked a cigarette and coughed gently, just to impose a sound upon the morning, to remind himself of himself.

He grimaced at the thought of his dream. Like witches or foreign tongues they made sense, but only to themselves. Someone in his family would have been able to decode it for him, were he able to tell them. Most of them loved nothing better than to sit over morning coffee and unpick the hem of a dream, to argue whether it was a vision from the future or the past or some dead soul reaching across the darkness. His aunt Mary was a merchant of dreams; she sold dreams to people in the neighbourhood who wanted a chance to fly, to have children or to revisit the countries of their birth one final time. He was never sure how this was done, but it seemed to involve an exchange of whispers and certain herbs, the pressing of amulets into wrinkled palms. Money as well, of course. Mary also claimed she could take people's dreams away from them, was able to bear the nightmares others found intolerable. When he was a boy, Josef would be woken in the middle of the night by her wailing in the next room, apparently lost in the cathedral of her dreaming, trying to outrun the madnesses that rightfully belonged to others. Those flocks of owls and crumbling teeth, the light that dripped like water. But then, like a fish in the shallows, his dream flickered and was gone.

Josef shivered. It suddenly seemed a long way to come in search of a little bastard like Lee. A lot of bother over such a pathetic sum of money. A snitch in the police department had told him about two men—who sounded a lot like Lee and his doctor friend—rolling a railway guard and jumping a train. It was the only clue Josef had been able to gather since leaving Sylvia's place that day, but it was enough. He was getting close. If Lee thought he was going to sneak off to his sister's, then he was dreaming. Josef would find him and stop him.

Aunt Mary would surely be dead by now, Josef realised. A lot of those people were probably dead. Dead or otherwise scattered like leaves. No way to track them, even if he wanted to—even if they wanted to be found by him. All those aunts and uncles and cousins: Leo, David, Drusilla. Little Carla, who wouldn't be so little anymore. Maybe even married. The family he hadn't seen for so many years.

He recalled his father trying not to cry as his mother pressed money into Josef's hand on the day he left more than twenty years ago. The day he went away to work and perhaps learn a trade, do things in the real world. His homecoming delayed, first by a ten-year sentence for armed robbery and then by shame. The only time his father and mother wrote to him in jail was to tell him he wasn't welcome in their home ever again. How quickly it had become too late, and for how long it had remained that way.

He wondered whether his parents were still in the same weatherboard house, crowded with relatives and their children, with their bramble of languages. There was probably still a glass jar full of wooden clothes pegs left on the lawn beside a saucer of milk for the cat. Josef's father had no sense of smell or taste because of an accident when he was young, but it didn't stop him leaning across to sniff plates of food in the hope that *this* meal, at long last, would be the one to rekindle this lost sense. Holding his tie back against his chest with his right hand to stop it trailing in the food, his other hand grasping the lip of the table for balance, eyes half closed in concentration. Once he found his father in the back garden handling an apple from their tree. His father was wearing a blue shirt that was frayed at the collar, with tiny strands of white thread waving loose around his brown neck. *Tell me, son. Does this have a actual smell?* he'd asked, and Josef, no more than ten years old, had closed his eyes and shyly brought the smooth, round shape right up against his nose. It was cold on his lips and large in his palm. At first there was nothing, but he wanted to please his father so he tried again, breathed in more deeply and discovered a scent of something sharp and tangy. What was it? How to describe such a thing? He'd never even noticed it before, had never thought apples had a smell at all, but it was unmistakably the smell of apple. Again he breathed in. It smelled of apple, that was all.

But *No*, he'd said with a shrug. *No smell. There's nothing you're missing here, Dad*, and his father had nodded and smiled and walked back indoors with his hands deep in his pockets.

He felt far from home, but this was nothing new. Running a palm across his chin, he decided he needed a shave. He sniffed at his brackish armpit. Needed a shower too. He hated travelling. Disliked being prey to the unfamiliar, having to improvise all the time. Why, he wondered, would anyone choose to make themselves a stranger? Those people who travel around because they got nothing better to do must be nuts.

Even up in this hotel room in the middle of the night, Josef felt conspicuous. He knew that a 53-year-old lone man was always considered sinister—a rapist or a terrorist. Pornographer. Even the old man who ran this hotel had seemed miffed by his lack of luggage when he checked in, as if its absence revealed something profound. He'd snuffled like a wombat and showed him upstairs without a backward glance. Like animals, people were suspicious of those abandoned by others. Josef needed to keep a low profile. Find out where Lee and the quack had gone next, and keep moving.

Holding it gingerly between thumb and forefinger, he smoked his cigarette right down. There should be enough time to catch a few more hours' sleep before morning, but he noticed a curious thing as he looked out over the small, remote town before returning to bed. The low clouds had begun to deteriorate and crumble. Small pieces of cloud fluttered, only a few at first but gaining in number until the sky was filled with white shards. They whitened the street and eaves and huddled in creamy drifts on roofs. They sprinkled without sound or apparent weight, utterly of their own magic. Josef wiped the window with his hand to see better and pressed his nose to the cold glass. A smile spidered across his lips. Snow.

He had never seen snow. Even the word was strange in his mouth. Snow, snow, snow. He laughed at the fairytale sight, and then again at his own laughter. Shaking his head in amazement, he walked away from the window and then returned to the glass again. Still the snow fell, like some great silent army. He flung open the window and put his head out into the muffled night. Flakes collected in his hair and on his shoulders. One snagged on an eyelash, hung for a second, then dissolved. Damn. What do you know about that? Snow. *Actual fucking snow.* Take a look at that. Take a look at that. Foolishly he looked around, hoping to see someone else enjoying the sight, but, of course, it was late and everyone else in this town was asleep. It seemed like something that children, at least, should see, but there was not a soul, young or old. Flakes sizzled on his tongue.

Josef's mother had told him of the snowfalls she had seen in her country when she was a girl: about the mineral crunch underfoot, the vast silence, the watery smell of ice. It had always seemed an impossibly distant phenomenon, of a sort that could never occur here. Her stories didn't prepare him for the unearthly sight of it. He dragged a chair to the window and leaned on the sill, exclaiming every so often and shaking his head. Despite the cold, he watched this secret carnival for an hour or more. Snowflakes clung to the glass and massed in shallow drifts along the outside of the wooden frame, their mathematical skeletons visible against the growing morning light. And as he watched, the town softened and almost vanished under a white pelt.

28

Wild tugged on the chain. The jolt of pain through his wrists was sudden but at least expected. He did it again. Then again. To take charge of one's own pain, at least that was something. A mockery of comfort. Tremors passed through his body like a mob of schoolboys running sticks along a corrugated tin fence. He yanked again at the chain until the skin covering his wrists broke and a bruise revealed itself quickly, as if it had been waiting beneath the skin for such an opportunity. A contusion. *Thou hast brought me to the dust of death.*

He shat in the bucket, squatting in one corner of the room with elbows on his thighs and his trousers bunched around his ankles. Picking at his hairy, twitching shanks. Everything was filthy, all surfaces in this room furred with dust. The walls were sea green, the paint cracked and scabbing loose in places. A huge brown cupboard stood against one wall. Inside it a pair of blue trousers on a coathanger and a ghostly smell. Over the fireplace hung a watercolour of a waterfront scene. In some war or other they pegged women spread-eagled to the ground and jammed sticks of dynamite into their cunts. He tried to remember what Jane's tits looked like. God, they were great tits. Breasts were the purest, warmest sort of flesh. Tears ballooned in his eyes and spilled over his eyelids. Pathetic.

He crouched and rocked and wept and his heart swung in his chest, tracing a pendulous arc like that of a chandelier on a listing ship. Again he yanked at the chain and the legs of the bed to which he was attached squealed across the floor. He found himself without trousers, the buttons on his shirt undone, cold, every hair on his body straining to break free, each part of him anxious to escape. How had all this happened? How had all this happened? If only there was someone to blame.

His body was a waxen thing, like something you'd find in a drain and prod with a stick. He flattened himself on the floor, felt the linoleum against his stomach and chest, became aware of every grain of grit crunching against him. Wondered if he could count them by feel alone. Got as far as fifty-two then stopped, just forgot what he was doing. What the hell? Snot leaked onto the floor. And always that wind, that wind scrabbling on all fours across his junkyard bones. The fire smouldered in the grate, the logs having turned to ash.

With the chain trailing behind, he staggered to the window and watched the rain pebble against the glass. In the distance, trees waved blurrily, as if bidding him goodnight or farewell. He looked at his watch, but both its crippled hands just dangled uselessly. He placed another log in the fireplace and waited, crouching, for it to catch. He poured whiskey straight from the bottle down his throat and vomited it straight up moments later into the metal bucket already reeking of shit. He took the final swig and again threw it up. It was hot in his throat. There are so many ways to be hungry. It is a sensation, he thought, that knows no bounds. An ocean, a desert. This great and endless hunger.

His hands shook furiously. Was this how life would be from now on? Was this his punishment? The endless chatter and interior disquiet, this bloody pack of crones rummaging through his body. Wild wondered what it would be like to die. Perhaps it was little more than making a decision. How hard would it really be?

It had almost happened when he overdosed once in his office several years earlier and had been disappointed at the lack of shining lights or warmth, or the benevolent face of God. He'd shrunk and scurried into the deepest parts of his body until there was only the faint sounds of his young nurse Anne calling to him and shaking the shell of his body, all of it as inconsequential as events on a remote planet.

An overdose of opiates wasn't exactly a peaceful way to go. There was usually circulatory collapse and cardiac arrest. An entire skirmish beneath the skin. The lungs clogged with blood. *Haemorrhage.* Was there a more frightening word in the language? *The escape of blood.*

Profound coma and death. But despite knowing all these effects and dangers, he had listened with mute detachment to Anne riffling through the cupboards for a narcotic antagonist. Thinking that he'd never heard her swear before now. That a pretty girl in a nurse's uniform saying *shit* was almost unbearably cute.

It wasn't that he didn't care whether he lived or died, it was just that suddenly it didn't really interest him. This was the beauty of it all: his own fate was no longer his concern. It had seemed to him then that death was no big deal, perhaps no more than stepping into another room of which you had previously been unaware. There was Mao's fifty million, the great plagues, untold massacres and the sudden death of his uncle James, each of them desperate and profound but worth little in the total scheme of things. Brueghel's Icarus forever tumbling to his death, unnoticed by the ploughman. The planet kept revolving, had not even blinked.

Then that jolt and a rude resurfacing: back to his office floor where he had slumped, back to life, to Anne leaning over him, still clutching the syringe she'd used to administer the drug that saved him. She'd laughed quickly with surprise and relief before berating him about how lucky he was that she'd happened to find him in time. *It's only because I happened to look in that you're bloody alive at all, you stupid man.* Disoriented, Wild had apologised and agreed about his luck, but knew already that it was in some way too late; learning is a one-way street.

Now he crouched on the floor, weeping. The evening wore on, grew darker, inevitably became night. He thought back to that night on his office floor. The memory of it was warm, almost a comfort. Was this how life was going to be from now on? Was this how it would be?

Save me from the lion's mouth. Deliver my soul from the sword.

29

J osef stood before the bathroom mirror. He wiped it free of accumulated steam with one palm and took a moment to stare at his own long features. He wore just dark-green trousers. His toes curled and uncurled on the cold, tiled floor.

He lathered his skin with shaving cream and applied his razor to his face, adhering to the pattern he had followed for thirty-five years. First he pulled his upper lips against his teeth to pass below his angular nose. Then the cheeks, along the hazardous jawline, and finally his chin and throat. He enjoyed the sensation of towelling off the frothy remnants and running his palm along his fresher, cleaner self each day. In defiance of his frugal nature, he used a new blade every morning. It supplied a small gratification, of the sort that only a private extravagance can provide. He splashed cologne onto his palms and applied it to his stinging skin before running lotion through his sleek but thinning hair. If he were the kind of man who hummed, it might be at this point that he would do so.

It was mid-morning by the time Josef picked his way across the bright, icy footpath. There was nobody else out on the street. The few shops along the main street were apparently closed or otherwise abandoned. Perhaps it was a holiday. The needling air smelled crisp, of wood smoke and winter.

Hard-packed snow had buried the lower half of his car's wheels overnight and he had to kick some aside to get in. The car door was stiff and creaked loudly on its hinge. The car interior offered only the slightest insulation; the leather seats were as cold as rocks. He rubbed his hands together and huffed and blew in an effort to generate some heat.

The car's windscreen was frosted and mounds of snow had gathered around the wipers, making it impossible to see. Josef sighed and stared for a moment at the webbing of ice on the glass. Reluctantly, he went back into the hotel, got a bucket of water and a rag, and managed to sluice the ice and snow from the windscreen. It took some time, and when he returned to the driver's seat, he felt even colder than before, his hands as unfeeling as planks. He paddled his feet on the floor and hugged himself. In silence, he rolled and smoked a cigarette but even that failed to warm him. He rubbed at his tattoo and ran a hand over his face.

Eventually he jammed the soggy cigarette butt into the ashtray, smoothed his hair and slotted the key into the ignition. He depressed the accelerator and turned the key. Nothing. Just the keys clanking against the steering column and the impotent gulp of the pedals. He paused before trying again, but with the same result. The engine gave no sign of life, might have been a solid block of ice. Something was seriously wrong with this car. It wasn't going anywhere. Shit, he muttered under his breath. Shit.

30

Even at night, the prison is never completely silent. There's always someone moaning or talking or laughing or threatening. The unhappiness of men waking in darkness makes an impression. And the building seems to possess sounds of its own apart from those of restless men. It shifts and sighs. The walls have their own things to say.

Although he has been awake most of the night, Lee is somehow taken unawares when morning scratches around the prison walls and peers through the high, barred window. When he does manage to sleep, he dreams of snapshot things with no apparent relationship to anything else: of a rusted tap; a grey wall worn and dirty at shoulder height; a scuffed kitchen floor. With disappointment, he realises it is prison he is dreaming of.

His eyes are gritty. After a short while he feels the bunk wobble as Simon jerks off furiously in the bed above, finishing with a small gasp that could be mistaken for surprise. Is there anything more disgusting, Lee wonders, as he turns to face the grimy wall. His own quickening breath bounces back at him, with the flavour of dreams and sweat and terror, like the remnants of something eaten long ago. He lies like a Z on its side with trembling hands clasped between his thighs. Like every other morning, Lee listens to Simon get down from his upper bunk and pad across to the toilet in the corner. The sound of his pissing is deep and frothy.

It's 6.00 a.m. Soon the cells will be unlocked, they will be counted off and file under escort to the showers, after which they will be counted off again and allowed to eat breakfast. There is a system here. There is nothing but system. Lee knows the habits of strangers. He knows how old Gerry likes his tea. He knows the way Lebanese Sammy shaves. He knows Simon will smoke a cigarette in bed and fall back into a heavy sleep for a short while longer. In fact, he is relying on it. It's 6.04.

How do you know you're doing the right thing? How can you ever know? Life should work backwards: at least then you could see the consequences of things first. He looks around the tiny cell. The light is pale and medicinal. Early morning was once his favourite time of day, but that seems a long time ago now. Breakfast at a wooden table, the clatter of voices and crockery, the slightly adhesive texture of poached eggs. The light just so. His father's voice always shone as he gazed down his nose at the form guide and prodded the newspaper at a particularly good bet. *That's the one*, he would say. *That's the one*. And all the while Lee's mother would stand behind, rolling her eyes dramatically and making faces at her husband's forecasting ineptitude. His father would then peer over the rim of his glasses to try to fathom the nature of his son's giggling before spinning to look at his wife, who would be suddenly straight-faced, blowing cigarette smoke from the corner of her mouth. Then Lee's father would return to his newspaper, allowing his wife to wink at Lee and swivel back to the stove. If love could be compressed into a single point, then it might be this ancient moment.

Everything seems a long time ago, his childhood thousands of miles away, enacted by strangers in foreign cities like Cairo or Prague, the language and place incomprehensible from this distance. He wonders what really happened in his life. He teeters. He has to show Morris and his cronies a thing or two or it will be the end of him. His heart is afraid. He worries it will, in fact, fail him altogether.

In the minutes before all the cell doors are unlocked by the central system, Lee dresses and sits on the very edge of his hard bed. In one hand is the tin of lighter fluid he stole from Simon during the night. The tin is full, having been smuggled in by Simon's brother the day before. Its surface is textured with embossed print. Lee picks at it with his thumbnail and manages to remove a curl of paint. He breathes through clenched teeth, is aware of cold air sliding down his throat. He stands slowly so as not to disturb the bunk, and peers over the lip of the upper mattress. He has rehearsed this for several days now. As always,

Simon is sleeping with his body curled towards the wall. His shoulders rise and innocently fall as he breathes. Men are beginning to cough in the cells around him. Toilets flush. Someone laughs like a squeezebox. In his other hand, Lee holds a box of matches. It's 6.28.

And then, as quietly as he can, Lee squirts lighter fluid on the mattress behind Simon. He soaks the mattress as much as possible, saving the last of the fluid for Simon himself. The smell of the fluid reminds Lee of dark back sheds during childhood, of rusty nails and broken wood. At exactly 6.30 a.m. there is a hum and click as the cell doors are unlocked remotely. Lee squeezes the tin and sprays fluid all over Simon's back, into his hair. The tin whistles as it empties and Simon wakes suddenly, making small sounds of bother and annoyance, wiping at himself and spitting. Lee fumbles with the box of matches. Simon turns and sits up. Lighter fluid is in his mouth. It runs down the side of his neck. Simon looks at Lee, one eye closed with sleep, or discomfort at the fluid, and opens his mouth to speak but it's at that moment that Lee strikes a match.

The small, pale fire of the match tumbles through the air. It inhabits the space completely, is the only thing happening anywhere. They both watch it cross the short distance between them. It makes no sound. What on *earth* are you doing? Simon asks. His voice is croaky. It's clear that he is struggling to assemble the smell of the fluid, Lee's presence, the fluttering match and the liquid spattered over him into some sort of coherent thought. And then a deep whump and fire slides across the mattress and the tangle of sheets and scrambles over him, fattening itself as it goes.

It isn't long before the fire takes hold, just a few seconds. It emerges from Simon's own skin, as if it has been sleeping underneath all along. At first, Simon swats at it with his hands, then backs against the wall. His mouth is set at a strange angle. Dark holes with glowing orange rims appear in the sheets and expand. There is the sharp and bitter smell of burning hair. A crackling. Simon has forgotten all about Lee, is yelling, swearing. Words fall from his mouth, half formed. Then not even words, just dark, volcanic sounds.

Lee tosses the empty tin of lighter fluid onto the bed and flees the cell. He slides the heavy door closed, but can hear Simon crashing about inside, the screams and roars. There might even be the low whine of an alarm sounding. Out on the tier, the screws are running around enquiring about the commotion and the other prisoners are looking around trying to figure out what is happening. Some of them grin; there is at least the promise of some sort of excitement.

Lee stands with his back to his cell and a little to the side. He hitches his trousers and hugs himself to himself. The cell doors each have a small oblong window of reinforced glass fitted into them for observation. Men on the opposite walkway are staring at him and peering into his cell. They point and bob around to see better. They must be able to see something. A man in flames.

Part Four

⌒⌒

31

Lee woke to find himself curled on the couch in the lounge room. He was fully dressed, crumpled, even wearing shoes. It was very cold and he was unwilling to move and disturb the cocoon of warmth he'd established during the night. His body was heavy and mute, telling him nothing of himself. For this he was thankful. The fire snoozed in the hearth.

He felt he was finally conscious after a lengthy period of time somewhere far away. He remembered the motel, and he remembered the crash and the night on the train, but it was almost as if they were another person's memories, or stories he'd read long ago. It was all too strange. He tilted an ear to the great silence, then shifted and pain flooded his torso. He winced and mentally examined the dressing over his wound, feeling for leakage or infection. It felt OK, just the usual persistent ache. Perhaps a slight humming itch as his body healed. A dream skulked like a burglar in the corner of his mind. Was this how it felt to be old, everything formless and bulky, memories so incomplete?

After a time, he sat up with a sudden urge to go outside and walk in the fresh air. He felt he had been cooped up for weeks in the stale and dusty air of this house. He pulled on his coat and shambled through the house; the old place smelled of cold lino and dried flowers. It wasn't until he stepped outside that he saw it had snowed during the night. When he saw the white, glittering blanket covering the garden and trees, he laughed with unexpected recognition. No wonder it was so cold last night. No fucking wonder.

Hugging himself, he crunched through the garden, allowing his fingers to linger over frozen railings, and pausing here and there to marvel at the billowing plumes of his own exhalation. He could feel his cheeks going pink, and his hands were thick and numb with cold. Everything dripped and shimmered, appeared both fragile and monumental. Awkwardly, he bent down, scooped a handful of snow and packed it into a ball. The snowball held its shape in his palm and he brought it close to his face. There was something about it that made him want to eat it, to see what it was like. Smiling, he nibbled gingerly at the snowball. It was harder than he expected, less satisfying. The granular burn of ice, the way he imagined a cloud would taste. The snowball left frosty crumbs on his lips and chin. His nose ran with the cold. He laughed at his own childishness and considered the snowball for a minute before lobbing it against the trunk of a nearby tree.

The garden was spectacular. With its sparkling eaves and white roof, even the dilapidated house looked more beautiful, as if designed for such a landscape. Against the dark and foaming sky, the old dump almost glowed. He negotiated overgrown paths. A trickle of icy water slid down his back. His memory of their arrival was vague—an old man on a cart, a village, a broken road—but he must have passed through this garden some days earlier with Wild. Wild. He'd forgotten about Wild. He'll love this, he whispered to himself and, grinning, shambled back up the steps, through the kitchen and down the hall to Wild's room. He listened at the door before entering. This will cheer the old bastard up.

He knew, of course. Somewhere deep in the bones of his knowing.

The air in the room was cold and brittle. Even in here, Lee could see his own breath. Wild was on his side, facing the wall, a mountain beneath the bunched sheets. One socked foot protruded from a blanket. The empty whiskey bottle was beneath the bed and the metal bucket was under the window. One of Wild's black shoes alone by the wardrobe. It appeared so lost. Even in the thin light, he could make out the angle of wear on one side of the sole, the knot of a broken lace.

The fire he'd built the previous night had burned down, was now mere ashes and coals in the grate. Lee crossed the room, jabbed at the coals with the poker and arranged more logs, crouching until they caught fire. Using the poker for balance, he stood companionably and faced the room. The backs of his knees grew warm and flames crackled and popped. He was reluctant to move. He waited, content to prolong the sensation of being the bearer of exciting news. The moment, he knew, was frail. Water dripped from an icicle over the window. It made a high-pitched plinking sound, like glass. Wild didn't move.

In hospital after the car accident, Lee was unable to attend his parents' funeral but his sister had told him all about it. He hadn't wanted to know the details, but Claire had been so talkative, at a heightened and manic pitch in this new country of teenage grief—perhaps even secretly enjoying the drama. Imprisoned by his injuries, he'd been unable to escape her ranting. She'd told him who was there and what they wore, that Uncle David was drunk and sat in a pew *crying*, that the church was full of strangers talking about their parents, that they misspelled his name in the funeral notice in the newspaper. *L-E-I-G-H*, she'd said, incredulous. *They're idiots. Leigh. Can you imagine?* She'd discovered things about their parents, as if death had released them from their private histories. With relish, she'd told him that their father had been in the merchant navy when he was a teenager and abandoned ship at Singapore. *I bet you didn't know that? Or that Mum was a swimming champion in high school?*

At the funeral, you could walk past the caskets and look inside and see them in their nice clothes. Dad in a suit and Mum in her red dress, you know the one with the clasp thing at the neck? Or at least see most of them, their faces and stuff. And you could see that they were calm, calmer even than when they were, you know . . . She was terrified, she'd said, but they made her file past. Said it would be good for her, God only knows why. Something about love and saying a final goodbye. She was crying and she wasn't going to look but she couldn't help it, and they didn't actually look too bad. Staring at the ceiling from his hospital bed, Lee had wondered what Claire could have meant, because he knew how ugly and crushed they had been.

Lee inspected the mantel above the fireplace. He idly ran a finger over the surface and rolled the accumulated dust into a ball between his thumb and forefinger. He picked up a bottle of ink, removed the cork and inhaled the smell of bottled schoolrooms. There was a clump of dried lavender stuck in a glass and a group of toy soldiers. The four thumb-sized figures clutched instruments, so crudely carved from wood that they had no hands as such. They each wore curling, painted moustaches and red uniforms with sashes of yellow. Their expressions were bland but stoic as they prepared to play their gold-painted instruments. Strangely, the figures all had a red dot on their pink foreheads. Indian soldiers, perhaps. He picked one up and examined it. A soldier preparing to clash two cymbals. The paint was cracked off one side of its face. Lee tested the glazed paint on its back with a thumbnail and balanced the tiny man in his palm. It weighed almost nothing. An old, dry thing, belonging to some child who was by now elderly or dead.

He wanted to go back outside into the garden and lie in snowy drifts. To bathe in the silence. He kneeled on the floor beside the bed and rested an elbow on the edge of the mattress. The bed sheets were as cold and hard as marble. He felt incomplete, as if being slowly dismantled. Some prehistoric sorrow bubbled in his throat. He gulped and swallowed. He groaned and shuddered. His face became wet and doughy. His tears were salty on his lips as they passed down to his chin and dripped onto the bed. There were hundreds of them, thousands, springing so readily from his eyes they might have been lurking just beneath the surface, swelling, waiting for this moment. Thus abandoned, he wept, kneeling on the floor, head in his hands, inconsolable.

He dug a grave for Wild at the higher side of the house, in a space surrounded by low bushes. The ground was frozen and it took most of the morning just to break the icy crust. He had to pause every few minutes to catch his breath, and took the opportunity to look down over the white countryside. Nothing moved, not even the clouds. There were no birds in view. A line of trees stood still, like a distant crowd of mourners.

Sweat dripped from his forehead and nose when he again bent to the spade. He put a foot on the top of the blade, pressed his entire weight into it and wedged out a clump of soil to add to the sodden pile. Then he did it again. And again. His whole left side, where he'd been shot, made itself known with each exertion. Later, when he removed the dressing, he knew it would be soaked in his own blood. He felt pale and old.

When Lee had finally stopped weeping and rolled Wild over, he'd discovered a dozen empty morphine vials gathered to the curl of his body like a clutch of glassy, misshapen eggs. There was also a handful of used plastic syringes, their metal tips jewelled with blood. The inside of Wild's arm was darkly bruised and smeared with blood, and the sheets were also stained with it. His lips were purple, his skin damp and cold.

Wild's face had been long vacated and contained no expression, the blue eyes like stones jammed into the cavities. There was a tiny mark high on Wild's left cheek, perhaps a chicken-pox scar. The straggling beard. In an otherwise unnoticed breeze from the window, a fold of Wild's grey hair had waved gently from the side of his head, giving the body a suggestion of mere dormancy rather than death. Lee had reached forward with one hand and smoothed the fold back into place. He half expected Wild to sniff and sit up and wonder what the hell was happening, but of course nothing of the sort occurred; nothing remained.

For some time he had deliberated what to do before unchaining Wild from the bed frame and dragging him still on the mattress into the garden. It took nearly an hour. The mattress snagged and tore on rusty nails that crooked from the floor. The guy had weighed a ton, surely heavier dead than alive.

And so Lee kept digging, spadeful by scratching spadeful, trying to determine a rhythm in the work. He sank into the grave up to his knees. His hands and feet became numb. Mumbling an apology, he covered Wild with a blanket and tried not to look at his shape as he worked. The black goat stood nearby eating some paper, apparently not bothered by the cold. It chewed and watched and chewed again. Every so often it bleated its expressionless, faintly comical bleat and the sound was carried away by the wind, over the rise at the back of the property.

The day wore on. The air grew harder and colder. Occasionally he clambered from the hole and went back into the house to smoke a cigarette and warm himself. He stoked the ancient kitchen stove. He trembled inside and out and was shaken every so often by sobs that bubbled to his surface. He tried not to think of anything. When at last almost done, he paused and looked up, panting heavily as he rested on the spade handle. Steam ballooned in front of his face. His lips were dry and cracked. In the hours he had been outside digging, the cold had stolen through his clothes and skin and then through his muscles until his bones were like ice. He squinted and stared. There, in the space between the bottom fence of the property and the distant crease of the horizon, something moved. A tiny shape by a jagged fence that was stitched across the landscape. He wiped the back of one filthy hand across his nose and watched. The dot was moving ever so slightly, almost not at all, like a dark satellite trembling across a milky sky.

The shape drew larger and closer. What on earth would be out travelling on such a day? Too big for a dingo or kangaroo, too slow for a car.

Eventually, Lee could make out the shape of—what? A bulky person? Perhaps a horse. A man. Hat. A man wearing a wide-brimmed hat. It was the old man who'd driven them here. And his cart. The old cougher with the horse and cart. Lee had to get the hell away from here as soon as he buried Wild. Had to hit the road and get to Claire's place. Needed to escape. Whatever he wanted, the old man and his cart might be perfect timing. The old guy was still a mile away and moving pretty slowly. Lee was nearly finished. His palms were blistered and sore, but he should be able to bury Wild before the old bloke arrived. Just a few more spadefuls.

Lee looked across at the figure of Wild under his blue blanket. There was no mistaking the shape—the higher peaks of the face and toes and the awkward, spreading sag through the middle. Yellow foam stuffing crumbled onto the snowy ground through a tear in a corner of the mattress. If Lee left him there, the snow would soon cover him and nobody would ever know. The crows would peck and the possums would paw. By the time spring crept across the landscape, the wind would be able to sluice through the very wreck of him. Maybe someone would find him in a year, when Lee was long gone. After all, it was unlikely anyone would come to this part of the garden anytime soon and discover the body.

He pondered this for a while, then bent and leaned his weight into the spade until another small portion of the ground gave way. The level of the earth was at his stomach. A little more and he could tip Wild into the hole and cover him. The earth at least would be warm. He could be done with this and get out of here. He kept digging, became contentedly enslaved to the circular rhythm: dig, press foot upon the spade, lever some earth and hoist it over the edge of the grave; dig, press foot upon the spade, lever some earth and hoist it over the edge of the grave. Dig.

Isn't it a bit cold for gardening?

Pausing with the heavy spade in midair, Lee looked up. He didn't need to because he recognised the voice. He licked his lips and swallowed. Josef.

Yes.

What are you doing here?

Dumb question.

Josef was standing near the back corner of the house, beside a glass-enclosed room probably designed as a sunroom for warmer months. Within, Lee could make out the silent, motionless tribe of long-dead ferns. Josef tapped the barrel of a pistol impatiently against his thigh, like he'd been waiting there for ages. Maybe he had been. Maybe he'd been standing there forever, waiting for the right moment to finally kill him.

A wintry current ran through Lee. He nodded and opened his mouth to say something, but had no idea what it could be. He thought of Simon, tried to remember if he had said anything. *What the fuck are you doing?* It was the moment, presumably, when he should make a—what? A *plea* for his life? Such a strange, half-formed noise. Plea, plea, plea. Plea. Plea. A meagre grunt. Words lose meaning when repeated, are reduced to lines and scratches. Plead for his life. When he should say *something*. Instead he sighed, held his breath and closed his eyes.

Lee waited for the shot, alone in his immense, private darkness. He waited for the sound and the sensation, for whatever would happen after that. He imagined tumbling end over end for a thousand years, as if through space. He felt his heart quivering against his ribcage and was surprised it seemed to make no sound. One blistered hand gripped the smooth wooden spade handle while his other arm instinctively crossed his chest. Otherwise, he made no movement to protect himself. Inexplicably, he recalled the warm smells of fresh laundry and toast, the sound of a springtime wind. He recalled hanging like a monkey from the bough of a tree and he remembered the scratch of his father's unshaven kiss upon his cheek. Just small things.

He clenched his teeth and pursed his mouth. At last, he thought. His neck shrank into the curling wings of his shoulders. The earth at least would be warm. At long last. But there was no sound. In fact, the silence became larger and more austere; a cathedral, a city, a kingdom. After a while, Lee opened his eyes again. He looked up and saw that nothing had changed and wondered if, in fact, he had merely blinked. The cold sang right through him. His teeth and gums felt like thick wadding. With difficulty, he swallowed. Was this relief or despair? He exhaled a pale cloud of his breath.

He and Josef observed each other for a long minute. Josef inspected Lee closely, probably trying to determine whether or not he was armed. Even with the gun, Josef looked different, more frail perhaps than the last time they had met at Lee's apartment. He was hunched against the cold. His trousers were ripped partway down, revealing a bony knee. It began to snow once more. Flakes drifted into the garden, making white again the area where Lee had been digging, which had become grey and sludgy.

Josef smiled his thin smile. Got to say, cold weather doesn't really agree with me, but I like this snow. It's . . . pretty. He approached, looked into the grave and then at the shape of Wild beneath the blanket. Oh, I see. Planting a *person*. I tried that once. What do you think will sprout?

Lee said nothing. He slowly straightened. Snowflakes caught in his hair. His body ached and was sluggish with exhaustion.

Not quite a gardener, Josef went on. More like a . . . sexton, I think it's called. A sexton. Again he peered into the grave. He sniggered and sucked at his gold tooth. Not burying any money, are you? It won't grow like that, you know. Doesn't, you know, grow on trees.

There's no money. You've wasted your time.

Josef pulled up the collar of his coat and hugged himself, evidently pleased with his own uncharacteristic wit. He indicated the house with his gun. Let's go inside, alright.

Lee hesitated. He pointed at Wild. What about him? I've got to . . . I've got to . . . Give me a hand, will you?

Josef's surprised gaze flickered between Lee and the shape under the blanket. He blinked and licked his lips before kicking back the blanket to reveal Wild's pallid face with its dark-blue mouth agape. This your doctor friend?

Lee averted his gaze. Wild. Yes.

You kill him?

No. Course not.

Yeah. Course not. What happened to him?

Killed himself, I think. Drugs. Overdose. Last night.

Josef nodded and looked almost pityingly down at Wild. Well, he's not going anywhere for now. Go inside, alright. We need to chat. Leave the spade.

I'm not armed, you know.

Where's the gun I gave you?

Threw it away.

Josef nodded. Get up here, slowly.

Lee allowed the spade to fall from his grasp, then hauled himself from the shallow grave on wet and muddy knees and allowed himself to be frisked. They went into the house.

32

Trembling with cold, Josef directed the dishevelled Lee to sit at the kitchen table and stood nearby with his gun trained on him. He clutched the collar of his jacket to his throat, but it was fruitless; this was not the kind of cold to be put off so easily. Thankfully, a fire burned in the stove. He stood next to it and shook snowflakes from his hair. They fell about his shoes and dissolved into dirty puddles. What a dump. After all this, to come out to a mouldy, old dump like this. For a few grand. Now that he had finally found Lee, Josef was unsure what to do, or couldn't be bothered doing what he was supposed to. Lee slumped with his blistered hands resting upon the wooden table like a pathetic schoolboy. The kid looked almost dead, like he was just going to let happen whatever was going to happen. His clothes were bloody and his hands were muddy. He stank like a butcher shop.

Had a good chat to your *sister* the other day, Josef said after a few minutes.

That got the punk's attention.

Lee looked up through his little black eyes. There were smears of blood and dirt over his face. My sister?

Yeah. On the phone. I was surprised to talk to someone who was supposed to be dead. She was surprised at the news, too. Seemed . . . put out, I guess you could say. Put out at the news. Sounded pretty hale and hearty to me, for now at least—

What's that supposed to mean?

Josef paused. You had all this planned, didn't you? Ditch us and make a run for it? Is that what you thought you'd do? Go and live your other life, the *honest* version?

Lee shrugged and inspected his right shoe where there was a hole in the leather sole the size and shape of a fifty-cent coin. The stitching on one side of the shoe was also coming away. It made Josef aware of his own cold feet. The kitchen had the old-dog smell of drying clothes. It was growing dark. It seemed to him that the dark was always closing in. The days lately were like heartbeats or breaths, they passed almost without registering. Another symptom of age.

For what? Josef added. Eight grand?

Lee let his foot go and stared at some point on the floor.

Might be worth it for a bit more, but eight grand? I had high hopes for you. Put my neck on the line for you, you know. Brought you in and talked you up. Marcel had to be convinced, Lee. It's not a game, you know. You can't—

Maybe you're losing your touch.

Despite himself, Josef started. Maybe he should just shoot the little bastard right now? Get it over and done with. If Lee still had it, the money must be here somewhere in the house. He sighed and scratched his tattoo. I been around a long time. I'm a pretty good judge of horseflesh.

Maybe not this time.

We chose you. *I* chose you.

You got it wrong, old man. And Lee finally looked up at him. His lips were blue and his eyes were damp and red. I'm not like you.

Josef smiled. What we heard. What we heard was you set a man on fire when you were in prison. Lee opened his mouth to speak, but Josef shook his head and kept talking. You set your fucking *friend* on fire, Lee. That's no insignificant thing. You can't pretend that didn't happen. You blew it. Anyway, you got nowhere else to go now. Your sister won't have you back if you tell her what happened. Nobody will have you. Except us.

They were going to fucking kill me. I had to do something. He wasn't my friend, anyway.

Josef grunted and took out his tobacco. Careful to stand back slightly in case Lee should try anything, he jammed his gun under one arm and began to roll a cigarette. With his now clumsy, numb fingers, it took some time. The thin paper was uncooperative and the nub of tobacco lolled about in the groove. This cold was incredible, prehistoric. The ride on the old man's cart had taken him an hour or so over rutted roads. His bony arse was sore and when he licked the gum of the cigarette paper, he could smell the sour leather of the reins on his hands. He felt miles from anywhere, marooned in a stranger's dream. He looked around. Whatever happened, he would have to stay in this dump tonight.

Is it true what they say about your tattoo? Lee asked.

Josef completed the lumpy cigarette. He lit up and the kitchen filled with pungent smoke. He coughed. Depends. What do they say?

That you were . . . born with it.

He picked a shred of tobacco from his bottom lip. Once he had delighted in this story but now he was appalled by it. Automatically he reached for his left forearm, feeling for the tattoo's soft thread. Don't believe everything you hear, alright.

Looks old anyway.

Well. I am old by now.

It's been there a long time, then?

Josef paused. Long as I remember, but then again, my memory's not too great.

Maybe it chose you?

Josef waved his gun to indicate the unseen parts of the house somewhere behind them. He was getting impatient. Where's the money? I'll find it anyway, so you might as well tell me, alright.

From his chair, Lee stared up at him. Why don't you kill me now then, if that's what's going to happen?

You in a hurry? Want to join your little friend out there in his snowy grave?

Isn't that the way you animals work? Just, you know, fucking kill whoever you need to?

Well, you'd know, wouldn't you?

Lee looked like he was going to cry. The fingers of one hand opened and closed. I told you, there's no money.

Josef raised the gun. Come on. What do you take me for? I went to see Stella. I went to see Sylvia. I heard a police report on you and your dead mate from some railway guard. I'm connected, Lee. Two men and a suitcase. Ring any bells? A *suitcase*, Lee. A suitcase of money.

But Lee didn't budge. Josef had to hand it to him; the kid had balls. And it was then he realised, as though the thought had all along been a bud within him now flowering under the heat of this exchange, that he didn't really intend to kill Lee. Maybe Marcel and Lee were right. Maybe he was losing his touch. He stared at Lee's ravaged face. Like a dog. He looked like a dog who didn't even know enough to cower. Despite himself, he admired Lee's—what? Innocence?

They remained unspeaking. Josef looked through the frosty kitchen window at the snowflakes tumbling past. Each one unique, apparently. He thought of the grave outside filling with soft, white snow. The kitchen was as grey and dim as a cave. It would be dark in another hour or two. Soon, the entire day would pass from view and never return. There was this, and nothing more. It was a cold and lonely thought. He stood back and lowered the gun. Make us some tea.

What?

Tea. Make some tea, alright. I see some on the shelf up there. Over the stove.

Lee sighed but did as he was told. He winced with obvious discomfort as he moved about the kitchen, and returned sullenly to the table when he was done.

Almost thawed out at last, Josef sat opposite. He sipped his mug of tea, felt the hot liquid descend into his frozen guts. That quack fix you up? Take out the bullet?

Lee nodded and moved a hand to his bloody side.

Josef watched him. He felt sorry for him. The kid looked like shit, like he wasn't going to last very long. I been shot twice, he volunteered, surprised at the companionable words coming from his mouth. Once in the leg and once up here, at my collarbone. Seventeen years ago. Broke it all over the place. It was like being punched by a fucking truck. Nearly killed me, thought I ... Thought that was it.

Lee coughed. I know how you feel.

Thought for a long time I was dead—for a few hours, I mean. Maybe a whole day. I thought I'd died. Everything was different, washed out or something. People seemed far away. Took me a long time to get over that. Weeks in bed. He shook his head at the memory.

Lee was staring at him quizzically. Josef felt embarrassed. Another silence. Where did the doctor come from? He always part of the plan?

Wild?

Yes.

I don't know. He was at the motel, I think. Staying at that crappy motel. What do you care?

No reason. Just wondered.

They sat again in silence, not really looking at each other. Josef fingered the chipped mug in front of him. Idly, he ran a thumb across his tattoo and detected its mournful thrum. His clothes prickled his skin as they dried. The fire in the grate was burning low, so he reached across and tossed in several lengths of wood.

My aunt could dream other people's dreams for them, he said when he sat back. Said people in dreams were sometimes people who'd died and were coming around asking for things and you just had to know how to talk to them properly. Not be afraid. She reckoned you could . . . bargain with them. Give them food or something, gifts. And that sometimes they had information for you.

Food?

Yes. Cakes and things. Something for the—you know—the journey.

Lee sighed and rolled his eyes. You think I give a shit about your crazy aunt?

Josef sipped his tea. God knows why he was telling Lee any of this. I got a proposition for you, he said finally. He tasted the word in his mouth. *Proposition.*

Lee bent forward and took a gulp of his tea, barely raising the mug from the table. Oh yeah?

Yeah.

What kind of proposition?

Give me the money and I'll let you go to your sister's place or wherever you want to go. I don't care.

You don't care?

Go away and never come back, alright. Stay with your sister and never show your face again. Go wherever you want, just don't come back. I'll tell Marcel it was all taken care of.

Why would you do that? I'm sure Marcel told you to, you know, kill me.

He did.

So why not just do it?

Josef shrugged. Beside him the fire wheezed.

Lee pulled out a crumpled packet of cigarettes and lit one. What if there *is* no money?

Josef paused. It was an old trick, always the final move you could make; you paused, waited until you had their complete attention, then slowly raised the gun and jammed it into their face, so close they could smell dry cordite in the barrel. Then I might as well shoot you in the face right now. For wasting my precious time.

Lee's lips moved, not in a tremble exactly, but with a flickering, as if he lacked the coordination to form actual sounds.

Josef waited. He felt sick, but he waited. One more killing, would it really matter?

Wait, Lee said at last.

Why?

Because.

Why?

How can I be sure you won't shoot me anyway?

I just want the money, Lee. If I don't get back with it, then *I'm* the dead man.

So what, I should take your fucking word for it? Trust you?

Something like that. But I tell you this: I *will* kill you if there's no money, if you made me track you all the way into God-knows-where for nothing. You can trust me on that. There's only one bargaining chip and you've got it. You need to play it now, son.

You'll never find it without me. You'll have to go back empty-handed if you kill me now.

So there *is* money? At least we're getting somewhere.

There's only money if we have a deal.

Josef sighed. This shouldn't be this complicated, he thought, and suddenly had the feeling he should just walk away, jump in the cart and go home to wait for his fate. Wait for Sammy—or whoever it would be—to come around and put a bullet in his brain. His heart really wasn't in it. Besides, his arm—the arm holding the gun—was tired. There's only a deal if there's money, he said at last. Otherwise you got nothing to offer me. You're in no position to be driving hard bargains. Besides, you're still on to a winner.

Lee laughed nervously. How do you figure that?

Josef shrugged, embarrassed. He ran his tongue over his capped tooth, its metallic surface so unlike his other teeth. Well. I just get money. Money that isn't even mine, money I got to hand over. You get . . . a second chance maybe. Got to be worth something. You should take this, you know. I'm doing you a favour. I wish someone had done it for me.

Again Lee was looking at him strangely. You said yourself nobody would have me.

Maybe I was wrong.

I don't know.

Yes, you do. Just decide.

And they waited like that, as day prepared for night, each looking into the face of the other, until Lee raised a trembling hand and pushed the pistol barrel aside with the back of his fingers. OK. Let's go.

Josef was unsure who might have been more relieved.

33

Lee had shoved the suitcase of money beneath one of the sagging couches in the lounge room, so that when he'd been lying on the couch, he could reach down and touch it, to reassure himself. Unsure of what else to do, he dragged it, now marbled with spider webs, from its hiding place and tossed it at Josef's feet.

Josef squatted on his heels in front of the suitcase. Yeah, I would never have found this without you. Very tricky hiding place. He thumbed down to release the metal clasps and raised the lid, releasing a waft of mildew. There, in rows, were the bundles of money. All here?

More or less.

How much?

Eight.

With the gun still in his left hand, Josef bent forward and scooped up one of the bundles. He tossed it up and down as if checking the weight. It made a light slapping sound in his palm. Jesus, he said. All this trouble for a lousy eight grand.

Lee realised this would probably be his only chance. In a sudden, fluid movement, he shoved Josef and tried to wrestle the gun from his hand. Josef sprawled forward with an earthy grunt but maintained his grip on the weapon. Lee struggled with the prone and writhing Josef, who was trying to push himself free but was unable to gain a hold on the wooden floor. His shoe slipped and slid. Lee could smell the damp wool of Josef's coat and his tart tobacco breath. Neither of them uttered actual words, just the occasional simian growl of effort or frustration. A lamp crashed to the floor. A stack of magazines collapsed. Josef kicked at Lee's shin then aimed higher, obviously seeking the area at his side where he'd been shot. He knew he would be finished if Josef made contact. Already the pain of his wound was excruciating. Josef's leg flew out and missed. He tried again. Then again. Each time, Lee arched backwards without loosening his grip on Josef's hand and the gun. Finally, he jerked back and landed a kick of his own in the middle of Josef's chest that sent him to the floor and weakened his grip on the weapon.

Lee clutched his side. His shirt was wet and warm. His stitches had torn apart and his wound was bleeding freely. He swore under his breath and stood over Josef with the pistol in his face. You can't have it. Josef made a move to stand up, but Lee shook his head and raised the gun. You want it for yourself, don't you?

This? The money?

Of course, the money. What else?

Josef glanced at the suitcase and then back to Lee. He shook his head.

That's it, isn't it? You want it for yourself? It's not for Marcel at all. You're going to take it for yourself. I can tell.

Josef sniggered and patted himself down. And where on earth would I go with it? Eight thousand dollars is hardly enough to start a new life for someone like me.

I don't know. Away.

Away? Right. It's a bit late for me. Put the gun down. You're making a big mistake, son. A big mistake. This isn't your thing. Look at you. You don't have the heart for this. Maybe you're right, maybe you're not like us. Just *go*. I'm serious, alright. I'm actually doing you a fucking favour. I'm trying to *save* you. If I return the money, Marcel will forget you as long as you never show up again. You'll never escape if you take it. You'll have to go back. Especially if you kill me.

What the hell does that mean?

Well. Where else could you possibly go? Show up at your sister's place with cash and a bullet wound? Nobody will have you, Lee. Believe me, nobody will have you. I'm actually the best chance you've got. Think about it. Just go. Leave the money and go. I'm serious.

Lee grimaced with pain. Would Josef really let him go, this man of God-knows-how-many murders? The old crow actually looked scared.

They stared at each other for a long time, until Lee could make out his own looming shape in the dull gleam of Josef's eyes. The gun shook in his hand. He smelled Josef's meaty sweat and could hear the faint whistle when Josef exhaled through his nose. Such a dumb, human sound. Like a leaking pipe. That's what his dad would have said. *You sprung a leak, mate?* He recalled Josef's whistling nostril from the time at his apartment. So much had happened since then and yet it all could probably be compacted into one tiny moment. He felt like a tree or rock, some mute and ancient thing. Now it was Lee's turn to hold the gun.

Well, Josef said, as if he'd read Lee's thoughts. The tables have really turned here, haven't they?

But not to your advantage.

Not necessarily to yours neither.

Lee decided not to ask what Josef meant by this; he was already learning too much. Strangely, now that the moment had arrived, he bore Josef no real malice. He allowed his gaze to drift to an indistinct point somewhere above Josef's head, as if his vision had suddenly become unhinged, then squeezed the trigger. Just like that. Josef slumped backwards, immediately dead. Blood spattered across the wall. It gurgled and pooled on the wooden floor and soaked into one of the patterned rugs at his feet. Lee stood there a moment longer before jamming the gun into a coat pocket. He was aware, dimly, of something draining from him.

34

The horse stood in the snow-covered drive attached to its cart, two even jets of steam emerging from its wide nostrils. Its head was lowered and the creature's flanks shivered like jelly in the crisp air. Occasionally it stamped a hoof and kicked at the drifts of floury snow gathering about its shaggy fetlocks. It looked up, shook its head and snorted as Lee approached in a stumbling run.

Lee had never been very close to a horse before, let alone touched one. Such a large animal. It seemed an old horse, with strands of grey in its mane. Its hooves were cracked, like wood. He placed a palm on the animal's brown, velvety chest. It was satisfyingly warm. A huge living thing, this muscular furnace.

Although he was unsure of exactly what to do, the horse would at least take him away from this place. He felt an urgency in his throat and looked into one of the horse's enormous cloudy eyes fringed by long lashes. The creature regarded him without interest. There was a slow, feminine blink. What's your name? What's your name, old timer? Heh? He brushed snowflakes from the horse's back and mane, then rested his cheek against the creature's neck. Don't worry. We'll be OK. We'll get you away from here. Where it's warm. Where there's grass and trees. Come on.

He gathered the bridle and led the horse around in a large circle until they faced the entrance to the property's driveway. Wracked by pain, Lee tossed the suitcase onto the cart, clambered awkwardly aboard, took up the reins and clicked his tongue. To his surprise, the horse lumbered off at a mournful pace. He dared not inspect the wound but could feel his waist warm and sodden with blood. He hunched against the continuing snowfall and jammed his hands under his armpits for warmth. As they went on their ramshackle way, he felt the grumbling jolt and shudder of the road through the wooden seat. The horse's hooves made a sound on the icy surface like an apple's damp crunch. Through a pale landscape they rattled and swung.

Although the ground was white with thick snow, there was a definite, albeit faint, shadow of road. The village had to be this way. He would get there and clean himself up and make a plan. That's what he would do. That's what he would do. Once he knew where he was, he could figure out where to go next.

He thought of Claire. Josef was right when he said that Lee couldn't show up on her doorstep with a bullet wound. But what did he mean by *Nobody will have you?* He shrugged it off. Dying people will say anything.

They hadn't travelled for more than ten minutes when the horse stopped with a shudder and again hung its head. Lee swivelled on his seat and looked around. He could see almost nothing through the dense snowfall. Just spectral trees with their spindly limbs raised as if frozen in the act of waving. A broken fence hovered to his left. He listened but there was nothing, only the murmur of blood flowing through his body. Snow accumulated stealthily in his hair and across his shoulders. His hands were stiff and grey with cold. Fear stirred somewhere deep in his body.

He slapped the reins against the horse's rump the way he'd seen people do in films. The horse raised its huge head, strained against the bridle and managed to move the cart a short way, but stopped after only a few more steps. It tried again but was unable to secure purchase on the icy ground. It was exhausted and the road's uneven surface made it difficult for it to establish any momentum. He jangled the reins. Come on, girl. Come on.

The horse pawed at the road. Still the snow fell. Clutching at his side, Lee stepped from the cart onto the icy ground. The air was so cold that he was losing sense of his own body in space. Even the brittle sensation of his feet hitting the ground was a distant one, almost an echo. Shivering, he went to the horse and nuzzled at its head and neck, inhaling its smells—of dust and sweat and mud, of sunshine and leather and wood. Its mane was coarse against his forehead and his eyes became unexpectedly hot with tears. He thought of all that had happened and wondered if he would ever make it home. Everything was taking so long. So very long. A lifetime. This massive animal with its earthen warmth. His shoulders trembled and he sobbed silently for several minutes. The creature bore Lee's sudden affection with stoicism.

Please, he said. Please. We can't stop now. Not now. We can't stay here on this road. We'll die here. We didn't get anywhere yet. And we can't go back to that house. He thought of Wild on his back staring at the sky, snow clogging his eyes and mouth. Perhaps he should have stayed to bury him but he couldn't bear to stay in that place any longer. He wiped tears from his face and patted the horse's sleek neck. Come on. We need to keep going. We need to keep moving.

Lee clambered again onto the squeaking cart. Trying to sound both stern and friendly, he clicked his tongue and slapped the reins. The horse staggered forward with the cart rolling behind, finally establishing a rickety momentum.

Lee laughed with relief. That's it. That's the way. Come on. He hunched against the cold and pinned his jacket collar at his throat with his free hand. But again, the horse only managed to continue for a few minutes before jerking to a halt. One of the cart's wheels had sunk into a pothole disguised by a cover of fresh snow. Shit. Fuck. He looked around. Behind them on the snowy road were the tracks of their meagre progress, two thick lines and a dark scrabble of hooves. This was no good. Still no sign of any town or farmhouse. No sign of anything. At his feet in the cart was a long, black whip. Lee considered it briefly before picking it up. The bound leather grip was smooth in his palm. He tried flicking it gently against the horse's side. Its ears twitched, but otherwise the horse didn't react. Lee did it again, this time harder. The horse tossed its head and stamped a hoof, but little else. Steam shot from its nostrils. The cart didn't move. Bracing himself with his left hand on a side railing, Lee stood up. He was breathing heavily now. A grim anger stalked through him. A dumb horse. A stupid, dumb horse. The final straw.

With a tight face, he regarded the horse for a long minute, then closed his eyes, raised his other hand and brought the whip down hard on the horse's rump with a rich thwack. The horse skittered and angled its rear away from the direction of the blow. Its tail swished and it tried to pull the cart from the pothole. Lee struck it again. And again. Again. He pounded at the horse, which tottered forward, slipped and staggered once more. Glistening streaks of blood appeared on its dark body and it turned its head as far as it was able to clack its teeth loudly back at him. A glimpse of lolling eye, like that of a harpooned whale. He struck again. He breathed through clenched teeth. A snowflake snagged on his cracked lower lip. Move, you fucking cunt, he hissed. *Move.*

The horse folded its head into its chest. Its flanks shuddered as it heaved against the weight of the cart. Lee stayed in a half-crouch with the whip in one raised fist. The horse and cart trembled from the pothole and progressed several feet. The horse staggered. It whinnied. There was a grunt and it slipped and fell onto its front knees with a hollow crack. It snorted and shook and tried to wrestle to its feet. As the cart lurched, Lee was barely able to stop himself from tumbling to the ground.

With the whip still in his hand, he stepped from the cart. The horse ignored him. It wheezed like a machine and shuddered and shook where it was in the snow, unable to stand. Its flanks were smeared with blood. Again the brute turned and snapped its great teeth as Lee neared. Get up. Stand up. Stand up. You think I've come all this way to be held up by you? After all that's happened?

He glared at it and wiped spittle from his lower lip. Warmed by his anger, he felt monumental and wide, like a swollen river. He raised his hand and whipped the horse. It jolted and bucked as much as it was able, hampered as it was by its attachment to the cart. He struck it again. The horse gave a huge, rattling sigh and attempted to stand. Its right front leg was obviously broken; partway along its narrow length was a bloodied smash of hair and bone. He no longer cared. He lashed it. The horse trembled and slid again to the sharp ground. It stretched its elegant neck. Blood flecked the snowy mush. It made unearthly keening sounds that could only be of terror and pain.

And as the snow continued to fall, he bent and thrashed the poor creature again. He wanted suddenly to kill it, to make a puddle of it. It had stopped making much sound, apart from the fierce cackle of its breath. Its body heaved and shook. Its head muzzled into the snow and occasionally its huge, flat tongue flickered out and in. Eventually Lee stood back, shaking. His side ached and his arm was sore. He felt sick and exhausted and allowed the whip to fall to the ground. Flayed skin hung in thick strips from the horse's back and rump. In the air was the murderous stink of hide and shit. With a filthy sleeve, he wiped sweat and blood from his forehead and watched the horse's panting shape. Still on its side, it made a scraping sound somewhere in its throat and scrabbled meekly at the snow. A dying thing, too fucking animal to know when to give up. A stupid dying thing.

Lee tasted warm blood on his lips. Meaty horse blood. He wiped it away and spat. He drew Josef's gun from his pocket, aimed it at the horse's face and pulled the trigger. Nothing. The trigger had jammed, perhaps from the cold. He inspected the weapon, fiddled with the safety catch with unfeeling fingers, then tried again. Steady, aim and shoot. Again nothing. He threw the gun clumsily at the horse. It struck the animal in the neck and clattered to the ground. He tilted his head back and looked skywards at the mass of fog and ice. Snowflakes landed softly on his face. They sizzled upon his eyeballs. He opened his mouth and screamed.

What now? What now? He loosened a wooden fence post from the packed snow at the roadside verge. Although partly rotted, the post was solid, about three feet long, with fine corners. A thick nail poked from one end. Lee slouched over to the horse, which was by now tangled among the various reins and straps securing it to the cart. The creature stared at him with one murky eye. It didn't really look afraid, certainly not as afraid as it should have been.

With both hands, Lee raised the post over his head and slammed it down across the horse's face with a dull grunt. There was the woody crack of bone. The horse roared and thrashed, each part of its body seemingly trying to escape in a different direction. Its upward-turned eye filled with blood. The momentum of the blow almost caused Lee to topple forward, and he was barely able to maintain his balance on the icy road. When he had recovered, he did it again. This time he made sure to strike the beast with one of the sharp corners of the post and was rewarded with the certainty that he'd managed to split its massive skull. Then he did it again. Blood pulsed from the wound in the horse's head, along with something flecked and creamy, the entire mess soaking into the surrounding snow. Although it had ceased struggling, the horse was still alive. It gazed straight ahead at whatever it could see from its vantage point on the ground—the mud, snow, a blackening sky—probably saying its horsey prayers.

Lee stood and watched until the horse died. It took a long time, but its back legs finally stiffened as if stretching after a lengthy sleep, before it shuddered and relaxed. He kneeled beside it in the crimson slush. His cheeks were spattered with blood. It was warm on his face. He could taste it on his lips.

He wouldn't know how long he stayed kneeling beside the horse, feeling its warmth drain into the earth. It might have been ten minutes or more. A year. Perhaps three seconds. Long enough for snow to gather about him and sprinkle down his neck. Long enough for him to have difficulty standing when he finally did so. Long enough for him to wonder what the hell had happened. He looked around and was amazed to see that nothing had altered. It was barren. Everything was as it had always been. He felt better. He felt worse. He had no idea where he was or what he was doing. This was just some blank, white place without obvious end. There was nothing and there was nowhere to go.

He had the urge to piss and fumbled at his trousers before abandoning the idea; he would never be able to undo his trousers with such frozen fingers. Perhaps he should piss his pants? Might at least warm him? He stood there debating with himself for a minute before shrugging and grabbing the suitcase of money from the cart that now yawed like a shipwreck in the snow and mud. He could barely feel his feet and his hands flailed at his sides like stumps. His ears stung and his eyeballs ached. He tottered away, the suitcase banging against his leg with every step. After a short distance, he halted. The snowflakes were heavier and larger than ever. Like pale coins, they fell to earth. He put the suitcase down to hug himself for warmth. He trembled. His teeth clattered uncontrollably. He sat on the suitcase and lit a cigarette, jamming his free hand into a coat pocket. Barely able to lift his head. The downy drifts of snow looked almost comfortable. He was so tired. Perhaps he could lie down for a few minutes to get his strength back before going on? A little sleep, a little childish sleep.

There was something small in his pocket and he lifted it out. It was the crumpled fragment of bullet Wild had removed from him. Lee held it in a shivering hand and stared at it for a long time. A pebble of metal. He remembered a woman with a gun. Her slow and deliberate blink. Was that where this had all begun, or was it even longer ago? By now his entire body was shaking. His cigarette fell from his fingers to the ground. Inexplicably he placed the bullet fragment upon his tongue and worked it around in his mouth, almost the only part of his body he could still feel. Like a stray tooth, the bullet clackered around in his chattering mouth. If it had a flavour, he was unable to detect it. He swallowed it. It rattled against his oesophagus and was gone.

He tried to move. He slapped at his face but could feel nothing. He slapped harder. Only with effort could he even waggle his sullen toes. He stamped his feet. Still perched on the suitcase, he folded himself against the cold until his face rested upon his knees. His nose ran with watery snot. One thing, at least. One thing was. Was one thing. At least the pain in his side was finally gone. That was one good. Thing.

At least. Something. Little thing.

By now it was nearly dark. While he'd been otherwise occupied, the horizon had crept closer until it now crowded around him. It muttered and sang. A wind flew across the plains, sank into a crouch and rent the air with a sound like the sharpening of knives. It keened through him. His heart drew breath and he raised his head to look about. Somewhere through the swirling snow was a dim and flickering light embedded into a thick, dark shape. In the distance. A boat. It was the shape of a boat. A thin smile softened his lips. He would be saved. A boat. A liner, churning through the foam. Any second now he would hear the lowing of its horn. He would be saved.

At last. Saved he would be saved he would.

Be saved.

ACKNOWLEDGMENTS

This novel would never have seen the light of day were it not for everyone at Scribe Publications—especially Aviva Tuffield, for making it happen in the first place; and Ian See, for his eagle-eyed editing. I would also like to thank the staff and students of RMIT's professional writing and editing course—particularly Olga Lorenzo, Steve Wide, Caroline Lee, Melissa Cranenburgh and Toni Jordan—who provided reserves of patience, respect, criticism and faith. Thanks also to the beautiful Roslyn Oades, who endured many questions along the lines of: 'Can you read this and tell me if it makes sense?'

ABOUT THE AUTHOR

Chris Womersley's fiction and reviews have appeared in *Granta*; *The Best Australian Stories* 2006, 2010, and 2011; *Griffith REVIEW*; *Meanjin*; and *The Age*. His debut novel, *The Low Road*, won the Ned Kelly Award for Best First Fiction. His second novel, *Bereft*, won the Australian Book Industry Award for Literary Fiction and the Indie Award for Fiction, and was shortlisted for the Miles Franklin Literary Award, *The Age* fiction prize, and the Australian Literature Society Gold Medal. Visit his website at www.chriswomersley.com.